Midnight Rider

Joan Hiatt Harlow

SCHOLASTIC INC.

New York Toronto London Auckland Sydney
Mexico City New Delhi Hong Kong Buenos Aires

No part of this publication may be reproduced, stored in a retrieval system, or transmitted in any form or by any means, electronic, mechanical, photocopying, recording, or otherwise, without written permission of the publisher. For information regarding permission, write to Margaret K. McElderry Books, an imprint of Simon & Schuster Children's Publishing Division, 1230 Avenue of the Americas, New York, NY 10020.

ISBN-13: 978-0-439-93266-0
ISBN-10: 0-439-93266-1

12 11 10 9 8 7 6 5 4 3 2   7 8 9 10 11 12/0

Printed in the U.S.A.   40

First Scholastic printing, March 2007

Book design by Sammy Yuen Jr.

Map by Chelsea Karitas

The text for this book is set in LombaBook.

Dedicated with love to:
Debbie, Lisa, Kristan, Scott, and Jennifer—
my best creative works!

contents

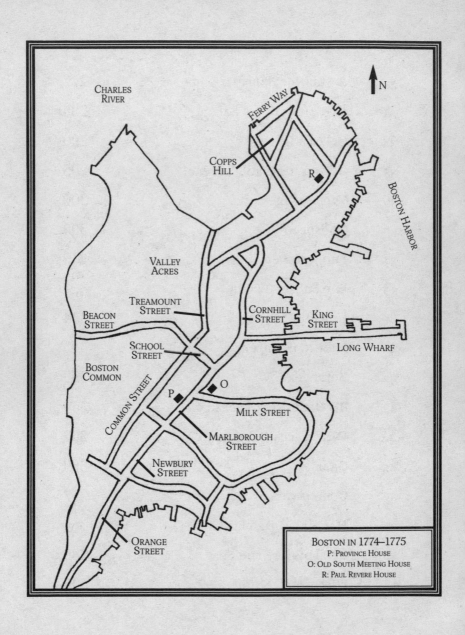

CHARLES
RIVER

N

FERRY WAY

COPPS
HILL

R

BOSTON HARBOR

VALLEY
ACRES

TREAMOUNT
STREET

BEACON
STREET

CORNHILL
STREET

KING
STREET

SCHOOL
STREET

LONG WHARF

BOSTON
COMMON

COMMON STREET

P

O

MILK STREET

MARLBOROUGH
STREET

NEWBURY
STREET

ORANGE
STREET

BOSTON IN 1774–1775
P: PROVINCE HOUSE
O: OLD SOUTH MEETING HOUSE
R: PAUL REVERE HOUSE

H ot wind blew through the open casement window. Hannah tossed on the bed, her legs tangling in the quilt. "Mama," she whispered. Was that her voice—hoarse and painful? Where was Mama? She wanted so much to curl up in her mother's lap.

"Your mother is gone," a voice said. "Don't you remember?"

Hannah opened her eyes. Aunt Phoebe was standing over her, her black hair pulled into a bun that made her dark eyes seem cold and sharp.

Then Hannah remembered.

Her mother had died of the smallpox. Mama was gone—like Papa. They were both gone forever.

Hannah pulled away the sleeve of her shift. Through the tears that blurred her vision she saw that her arm was covered with angry pustules. Sores oozed and burned with each movement of her body. She had the pox too! She closed her eyes as Phoebe pressed a cold, wet cloth to her face. "Thank you, Aunt Phoebe." She spoke painfully. The sores from the smallpox crusted on her throat.

Hannah turned her face to the window to see the green pasture rolling across the Salem hillside. Her black gelding, Promise, was grazing near the old elm tree. Promise had been left outside all summer. Since Aunt Phoebe was afraid of horses, there was no one to put him in the barn. Hannah wondered if she would ever ride again with the wind in her hair and Promise beneath her.

With her fever, headache, and terrible sores, days and nights intermingled. There were fleeting visions of Aunt Phoebe standing over the bed.

One morning when Aunt Phoebe brought Hannah her usual tea and slice of molasses bread, she said, "You've passed the crisis. You'll recover, Hannah." Aunt Phoebe then bathed her with herbs, shaking her head over the number of scabs on Hannah's body. "At least your face has been spared. Only this one scab embedded on your cheek will leave a scar. It will serve as a reminder that outward beauty is only vanity," she muttered.

When Phoebe left the room, Hannah turned to the open window. Promise must be out there waiting for her. She could hear a lark singing from the common pasture, and she could see Farmer Anderson's cows. But Promise was not in his customary grazing place.

Hannah threw back the quilt and climbed out of bed to get a better look. Her legs felt as weak as bent reeds as she made her way unsteadily to the casement window. Pushing the window open wide, she thrust her head outside. "Promise!" Usually, at the sound of her voice, Promise would stop grazing, prick up his ears, and look around eagerly to see where Hannah might be.

Hannah scanned the entire pasture. Promise was gone!

"Aunt Phoebe!" Hannah called. "Where is Promise?"

Aunt Phoebe, her hands folded in front of her, was standing in the doorway, her face without expression. "I sold the horse."

"No! You didn't! Promise is my horse—Papa's gift to me." Hannah's knees buckled and she fell to the floor. Through a sea of tears she looked up at her aunt, who now towered above her. "Please, Aunt Phoebe," she sobbed. "Please tell me you didn't sell my horse."

The woman took hold of Hannah's arm and pulled her to her feet. "Get back to bed," she said.

"No!" Hannah pulled away. "Tell me what you've done!"

Aunt Phoebe took a deep breath. "I cannot afford to keep a horse. Farmer Anderson has helped me take care of Promise since you and your mother got sick, but I cannot ask him to continue feeding that animal for you. In a few months it will be winter. Who will pay for oats or hay?" She smoothed her apron. "It costs enough for both of *us* to eat, without feeding a horse as well."

"But Promise helped with plowing and the carriage . . ." Hannah stopped. She knew only too well from the way Aunt Phoebe's eyes narrowed and her lips tightened into a thin line that the matter was settled.

Aunt Phoebe continued. "I've taken care of you

and your mother until my back is broken. The least you can do is be grateful and not complain about the decisions I make." She headed for the doorway.

Hannah climbed into the bed and closed her eyes. Tears squeezed out from under her lashes, stinging the still-red pockmark on her face.

"Dear Lord," she prayed. "Please help me to be grateful. Please help me to be strong. And please, please bring Promise back to me."

After she recovered, Hannah visited her mother's grave nearly every day. It had been almost two months now since that dreadful day in May when her mother died. The morning fog was lifting as Hannah brushed her hands across the granite headstone with its ugly skull. Once again she read the engraved words:

Here lieth Luvena Andrews, wife and mother,
who awaiteth the resurrection trumpet
                    Born 1740   Died 1774

Hannah knew about the resurrection, for Mama, who came from a Puritan background, had diligently read the Scriptures with her. The minister, Thomas Barnard, reminded Hannah that Elijah, Elisha, and Jesus raised people from the dead and brought them back to their families. Mr. Barnard said that God would raise her mother, too, but not until the resurrection trumpet sounded on the "last day" spoken of in the Bible. It seemed like a long time to wait.

A rooster crowed in the distance and a horse neighed. Hannah saw a boy galloping across the meadow. Until recently the meadow had been a muddy marshland due to the heavy spring rains. But the hot July sun had dried the soil, and today, as the sun broke through, the damp marsh was transformed into an emerald sea of grass where sparkling wildflowers became rubies and topaz. On a day as beautiful as this, Hannah longed to race across the fields with Promise. But Promise was gone.

Now Hannah rejoiced at the sight of the boy riding bareback through the meadow, his sun-streaked brown hair blowing in the breeze. That horse he was riding looked so much like Promise! She scurried to the stone wall that marked the common pasture and the town graveyard, then ran alongside it, her attention on the ebony horse.

Hannah scrambled over the wall and onto the field, waving her hands and calling, "Promise! Promise!"

The horse stopped suddenly, then turned, his ears twitching. Startled, the boy almost slipped off, and he yanked the reins angrily. The horse reared and headed in Hannah's direction. "Stop! Stop, Midnight!" the boy yelled, trying to turn the horse back. But the animal continued to make his way to Hannah.

"How dare you frighten my horse!" the boy yelled as he came closer. "Don't you have a brain? I could have been killed!"

"Promise is *my* horse," Hannah retorted as she ran and threw her arms around Promise's neck. "Nothing could keep him away from me." Hannah stroked the horse's shining mane. "I have missed you, my darling boy."

"He's not yours," the rider said. "My father bought him for me."

Hannah drew herself up tall to look up at the stranger. "My father gave *me* this horse, and his name is Promise. He knows my voice. That's why he stopped when I called him."

"Ah, perhaps that's why the horse has been so skittish. He misses you. He hasn't been eating much either." The boy slid off the horse. "We bought this gelding from that Andrews lady. She said the horse was hers."

"That Andrews lady is my aunt Phoebe," said Hannah. "My name is Hannah Andrews."

"I'm Will Samson. We moved into the farm over near the willows."

So this was why Aunt Phoebe had explicitly told her not to speak with the new family that moved into that farm, Hannah realized angrily. Aunt Phoebe didn't want her to know that Promise was somewhere in Salem.

"We paid good and true money for this horse. So he's mine now."

"How much did you pay?" Hannah was curious.

"Eighty pounds sterling." Will cocked his head. "Didn't your aunt tell you?"

"No." Hannah stroked Promise, who nuzzled her arm.

"If this horse is yours, then the money is yours."

"Aunt Phoebe will keep the money, I'm sure."

"Where did you ever get a name like Promise?"

"Papa brought him to me when I was ten. Papa said, 'I promised you a horse of your own.' Right then and there, I named him Promise." Tears welled in Hannah's eyes, and she turned away.

"Where's your papa now?"

"He died two years ago." Hannah paused, recalling mornings riding behind her father along an Indian trace by the Merrimack River in Chelmsford. They'd stop to pick daisies for Mama while Promise grazed in the meadow. "We came to live in Salem after he died. Now my mother is dead too."

"My pa said that lots of families around here were struck with the pox. Is that what happened to you and your ma?" His gaze fixed on her cheek.

Hannah flushed and pulled a strand of hair over the pockmark. "Yes. Mama was the first to fall ill. Then I got it and almost died too. Sometimes I wish I had." She nodded toward the burial ground. "Mama's grave is over there."

"I'm right sad to hear that," he said. "You must be greatly sorrowed."

Hannah nodded, but then smiled. "To see Promise again is a joyful thing."

Will stroked the neck of the horse. "He's a beauty."

The horse seemed to sense that they were talking about him and tossed his head. Hannah stroked his black neck again. "Aunt Phoebe told me not to speak with your family nor trespass on your land."

"She probably doesn't want you to know where the horse is, or how much we paid for him. She's a fox when it comes to money." Will shook his head. "And she's not a pleasant woman—in fact, if she'd been living here in Salem a hundred years ago, she'd have burned as a witch." His lips twitched into a grin.

Hannah stifled a laugh, then said solemnly, "Aunt Phoebe was good to us when we were sick. She tells me often how"—Hannah wrinkled up her nose and mimicked her aunt's self-righteous speech—"'I've given up everything to help you and your mother! My whole life has changed. And not for the better, I might add.'"

"You sound just like her!" Will said with a laugh. "But why are you here talking to me and disobeying your aunt's wishes? If she finds out, she'll give you a whipping."

"When she sold Promise, she hurt me more than any whipping." Hannah put her arms around the horse's neck. "Will, perhaps you should keep his name Promise. He's not used to Midnight."

"I'll do some thinking on it," Will agreed.

"I hope you're good to him." Promise nuzzled his soft nose into Hannah's face and nickered softly.

"Of course I'm good to him." Will smiled. "Would you like a ride?"

"Oh, indeed I would!" Hannah exclaimed.

Will held his hands together for Hannah to mount, which she did in a flash, pulling her skirt above her knees.

Will handed her the reins and was about to climb on the horse behind her, but Hannah clicked her heels into the horse's flank and yelled, "Giddap, Promise!"

As the horse bounded away, Hannah waved at Will, who was left behind, his hands on his hips. She and Promise galloped across the meadow, around a stand of white birches, and to the top of a small hill from where she could see the sapphire Atlantic Ocean sparkling in the distance. Down the hill they flew, into the north fields, where they came across a rapid brook. Promise slowed momentarily to keep his footing, then splashed through the water. Hannah laughed as the cold water splattered on her bare legs. They darted back across the meadow to the stone wall where Will was waiting.

Before Will could speak, Hannah pulled the reins and slid off the horse. "Thank you for letting me ride my horse again."

Will's mouth opened and shut in astonishment. "You ride like a wild thing!" he finally said. Promise nudged Hannah with his nose, as if inviting her to ride again. "He likes you," Will said.

Hannah stroked the horse's neck. "He *loves* me."

"Would you like to ride another day?"

"Oh, yes!" Hannah nodded eagerly. "I visit my mother's grave every morning."

Hannah's gloom diminished over the next few weeks, and sometimes she even sang as she helped Aunt Phoebe in the gardens and around the house. Hannah could sense her aunt watching her closely.

Almost every day she secretly met Will at the graveyard wall and rode Promise.

One late July morning they sat on the stone wall and talked. "I'm going to ride into Boston one day soon," Will told Hannah.

"Why?"

"I want to help the cause of freedom in Boston Town. Haven't you heard about all that's happening there? England has been unfairly sticking taxes and laws on Americans."

"Everyone's heard how Bostonians masqueraded as Mohawk Indians and dumped all the tea into the harbor rather than be taxed on it," Hannah broke in.

"It's not that Americans won't pay taxes," Will explained. "It's that we don't get representation. Parliament over there in London doesn't give an owl's hoot about us. They've left us alone all these years, and they've suddenly realized that *we're* thriving and *they're* in debt. Now they want our money—and we don't get a say about anything!" Will's voice rose. "They're even forcing Bostonians to quarter redcoat soldiers in their homes—to feed them and give them beds."

"It sounds dreadful in Boston," Hannah said.

"I want to help the Whigs work toward freedom from England."

"We have Whigs here in Salem, don't we?"

"Indeed we do. My father's a Whig. Whigs are trying to work peacefully with England for our rights," Will told her. "But lately most want freedom from England."

Hannah had heard Aunt Phoebe speak with loathing of Whigs and Patriots. She spoke of herself as a Loyalist. "What do Loyalists want?" Hannah asked.

"Loyalists want America to stay loyal to King George and England," Will explained. "They're also called Tories."

"Aunt Phoebe is a Loyalist—a Tory," Hannah said.

"I heard tell that General Gage is heading back to Boston." Will went on. "He's the one who closed off Boston Harbor so no ships or supplies can get into that town. That's why Salem's the main port for shipping now. But people say he's in danger living around these parts, so he's moving back to Boston to keep order there. He's not well liked, no matter where he goes."

"I would think he'd be in more danger in Boston," Hannah said. "Especially after the Boston Massacre."

"Right. Can you believe British soldiers killed five Bostonians in that riot? One of them, Christopher Seider, was just a boy. Bostonians have never forgotten it."

"I wouldn't want to go to Boston if I were you, Will. Besides," Hannah added hesitantly, "I'd miss you."

Will's face flushed, and he looked down. "Oh, you'd miss the horse, not me."

Aunt Phoebe suddenly came up behind them. "So this is what you've been up to, you ungrateful child! I saw you astride that horse with your skirt up and bare legs showing!" She pointed a long finger at Hannah. "I'm not putting up with this!"

It was only a matter of days. Aunt Phoebe stood with her hands on her hips and said, "I've arranged to send you away." Her thin lips stretched into a half smile. "You will be working for the Gages, the most important family in America. General Gage and his wife will be moving back to the Province House in Boston."

"Oh no, Aunt Phoebe, please don't send me away!" Hannah was trembling. "You promised Mama on her deathbed that I could stay here in this house. You promised!"

"I assured your mother that you would be well taken care of and that I would be your guardian. I've kept that vow." Aunt Phoebe pulled a rag from her pocket and began dusting the furniture.

"But this house is my home."

Aunt Phoebe scowled at Hannah. "No, this house is *my* home. My father built it! When you and your mother came to live with me two years ago, I opened it up to you both. Then I nursed you and your mother through smallpox—with no fear or thought for my own health. But now I'm done with that. I intend to go on living in this house until I die." Aunt Phoebe dusted faster and faster as she spoke. "Besides, you'll be clothed and well fed at the Gages' for the next seven years."

"Seven years?" Hannah felt tears of hot anger rising up. "You never once asked me if I wanted to go to Boston, or if I wanted to work for the Gages."

"You didn't care about what *I* wanted when you disobeyed me. We will not discuss it again. It's been arranged for you to leave tomorrow."

The next morning Hannah stuffed a carpetbag with the few items of clothing she owned.

She should have known this might happen. Aunt Phoebe had said many times that she was too old to care for such an "unruly" child. Hannah lay across her bed for the last time and pounded her fist into the pillow. Just because she liked to ride

Promise didn't mean she was unruly. Aunt Phoebe could never understand the joy of sitting tight in the saddle with Promise's powerful muscles under her thighs. When Hannah rode Promise, they were not separate beings; they were one with the wind and the sky. Now Aunt Phoebe had taken Promise from her and was sending her to Boston, where she knew no one.

She sat up and glanced around the room she had shared with her mother. There were many things here that Hannah loved, but Aunt Phoebe had said she could take only one item to Boston. What she wanted to take most of all was Mama's wedding ring, but Aunt Phoebe had taken it and put it in a box by her own bed. "You'll only lose it. I'll keep it here."

An ivory brush on the bureau still held wisps of her mother's raven hair, and on a little table by the window was her hornbook. Mama had been so proud when Hannah learned to read. How could she choose just one item when so many connected her to the past?

"Hurry!" Aunt Phoebe called from the kitchen. "Get your bag and be on your way. The carriage will pick you up at the general store at eleven o'clock."

Hannah stood, gathered up her carpetbag, and headed for the door. Then, with sudden determination, she ran into Aunt Phoebe's room and retrieved her mother's ring, stuffing it into the pocket in her skirt.

In the kitchen, Aunt Phoebe was trimming the wicks on the oil lamps. "Now, you remember your Christian upbringing and get yourself to a church in Boston. You're only fourteen and you must—"

Hannah had a strong urge to imitate her Aunt Phoebe's sermonizing words. Instead she asked in an accusing voice, "If you're so concerned about my upbringing, why are you sending me away?"

"You'll be just fine if you stop your mimicking and making fun of people," Aunt Phoebe stated. "I've heard you impersonate people in your brazen and disrespectful way. And don't go riding on horses with your skirt up above your knees. A proper young woman would only ride sidesaddle."

Hannah swallowed back an angry answer and started for the door, only to be blocked by a neighbor, Sarah Tarrant.

"Phoebe, you are making a mistake sending

Hannah off to Boston," Sarah said. "There could be an uprising in that town. The Whigs and Tories are so close to a confrontation—it's not safe for a young girl."

Aunt Phoebe cut her short. "She'll have a good home with the other servants at the Province House," she said virtuously. "And she'll be among firm Tory Loyalists!"

"Firm Tory Loyalists, indeed. Yes, she'll be among those who would make this entire country slave to the Crown." Sarah's face was flushed, almost matching her red hair.

"At the Province House she'll learn to be a loyal subject to her king. I've been patient and kind to her, but she's unthankful and disobedient. Loyalty! That's what she needs to be taught."

Sarah gave her a withering look. "Oh, I know the real reason you're sending her off. The Gages—"

"Stop!" Aunt Phoebe cast a meaningful glare at Mrs. Tarrant that was not lost on Hannah. "It's for her own good."

"It's for *your* own good, you mean." Sarah's eyes narrowed as she faced Hannah's aunt. "Everyone in Salem knows."

"Whist! Hush!" Aunt Phoebe warned. "Everyone in Salem should commend me for all I've sacrificed for Hannah. Moreover, this is no one's business but mine."

"It's Hannah's business!" Sarah left, shutting the door loudly behind her.

"What did Mrs. Tarrant mean?" Hannah asked. "What does everyone in Salem know?"

"They know that you'll be living at the governor's mansion with General Gage and his wife. What more could a girl ask for?" Aunt Phoebe opened the door. "You need to get to town right away. It's almost eleven o'clock." She took Hannah by the shoulders, turned her around, and peered into her eyes. "Be grateful for all I did for you and your mother. You'd probably be dead if it weren't for me." She took a loaf of bread from the cupboard, wrapped it in brown paper, and shoved it toward Hannah. "Here's something to eat on the way. Now kiss me good-bye and be gone."

Hannah tucked the parcel under her arm and pecked her aunt's thin, wrinkled cheek. "God be with you, Aunt Phoebe."

Hannah walked down the street toward the

center of town. The village was quiet, and the August sun was hot and oppressive. As she approached the village green she heard someone call her name.

"Hannah!" Will was riding Promise and heading her way at a full gallop. Hannah waited, glad to see Will and Promise once more before she went off to Boston.

"I have something for you." Will pulled the reins, and Promise stopped smoothly. He reached down and handed her a small bouquet.

Hannah smelled the flowers. "Mmm. Lilies of the valley," she said. "Thank you, Will."

"Your aunt Phoebe is cruel to send you away. Why doesn't she want you to ride Promise?"

"She doesn't want me around, and my riding the horse was just an excuse. 'No lady rides a horse like that. You are so brazen, exposing your bare legs for everyone in Salem to see!'" Hannah imitated Aunt Phoebe's berating words.

Will's worried expression softened into a grin.

"I'm to meet Mrs. Gage's carriage downstreet at eleven." She reached up and stroked Promise's nose. "I'll miss you, Midnight," she whispered. "Be a good boy for Will. You are Midnight now. We must forget that you were my Promise."

The horse nuzzled her neck and whinnied softly as if he knew they were saying good-bye.

"No, Hannah," Will said. "His name will continue to be Promise. That's the name he knows best. And he'll always belong to you in his heart."

Hannah blinked as the tears she had been holding back cascaded down her cheeks.

Will coughed and looked away. "I hear they're looking for stable boys to help out with the king's horses. Maybe I'll see you in Boston."

"You'd be right good as a stable hand," Hannah told him, the horse leaning against her. "No one knows horses better than you. And no one rides better either."

Will grinned. "Except you, Hannah."

"What will your folks do if you go to Boston?"

"Father has lots of help at the farm."

"But you're their only son," Hannah reminded him.

"If I can work with the Boston Whigs in their pursuit of freedom from England, Father would be right proud."

Hannah squinted at the sun, which was almost overhead. "I'd better go. Come to Boston and find me, Will." She climbed off the wall and picked up her bag.

"I shall," Will promised. "God be with you, Hannah."

"And with you." Hannah walked away, but as she crossed the village green she looked back once more. Will, sitting tall on Promise, was still watching her.

"Good-bye, my sweet horse. We will be together again. That's my promise to you."

H annah sat on a bench outside the general store, where she was to meet the Gages' carriage. She inhaled the fragrance of the flowers Will had given to her. It wasn't long before a wagon drew up and stopped. Two women were seated together in the back seat.

The driver climbed down. "Are you Hannah Andrews?" he asked.

"Yes, sir."

"I'm Isaac Monroe. I work for General Gage. We've come to take you to Boston." He tossed Hannah's carpetbag in the back with some other luggage. "Climb aboard."

Hannah took the only empty place, behind the driver, facing the rear.

Back in his seat, Isaac clicked the reins, and the

carriage moved down the hard-packed dirt street. The bouncing dray and the horses' hooves seemed to beat out the rhythm of Mrs. Tarrant's words over and over again. *Everyone knows the real reason . . . the real reason . . . the real reason . . .*

One of the women sitting opposite Hannah nodded stiffly. She was a large-boned woman with dark auburn hair and a long, thin nose that came to a point precisely at the bow of her top lip. "I am Lydia Perkins, the one who arranged for you to come with us to Boston. I am an old friend of your aunt Phoebe. General Gage employed me while he was living at the Hooper House in Danvers and working in Salem. I am the household overseer, and now I will be in charge of all the servants at the Province House."

Hannah nodded and smiled faintly.

The other woman leaned over and touched Hannah's hand. "Catherine Squires is my name. I was a cook for the governor at the Hooper House, but now I'll be working at the Province House." She was plump and soft-looking. She gazed at Hannah with kind gray eyes. "Is this the first time you've been away from home? You seem so young."

"I'm fourteen."

"She's old enough to be indentured," Lydia snapped defensively. "I would have never arranged this if she were under fourteen! We need someone who is old enough to work."

"Oh, of course you wouldn't, Miss Lydia," Catherine said quickly.

"What do you mean, I'm 'indentured'?" Hannah asked.

Catherine gasped. "Oh, my! Didn't your parents tell you?"

"My mother and father are both dead. I have only an aunt. She's the one who arranged all this." Hannah looked down at her hands.

Lydia frowned. "You are under obligation to work for General Gage and his wife for seven years." She reached into a satchel and pulled out a packet of papers, which she thumbed through. Then she thrust one at Hannah. "Read this. You can read, can't you?"

"Of course I can read," Hannah said hotly. She unfolded the document. *The contract is between Miss Phoebe Andrews, guardian of Hannah Andrews, a niece and minor destitute orphan having no estate for her maintenance and education . . .*

Hannah looked up. "Destitute? Having no estate? Does that mean I have no money?"

When Miss Lydia nodded, Hannah said, "But my father left money for my mother and me. Aunt Phoebe knows that, and when Mama was dying, she said Aunt Phoebe would take care of me! What did she do with that money?"

"That's no concern of mine," Miss Lydia said. "Your aunt said you had no money."

Hannah frowned and read on. . . . *between Miss Phoebe Andrews, guardian of Hannah Andrews, a niece and minor destitute orphan having no estate for her maintenance and education, and Miss Lydia Perkins, overseer of the household of His Excellency the Governor of Massachusetts.*

Her eyes skipped over the legal terms such as *witnesseth* and *aforesaid* and focused on *does hereby put, place, and bind Hannah Andrews to Lydia Perkins to learn the art of housekeeping, cooking, washing, ironing, sewing . . .*

"Why do you need to teach me these things? I already know them!"

"Not to the satisfaction of your aunt, evidently," Miss Lydia said. "If you keep reading you'll see where it says, 'until she reaches the age of twenty-one.' Now you understand. You are fourteen and you are indentured until you are twenty-one." Miss Lydia pointed to the next paragraph. "Read this part."

Hannah read again. *During all of which time the said Hannah Andrews shall well and faithfully serve the household of Governor Gage and everywhere and at all times obey his lawful commands. She shall do no damage to General Gage, nor willfully suffer any to be done by others.* "What kind of damage could I do to General Gage?" Hannah asked.

"Steal. Lie. Shirk your duties," Miss Lydia said sourly.

Hannah read on. *She shall not absent herself from the service of her master, but shall in all things behave and conduct herself as a good and faithful servant during the term aforesaid.*

"This is all well and good for the Gage household and for Aunt Phoebe, but what advantage is it to me?"

"Such impertinence!" Miss Lydia snapped.

"Don't you feel that's a fair question?" Catherine asked.

Lydia gave Catherine a cold look. "Keep reading and you'll see that you will be well provided for."

Hannah continued, this time reading aloud: "'And Lydia Perkins, as household overseer for Governor Gage, does hereby promise and agree to teach and instruct the said Hannah Andrews or cause her to be taught and instructed in the art and business of housekeeping as well as in reading, writing, and arithmetic, and to well and faithfully provide sufficient meat, drink, clothing, lodging, and all other necessaries during the seven years of Hannah Andrews's servitude.'"

"You see?" Miss Lydia said haughtily. "You will be well provided for. And you will gain an education by working in the Gages' household."

"I already know how to read and write and sum," Hannah said.

"Then things should go easier for both of us," Lydia said.

The document was signed by both Lydia and Phoebe and dated August 10, 1774—only one week ago. How Hannah's life had changed in such a short time!

"No one asked me if I wanted to go away and

learn the 'art of housekeeping,'" Hannah said. "I didn't sign this document."

"Of course not," Miss Lydia snapped. "You are a child, and your aunt is your guardian. She signed this indenture and received fifty pounds as a fair binder to seal the contract."

Fifty pounds? So that was the real reason Aunt Phoebe did this. That's what Mrs. Tarrant had meant! Aunt Phoebe had sold Hannah just as she had sold Promise, and she was keeping the money for herself.

"Am I a slave?" Hannah asked.

"Of course not! This is a business arrangement, and there are many benefits. You will have a place to live, food to eat, clothing, an education—and you will work for General and Mrs. Gage until your time is finished." Miss Lydia snatched the document away from Hannah and folded it back into the packet. "Then you can do whatever you want."

Catherine reached over and patted Hannah's hand. Hannah looked away. She wanted to cry. She reached into her pocket, pulled out her mother's ring, and placed it on her finger. It was comforting to wear it.

Catherine seemed to read Hannah's thoughts. "God is watching over you, Hannah. Be strong, and he will help you and show you the way."

As they passed through the town, Hannah saw the carriage maker, Mr. Skidmore, whom everyone called "Old Skid," talking with Parson Barnard. Hannah had played with his children. He and the parson looked up as the carriage approached.

"Good-bye, Hannah," Old Skid bellowed. He pointed to Hannah and said something to Parson Barnard.

"God be with you, my child," Parson Barnard called.

As they came closer to the bridge that crossed the North River, Miss Lydia pointed to a cannon on a grassy knoll. "I hope that cannon will never turn against our mother nation, England."

Mrs. Tarrant lived in the last house before the bridge. As the carriage neared her house, she ran out with a bundle. "Here, here! Stop!" she called out to Isaac, who pulled back on the reins. She handed the bundle up to Hannah. "For you, my dear," she said. "To eat on the way."

Isaac clicked his tongue and the horses started up again. "Thank you, Mrs. Tarrant. Good-bye," Hannah called. She opened the muslin and found slices of plum cake, which she offered to the women in the carriage. Miss Lydia took a portion and ate it daintily, but Catherine declined the cake Hannah held out to her. "You keep it. You may be hungry later," she said.

Hannah broke off a piece of the heavy cake, but even the luscious plums seemed bitter to her.

They rode along in silence for a long while. "What did your father do?" Catherine asked.

"He was a fine cabinetmaker," Hannah answered proudly. "He made lovely tables and chests, and his work is well known in the colony."

"I've never been to the Province House, but I've heard the building is quite glorious," Catherine said.

"It is magnificent indeed," Lydia answered. "It was built a hundred years ago."

"I suppose Governor Gage will be having formal dinners and parties," Catherine said.

"General Gage is the governor as well as a general?" Hannah asked, attempting to sort out

General Gage's position in her head.

"He is the royal governor of Massachusetts, appointed by the king," Miss Lydia said, "as well as commander in chief of British America. Don't you know anything?"

Hannah slouched into her seat. *Don't you know anything?* She was tempted to imitate Lydia's nasal voice but knew better than to provoke the woman, whose tongue seemed as sharp as her pointed nose.

Instead, she watched fences, milestones, forks, and signs, trying to seal them in her memory. Someday she might escape and find her way back to Salem and to Promise. She listened for a time as Lydia chatted idly to Catherine about Mrs. Gage. Margaret Kemble Gage was American, born into a wealthy family in New Jersey. Even though Mrs. Gage was married to General Gage, who was a British nobleman, the British repeatedly gossiped about her. And the Americans often belittled her husband.

"I'm sure it's difficult for an American to be married to a British general," Catherine commented.

Hannah yawned and leaned back. The warm

sunshine, the clomping of the horses' hooves, and the swaying of the wagon soon lulled her to sleep.

The sun was at a different angle when Hannah felt someone nudge her. "Wake up," Miss Lydia ordered. "We're going to be taking the ferry. From now on, don't think you can nap whenever you wish. Laziness will not be tolerated."

The wagon wobbled its way across a bridge to a cluster of buildings.

"This is Charlestown," Isaac said. He pointed to the sparkling river. "And that's the mouth of the Charles River. Boston Harbor is just over there around the bend."

Hannah felt a prickle of excitement. Large frigates and longboats lined the harbor and bobbed on the blue waves. She smelled the open sea, and she could see the roofs of houses and the spires of churches on the other shore.

"Take a look at what's ahead, but don't cringe." The driver gestured to a rusting iron cage at the side of the road. "If you're afraid, then Boston is no place for any of you!"

A black crow cawed, and its shadow fluttered over them.

"What is it?" Catherine peered across the road at the cage. "Good Lord!"

"It's an evil omen!" Lydia gasped.

As the horses brought the wagon closer, Hannah strained to see.

On the floor of the cage were the white bones of a skeleton!

"That skeleton was once a slave who ran away from his master," Isaac explained. "He was hanged and his bones remain here as a warning to others who might try the same thing."

Hannah felt weak and covered her eyes from the sight. As an indentured servant, she was not free to choose where she wanted to live or work. If she tried to run away . . . she peered back at the cage and shuddered.

Catherine sensed Hannah's horror. "There's nothing for you to fear, my dear," she said, patting Hannah's hand.

"As long as you don't try to run away," Miss Lydia added.

Hannah concentrated on the ring that glistened on her finger.

Isaac clicked the reins and the horses made their way down the hill to the waterfront. "Boston Town is almost an island. By land, folks can only enter through Boston Neck on the south-side. And over there they'd be greeted by a gallows. The town-born Tories of Boston don't want strangers comin' in and causin' trouble."

"I was born in Massachusetts, so I'm an American," Hannah objected.

"Yes, to be sure," Isaac agreed. "But in Boston there is bad blood between Tories, who support King George, and the Whigs who complain about the British taxes. The more taxes and soldiers King George sends, the more talk there is of rebellion. I pity the British soldiers that have been sent over here. They'll have a hard time in Boston Town."

"What about General Gage?" Catherine asked. "I've heard he has not been received well."

"They've written songs about him—and not a bit flatterin', to be sure." Isaac laughed. "I'd sing them to you, but they're not somethin' ladies should hear."

"General Gage is a kind gentleman," Miss Lydia protested. "He's fair and he's honest."

Isaac pulled on the reins, and the horses stopped at a wooden wharf that jutted out into the river. He climbed off the wagon and heaved the baggage to the ground. Hannah picked up her carpetbag and tucked the rest of the plum cake, along with Aunt Phoebe's bread, under her arm. She was about to slip Will's bouquet into a buttonhole on her vest, when Lydia snatched it. "The flowers are wilted. No sense in bringing them along." She tossed the bouquet onto the road and shoved Hannah toward the wharf. Hannah was about to object when she caught a warning glance from Catherine.

Isaac pointed to a gray wooden flatboat tied to the dock. "That boat will take you across."

He carried Catherine's and Lydia's baggage to the small vessel. "These women work for General Gage," he told a man with a sailor's cap. "See that they get a carriage to the Province House." Isaac turned to the women. "Here's where I leave you. God be with you." Then with a chuckle he added, "You'll need his protection if you're workin' for the general in Boston!"

Catherine and Hannah called their good-byes

and thanks to Isaac, and then Catherine and Lydia climbed into the long boat and settled on the plank that served as a seat. Hannah stepped aboard after them and sat on a bench in the bow. Miss Lydia took a purse from her pocket and handed some coins to the skipper who would be rowing them across the river. "General Gage himself is paying for our passage," she said, her nose pointed in the air. Hannah held back the powerful urge to mimic her, but was unable to suppress a giggle, which she muffled with her hand. When the woman gave her a contemptuous stare, Hannah gazed innocently at the church spires in the distance.

The man took the money and untied the boat. After adjusting the long oars, he began rowing to the opposite shore.

A welcome breeze stirred the water and cooled the August air. The sound of church bells drifted over the waves, and Hannah could smell the sea. Surely that peaceful, God-fearing town ahead could not be a dangerous place.

When they pulled up to the wharf, a boy ran out to grab the line that the skipper tossed to him.

Soon the women were bouncing over the

town's uneven cobblestone streets in a carriage. Carved signs identified the shops along the way. A large wooden fish hung outside a market; a plumed pen identified a calligrapher; a horseshoe hung over the door of a barn where a blacksmith was shoeing a bay mare.

On the peak of a stately building a shiny weather vane in the shape of a grasshopper glistened in the late afternoon sun. The town had many weather vanes, and Hannah found herself looking up to admire them. At Union Street they passed a grand brick building with a carved dragon sign and a matching dragon weather vane.

"That must be the Green Dragon Tavern," Catherine said. "I've heard rumors about that place."

Hannah caught sight of the street signs. A painted finger sign on the right pointed to King Street and Long Wharf. The carriage continued through the town past School Street, then paused at the entrance of a magnificent mansion. A wrought-iron gate was open, and stone walkways flanked by flowers wound through the lawns of the estate.

"The governor's house," Catherine whispered in awe.

As they passed the mansion, Hannah could see a courtyard and a garden of pink and white roses, deep blue larkspur, and yellow and spotted-orange lilies. The manor would have seemed welcoming had there not been guardhouses with redcoat soldiers posted at each entrance. The front of the mansion had a spacious porch and a balcony over which hung the royal coat of arms of King George III. Hannah could make out the words *Dieu et Mon Droit.*

"What do those words mean?" Hannah asked.

"They're French for 'God and my right,'" Catherine answered.

Miss Lydia spoke up. "God himself has given the king the right to rule the empire. So anyone who rebels against the king is rebelling against God."

The carriage turned up a side street to an alley that led behind the mansion. Hannah raised her eyes to the immense cupola, where a gilded weather vane adorned the roof. This one was in the likeness of an Indian with a bow and arrow.

Catherine leaned over to Hannah. "I've heard a

tale that one day at noon the Indian will shoot his arrow—and that that's when the British redcoat soldiers will leave."

"Maybe it will happen while we are here," Hannah replied. "I hope we see it!"

"Nonsense!" Miss Lydia said with a snort. She drew herself up in her seat. "That's rebel talk! Be careful of what you say."

The carriage passed another guardhouse and stopped between the rear of the manor and a long wooden building. The doors were open, and Hannah could smell horses and hay. *Horses!* She strained to see inside.

As the women climbed down from the wagon and the driver began removing their bags, Hannah ran to the stable door. She glanced back to where Lydia and Catherine were talking to another woman; then she darted boldly into the shadowy stable. Dozens of stalls lined both sides of a central dirt passage. She tiptoed farther into the building, treading softly and pausing at each stall. They were all empty! Where were the horses?

Suddenly she heard a neigh, followed by a snort. Peering out at Hannah from the opening of the farthest stall was a pale golden horse with a mane the color of corn silk. Was this a real horse? It looked like the foal of a unicorn, except that there was no horn protruding from its fine-boned head.

The horse snorted again and pulled back into the stall. Hesitantly, Hannah walked closer and peered inside. The horse circled the enclosure and then turned to watch her.

"Hello, beauty," Hannah whispered. "Come see me. Don't be afraid. You are a fairy creature, I'm sure!"

The horse sidled closer toward her. Hannah was about to reach out her hand when someone bellowed, "What are you doing in here?"

Hannah spun around. A tall, gangly boy was standing behind her, his hands on his hips and his dark eyes filled with anger.

"What are you doing in here?" the boy demanded again.

"I—I work here . . . in the house, I mean," Hannah stammered.

"Then you must be new. You are not allowed in the stables. The horses here are owned by His Majesty King George."

Without thinking, Hannah mimicked the boy's words. "'His Majesty King George' is in England."

The lad bristled. "Well, ain't you the sassy one. You'd better respect those of us who work for King George, or you'll be in trouble here."

Hannah nodded. "I'm sorry." She sighed. "But this horse is so handsome. And I *am* new here."

"Keep out of the stables!" The young man turned to walk away.

"Wait!" Hannah tried to explain. "I've never seen a horse like this."

"He's from Spain—a descendant of Queen Isabella's personal horses. Gabriel was a gift to General Gage." The boy's anger slowly faded. "What's your name?"

"Hannah Andrews."

The boy took off his hat, revealing his unruly brown hair. "My name's Caleb Gibbs."

"Could I come by now and then, just to visit Gabriel?"

"Not when the reg'lars are here," the boy answered.

"Who are the regulars?" Hannah asked.

"British soldiers—the redcoats," Caleb explained. "And don't come in when Joseph, the Gages' coachman, is here either. He reports everything that goes on."

"Where are the regulars and their horses now?"

"The chargers are out on the Common. The reg'lars put them through their paces there. In fact, with all the trouble here lately, some of the troops are camped right on the Common. There are fewer officers' horses in here lately, but this is where they're groomed and shod." He gestured to a section of the stable where blacksmith's tools hung on a stone wall alongside a fireplace. "The work horses that pull the carriages, they're at the other end of the stable, where the chaises and wagons are kept. That's where Joseph stays most of the time."

"Why isn't Gabriel out on the Common?"

"He's special. Like the Gages, he don't mix well with the common folk!" Caleb joked. "No, the real story is that this breed of horse shouldn't be out in the sun much. His eyes and skin are too delicate."

"Have you ridden him?"

"Of course not! I'd be whipped if I dared. Besides, he's a wild one. Anyone would be crazy to take a chance."

Hannah put her hand out to the horse, who watched her curiously.

"Don't touch him! He bites," Caleb warned.

"I'd like him to be my friend."

Caleb laughed. "Aye, and I'd like to sit on King George's throne."

Hannah reached to touch the horse's neck, but he snorted and moved away.

"Careful!" Caleb warned.

Hannah pulled her hand back but continued to hold it, palm outward, through the open top half of the stall door. The horse just tossed its head, as if shunning her.

"I warned you—" Caleb started to say.

"Whist! Hush!" Hannah whispered, keeping her hand outstretched. The horse eyed her curiously and whinnied nervously.

Hannah echoed Gabriel's neigh, then clicked her tongue. "Come to me, Gabriel. Good boy," she said softly, not moving her hand.

The stallion again tossed his head rebelliously.

"Come," Hannah whispered. "Come."

Gabriel took a step toward her, then hesitated.

Hannah imitated Gabriel's whinny once more. "Come, boy."

This time the horse came closer and cautiously stretched his creamy head toward her hand. Hannah did not move. Gabriel sniffed, then rubbed his soft pink nose against her palm.

"I've never seen the likes," Caleb whispered.

"Whist!" Hannah said. Slowly she turned her palm and gently stroked Gabriel's nose.

"Hannah!" Miss Lydia called. "Hannah!"

Startled, Gabriel backed away. "I've got to go," Hannah said.

"You can visit Gabriel when I'm around, but don't come when the soldiers are here. It's no place to be, let me tell. They're not in good humor lately."

"Thank you, Caleb. I'll be back, Gabriel." Hannah turned to leave, when Lydia appeared in the open door and stomped toward her.

"So this is where you are!" Before Hannah could say a word, Lydia grabbed her by the ear and pulled her out of the barn and into the courtyard. "Don't you *ever* go into that stable again! You'd better behave yourself, or I'll have you doing nothing but scrubbing pans!"

Hannah wanted to pull away, but Lydia had such a strong grip on her ear that she thought better of it. Caleb watched in alarm, his mouth open. Then Catherine, who was waiting in the courtyard, spoke up. "Miss Lydia, please. Hannah didn't know the rules."

Lydia let go of Hannah's ear and pushed her toward Catherine. "Here, she can be your responsibility, then. You'll have your hands full with this one!"

Catherine put her arm around Hannah's

shoulder and turned her toward an elderly, gray-haired woman who stood by a red-painted wooden door in the courtyard. "Mrs. Dudley, this is Hannah Andrews."

"Welcome to the Province House, Hannah. I'm Esther Dudley, the housekeeper." She smiled kindly. "You'll soon learn what's required of you, my child, but I'm sure you're tired from your long trip. Come along. I'll show you to your room." She led them through a huge kitchen that jutted out from the main house. At the end of a hallway, Hannah and Catherine followed the housekeeper up a narrow stairway to the third floor, where they were ushered into a room with two beds. "It's hot up here in the summer," Mrs. Dudley said as she opened a window behind each bed. "There, now you'll get a breeze in from the sea."

Hannah looked out the window and was happy to see that it overlooked the stables.

"Catherine, you and Hannah will share this bedchamber," Mrs. Dudley said.

Catherine placed her bag on a bed. "Thank you. This is a fine room."

"Please come to the kitchen after you have

rested for a while. We will need your help preparing supper for the family at candlelighting. There is fresh water in the pitchers for you to wash up." She pointed to the two plain white pitchers and washbasins on a stand. Mrs. Dudley went to the door. "After today you'll bring your own water up each night from the well in the courtyard."

Hannah placed her bag on the other bed, opened it, and removed a plain everyday dress and two extra pinafore aprons. Sadness flooded over her as she took out her one Sunday-go-meeting dress; her mother had used the handmade lace from her own wedding dress to trim the collar and sleeves. Then Hannah pulled out the dark-red woolen cloak that had been her mother's. It was hers now, and she would need it when winter came.

Hannah removed the dusty calico dress she was wearing, then washed her face and hands in water she poured into a bowl from one of the china pitchers. She felt Catherine's eyes on her and paused, pulling the dress around her again, trying to cover the deep scars on her body. "I am covered with the pox," she murmured.

"But you're alive, my dear," Catherine said,

turning away. "I had a son. Simon. He died from the pox, as did my husband."

"I'm so sorry, Catherine."

Catherine began emptying her own satchel and pulled out a small leather-bound book. "This book was my grandmother's. It came from England." Catherine opened the soft cover. Each parchment page held a pressed flower with a handwritten inscription beneath it. "It's the ancient language of flowers," she said. "A rare and lovely book."

"It is lovely," Hannah agreed. As Catherine turned a page, Hannah caught sight of dried lilies of the valley. "What do they mean?" she asked.

Catherine peered at the writing. "A return of happiness," she said. "Whoever gave you that bouquet today wants you to be happy again." Catherine placed the book in a drawer by her bed.

Hannah wondered if Will knew the language of flowers. Probably not, she decided. She placed the calico dress, along with her few other garments, on the wall pegs. Then she pulled out a plain linen shift with drawstring at the neckline and wrists. "What will I be doing here?" she asked, wondering what she should wear. "Miss

Lydia said I'd be doing pans in the kitchen."

"If so, I'm sure they will have an apron for you," Catherine said.

Hannah put a pinafore on over her shift, pinned a kerchief around her neck, and then pulled a white clout over her thick hair. "I'm ready," she said.

"You go on down to the kitchen, Hannah. I'll be there soon."

Hannah paused in the hall. The stairway she had climbed earlier was at the far end of the corridor. But she noticed another flight of stairs off to the left and decided to see where it would lead. She tiptoed down the winding stairs to the second floor.

Hannah stepped onto a multicolored hooked rug that stretched across the gleaming wood floor like a flowered pathway. She followed it to a large open hall. Crystal and brass chandeliers sparkled in the late afternoon sunlight that streamed through the tall windows. A wide stairway led to the floor below and circled to the cupola above.

On one wall was a large portrait of an exotically beautiful woman reclining on a brocaded chair. A similar painting of a fine-looking British officer hung on the opposite wall. Both portraits were encased in gilded frames.

Suddenly Hannah heard men's voices. Perhaps she should not be here! Where could she hide? Quickly she raced to a large reception room. Trembling, she hovered in a corner. After a time she peeked cautiously into the hall. Two men stood at the head of the stairs and spoke in low voices. One of them was dressed in a gold-braided jacket; Hannah recognized him as the officer in the portrait. He was shaking hands with a tall, lanky man who glanced nervously over his shoulder. As he turned in Hannah's direction, she pulled back into the shadows. The two men went into another room and closed the door.

"Who are you?"

Hannah spun around. A girl was staring defiantly at Hannah. "Obviously you are a servant."

"Yes, I—I am a servant here," Hannah stammered. "My name is Hannah Andrews."

"I've never seen you before."

"I arrived today. I'm on my way to the kitchen. But I've become lost."

"This is not the way to the kitchen," the girl

said. "Servants must use the back stairs. I'll show you." She led Hannah past the grand staircase and down the hall to the servants' stairway. As she guided Hannah, her white lawn dress made a soft fluttering noise and her golden ringlets bobbed. "I live here with General and Mrs. Gage."

"Are you their daughter?" Hannah asked, trying to keep up with her.

"No. My father is one of General Gage's officers. He is back in England now. My mother died a while ago, so the Gages took me in." The girl had green eyes, and her skin glowed like a pink rose petal. Hannah instinctively pulled a strand of hair from under her cap and arranged it over her cheek. "My brothers and sisters are living with relatives, but they couldn't—or wouldn't—take me in. I'm glad of that. It's much nicer to be living here in the governor's house." The girl went on in a boastful voice. "I'm practically a member of the Gage family, especially since the Gage children are all back in England. My name is really Margaret, like Mrs. Gage's, so to avoid confusion, I am called Meg." She stopped at the back stairwell and turned to Hannah. "This is the way to the kitchen." She stood back and looked Hannah up and down. "I think we are of the same age, or thereabouts," said Meg. "I'm fifteen."

"I am fourteen," Hannah said. "Soon to be fifteen."

"Perhaps we will be friends," said Meg. "But of course, you are a servant," she added hastily. She started to turn away, then said, "I'll see you at supper, if you will be serving."

"I don't know what Mrs. Dudley will want me to do."

Meg frowned slightly, and then her face lit up. "Perhaps . . ." But she didn't finish what she was about to say. Instead she nodded, turned on her heel, and marched away, her brocaded silk slippers pattering softly and the white satin sash of her dress swinging behind her.

Hannah hastened down the back stairs to the kitchen, where a short, stocky girl was washing vegetables in a slate sink.

Mrs. Dudley looked up from the large oak trestle table where she was sorting a stack of damask linens. "Ah, Hannah. This is Annie, one of our scullery maids." Annie nodded and wiped her nose with her sleeve. Mrs. Dudley piled napkins in Hannah's arms. "Take these into the dining room, please." She pointed to a door. "In there, my dear."

Hannah gasped as she entered the magnificent dining room. A life-size portrait of a solemn King George hung on a paneled wall above the fireplace mantel. Long, paned windows captured the summer sun as it glistened on the immense crystal chandeliers, each of which held dozens of white candles. There were twelve chairs at the mahogany table, on which lay porcelain dishes displaying the royal crest and silverware shimmering in a velvet-lined tray.

Hannah started to fold the napkins, then stopped. Did the napkin go on the left or right? Should it be folded in a special way?

At that moment Miss Lydia came into the room. "Fold those linens up prettily and neatly."

"I—I don't know . . ." Hannah stammered.

"You don't seem to know much," Miss Lydia said.

Mrs. Dudley entered the room with a basket of yellow and red roses. "She's been here only a few hours, Lydia. She'll learn." Miss Lydia sniffed and then disappeared into the kitchen.

"Thank you," Hannah whispered to Mrs. Dudley. "I don't know how to set a table this grand. We had a humble home, Mrs. Dudley."

"I understand," the housekeeper said. She arranged the bouquet in a china vase and then showed Hannah how to fold the napkins. Mrs. Dudley explained the order of the place settings as she set one place. "Forks, tines down, on the left of the plate. Knives to the right. Spoons lie horizontally above the plate. There, see?"

Hannah enjoyed setting the table with the beautiful silver. When she returned to the kitchen, several servants, including Catherine, were busy preparing various courses of vegetables and fruits.

"Come, Hannah," Catherine beckoned her. "You can help make the tarts." She slipped an apron over Hannah's head and fastened it at the back.

Hannah plucked stems from blueberries until her hands were stained with juice. Catherine rolled dough, filled the delicate pastries with berries, and then used a long-handled pan to place them in one of the ovens. The time passed quickly, and Hannah didn't realize how late it was until someone lit the kitchen's oil lamps and she heard laughter coming from the dining hall.

Mrs. Dudley clapped her hands and announced softly, "The governor's family and his guests are being seated. Be as quiet as possible."

Three servants took platters of stuffed capons, roasted ham, and baked fish into the dining room.

Hannah helped fill china bowls with summer squash and hot spinach with currants.

When things had quieted down and the family was eating, Hannah peeked through the door. She recognized the people at the head and foot of the table as the handsome man and woman in the portraits at the top of the stairway. The other guests she did not know, except for Meg, who was chatting coquettishly with a young British officer sitting next to her.

Hannah noticed a stylishly dressed Negro girl seated next to an older white lady who patted her hand in a maternal way. Most Negroes were servants, but this girl was being treated differently—as if she were royalty.

Miss Lydia tugged at Hannah's apron. "Don't be dawdling! Get to work!" she hissed.

"The dinner plates have been removed," Mrs. Dudley said. "Would you like to serve the tarts, Hannah?"

Hannah hesitated. Suppose she stumbled, or dropped them? She was relieved when Miss Lydia protested. "She should not serve! You said yourself, she has no experience."

"Thank you," Hannah said to Mrs. Dudley, "but I'm fearful I might drop something."

"First time I've heard anything sensible come from your mouth," Miss Lydia said with a nod.

Mrs. Dudley thought for a moment, and then said. "Walk behind me, Hannah. You carry the tray of tarts and I'll set them on the table for each guest." Mrs. Dudley untied Hannah's apron and tucked the hair that covered her pockmark under her clout. "There, you look fine."

Hannah wanted to pull the hair back over the flaw on her cheek, but she lowered her gaze and followed Mrs. Dudley into the dining room, carrying the platter of tarts.

Mrs. Dudley took a plate from the tray and placed it in front of Mrs. Gage. Hannah felt her hands shake as Mrs. Gage scrutinized her with dark, intense eyes.

"And who is this?" she asked.

"Madam, this is our new serving girl, Hannah Andrews," Mrs. Dudley said. "Hannah, this is your mistress, Mrs. Gage."

Hannah struggled with the heavy tray and

tried to curtsy, remembering Aunt Phoebe's orders. *Always curtsy when you meet someone— especially someone of importance.*

Mrs. Gage was about to speak when Meg interrupted. "Oh, Aunt Margaret, this girl is about my age, and I'm in desperate need of an upstairs maid."

"You don't need an upstairs maid," Mrs. Gage answered.

With Hannah following closely at her heels, Mrs. Dudley put a dish at each setting. Hannah, intent on the conversation between Mrs. Gage and Meg, didn't see Mrs. Dudley suddenly stop. *Crash!* Hannah bumped into the housekeeper and a plate fell from Mrs. Dudley's hands, clattering onto the table. Mrs. Dudley quickly retrieved the tart and the dish.

"I'm sorry," Hannah apologized.

"You see?" Meg exclaimed. "She should not be handling delicate china, but she would serve very nicely as my maid."

"Please discuss this at a later time," General Gage said.

Meg's face fell. "I'm so lonely for my brothers and sister, and my poor dead mother. I would so like to have someone my own age to . . . befriend."

General Gage's expression softened. "We shall find a companion for you. But certainly not a servant girl, Meg."

Hannah felt her face flush. If she had dared, she would have raised her nose in the air and mimicked his arrogant statement and scholarly English accent. *Certainly not a servant girl!*

"As the general said, we'll talk about this later in private." Mrs. Gage looked apologetically at her guests.

Once everyone was served, Hannah followed Mrs. Dudley back to the kitchen, where the servants were settling down for their supper. Catherine motioned for Hannah to join her at the table, which was already set with ham and fish and a large crock of beans.

Hannah settled in by Catherine, and Mrs. Dudley sat on the bench next to her. Caleb came in from the stable, smelling of horses. He sat at the other side of the table, next to the butler, who had introduced himself as Edward.

"Who is that young Negro girl seated at the dining table?" Hannah asked.

"Oh, that is Miss Phillis Wheatley," Edward said.

"The young woman is a famous poet," Mrs. Dudley explained. "Her verses are in demand both here and in London. She's talented and quite intelligent."

"I'm surprised that the Gages have condescended to have a Negro slave dining at the Province House," Sally, a young upstairs maid, said.

"She's no longer a slave. Mr. and Mrs. Wheatley have set her free," said Edward. "In fact, she is Mrs. Wheatley's protégé. When she was about seven years old, Mr. Wheatley purchased her from the slave market as a maid for his wife. It was only a matter of weeks before the Wheatleys discovered her amazing talents. Why, the child was already reading and writing in English, and within sixteen months she was reading Greek and Latin classics!"

"The Wheatleys encouraged her and sent her to London, where she had a book of poetry published," Mrs. Dudley added. "She was received like nobility in London."

There was silence at the table for a short while, and then Edward spoke up again. "When I was pouring wine in the dining room, I heard Miss Meg begging to have Hannah here as her personal maid."

"That girl is always after something—or *someone*," Caleb said with a wink at Edward.

Edward chuckled. "As long as he wears breeches!"

"From what I've seen, that spoiled child can wind the general around her little finger," Sally whispered.

"Mrs. Gage, on the other hand, does not approve of Miss Meg's dallying," Edward said.

"Whist! We shouldn't discuss the family," Mrs. Dudley warned as Miss Lydia entered the kitchen.

Mrs. Dudley got up to make a place for Miss Lydia. Hannah finished her meal without saying a word, and then climbed from the bench, careful not to touch Miss Lydia, who ate ravenously and seemed, for once, oblivious of her.

"You can help clear the dining table, Hannah," said Mrs. Dudley, handing her a tray.

The family and guests had moved into the great drawing room on the opposite side of the house. As Hannah did her work she could hear laughter and loud voices.

"Usually the women go into the parlor together, but tonight everyone will be hearing Miss Wheatley recite her poetry." Mrs. Dudley led Hannah to the center hallway. "You can listen quietly from here for a short while, dear." She took the tray from Hannah and went back to the kitchen.

In the drawing room the guests took their seats, and Mrs. Gage introduced the pretty poet, who stood with her head bowed.

"We are blessed to have dear Phillis Wheatley here in our midst," Mrs. Gage said with a gracious gesture to the small young woman. "She will recite her poem 'On Being Brought from Africa to America,' which she has read for the nobility of London. You will, perhaps, understand through this poetic work how what seemed to be an abduction from her birthplace was truly a release from pagan worship and a revelation of Christian salvation."

Miss Wheatley nodded her head, smiled briefly, and then, clasping both hands to her breast, she spoke in a clear, soft voice:

'Twas mercy brought me from my Pagan land,
Taught my benighted soul to understand
That there's a God, that there's a Saviour too:
Once I redemption neither sought nor knew.
Some view our sable race with scornful eye.
"Their colour is a diabolic die."
Remember, Christians, Negros black as Cain
May be refin'd and join th'angelic train.

Miss Wheatley curtsied as the guests applauded. Mrs. Wheatley smiled benevolently at the gathered crowd and then motioned for Phillis to sit next to her.

At this point General Gage made a toast. "God bless our beloved sovereign, and our motherland."

"And may the rabble-rousers in Boston learn to be loyal subjects," added the young officer who had been sitting next to Meg, "or all hang from their Liberty Tree!"

"Aye, Lieutenant Pratt!" The others applauded and laughed—except for General Gage, who looked more troubled than amused. Someone then began to sing "Yankee Doodle," the song that made fun of the Americans, and before long everyone in the party joined in.

Caleb slipped into the hall and stood next to Hannah. "Redcoats! Cowards!" he whispered in Hannah's ear.

"This is shameful!" she whispered back. "'Hang the rabble-rousers'? How dare they speak so rudely of American colonists?"

"They forget that we are British subjects just as they are. They want our taxes and our loyalty, yet they don't treat us equally." Caleb pulled Hannah into the empty dining room. "Tomorrow night, at North Square, there will be a different type of entertainment. Would you like to come with me?"

"I don't know."

"You're American-born, aren't you? And from Massachusetts Colony?" When Hannah nodded, Caleb continued. "Then it's your right to know what's going on in Boston."

Hannah had already heard about the unfair taxes, the infamous Tea Party, and the Boston Massacre, and she knew that Boston Harbor was under siege. British warships and merchant ships were forbidden to land to bring in provisions, yet the colonists were receiving ample food and supplies from secret sources outside the city. What more could be happening in Boston? Did she dare go with Caleb to find out?

"Meet me at the stable tomorrow night after you're finished with work," Caleb coaxed.

Hannah hesitated. "I don't know if I'm allowed to leave."

"No one needs to know," Caleb said.

"What about Joseph? Won't he see us?"

"He stays in the carriage house at night, unless he's driving the Gages somewhere. He won't notice us leave."

Hannah looked toward the parlor where the guests were milling about. Yes, she decided. She would try to go with Caleb tomorrow night. But when she turned to accept his invitation, he was gone.

Hannah undressed and collapsed onto the bed before Catherine was finished in the kitchen. It was still light outside, and the room was hot. Through the open window Hannah could hear the whinny of a horse in the stable below.

She fell into a deep sleep, and in her dreams she was riding Promise through the fields in

Salem. Will was there too, waving her on.

When Catherine tiptoed into the room late that night, Hannah woke briefly. Realizing sadly where she really was, she gathered her pillow in her arms and returned to dreams of Promise, the meadows, and the wind through her hair.

When the morning sun drifted across her pillow, Hannah awoke. Catherine had dressed quietly and was already gone from the room. Hannah pulled her pinafore on over her nightclothes, picked up the heavy white water pitcher, and trotted down the servants' stairway to the back of the house to get fresh water. The aroma of newly burning fires drifted from the kitchen as she passed by.

Hannah stepped out into the courtyard, held the pitcher under the spigot, pumped the handle, and then shrieked as the icy water splashed over her hands and onto her feet. From the stable came a shrill whinny. Hannah set the pitcher down near the well, and peeked inside the barn. It was empty except for Gabriel, who tossed his golden head and looked out at her from the stall.

"Are you mimicking me, you naughty boy?" Hannah called. The horse whinnied again.

Hannah looked around for Caleb, and after glancing over her shoulder for any sign of Miss Lydia or Joseph, she cautiously made her way to Gabriel's stall.

"You are so fine-looking," she whispered to the pale golden horse. "I would love to ride you, but I've heard you're a wild one."

The horse snorted and tossed his head, then backed away, all the while keeping his gaze on Hannah.

"Don't you ever go out to the Common like the other horses?" she said with a frown. "Oh fie! Fie on General Gage for leaving you here like this. You need exercise. You'd be much happier running free in the fields than in this dark place."

"And who are you to be voicing your opinions about the care of my horse? A soldier? A horseman?"

Hannah whirled around to face General Gage,

who was dressed in riding gear and boots, a whip in his hand.

Hannah gasped. "Oh! I—I didn't know anyone was here! I . . ."

"What are you doing in here?"

"I came in to see your horse. He's handsome."

"Yes, he is," the General agreed curtly.

Hannah looked down and shuffled her bare feet. "Sir, I am sorry that you overheard my concerns. You see, I had a horse once, but he was sold when my mama died. His name is Promise. I miss him."

General Gage said nothing.

"I . . . thought your horse might be lonely, like me."

The General stared at Hannah for a long moment. Then he said, "I do not allow him to graze with other horses. He must be kept separate and disciplined, for his own good."

"Like servants and masters, I suppose," Hannah said. "Oh!" She put her hand to her mouth, wishing the words back.

General Gage's brows furrowed, and Hannah could see his fingers tighten on the whip.

What had she done? How could she speak to the governor of Massachusetts Colony with such brash, foolhardy words? "Please forgive me, sir," she begged. "Sometimes words come out of my mouth before I think." Slowly she backed away toward the door of the barn.

"Stay where you are!" General Gage ordered. "I have not dismissed you."

Hannah stopped, took a breath, and tried to compose herself.

The General tapped the whip against his thigh. "I have a daughter your age in England." He looked down at Hannah's bare feet. "Who indentured you?"

"My aunt Phoebe. For seven years."

"Why did she send you away?"

"For riding a horse." Hannah's voice trembled.

General Gage raised his eyebrows. "Seven years of indentured service seems like a harsh punishment for riding a horse. Do you ride well?"

Hannah nodded.

"'Tis a favorable thing for a young woman to have the ability to ride."

"Hannah!" crowed a shrill voice. Miss Lydia stood in the doorway, her fists on her hips. "I warned you about sneaking into the stable!" The woman gave a simpering smile at General Gage. "Please accept my apologies, Governor. This minx has disobeyed my orders—again." She stomped over to Hannah. "Get into the kitchen! I'll deal with you there," she said, dragging Hannah by her ear.

"Ow!" Hannah yelped.

"Here, here!" General Gage exclaimed. "This girl is just a child."

"Yes, sir." Miss Lydia let go of Hannah's ear, then muttered under her breath, "And a wicked child she is."

"I am *not* wicked," Hannah said defiantly.

"Whist! Don't you speak another word," Miss Lydia warned. Grabbing hold of the neck of Hannah's nightdress, the woman pulled her back toward the kitchen.

Hannah turned once to see General Gage, still grasping his whip, watching from the stable. She would not let these people treat her like this! She would run away the first chance she had!

Once inside the kitchen, Lydia let go of Hannah's nightdress and shoved her into a corner. "You little wretch! Putting me in a bad light with General Gage. I told you not to go into that stable, and you disobeyed!" She stood back, and her mouth wrinkled into a cruel smile. "Well, I'll fix you. From now on you'll work in the scullery and do the pans with Annie. Just as I promised!"

Hannah stood stiffly in front of Lydia, sorely tempted to pummel the woman with her fists. Instead she put her mind toward planning ways to escape from the Province House and her servitude there.

Miss Lydia looked down at Hannah's nightclothes and bare feet. "Get dressed and come back here quickly!" She shoved Hannah toward the stairway. "Shame on you, running around like this. It's a wonder General Gage didn't flog you!"

Hannah raced up the stairs to the servants' quarters and dashed into her room. She threw herself onto her bed and pulled a quilt around her. It was soft and comforting, like her mother's arms. "Mama," she whispered through her sobs.

Mama had always said, *God is nearer than we think, and he answers prayers.*

Hannah sat up and bowed her head. "Our Father in Heaven," she began, "I am truly sorry for being disobedient and going into the stable. I just wanted to have a friend."

"Hannah." Catherine stood in the doorway. "Miss Lydia sent me to find you. You must go to Mrs. Gage's chamber right away. She has asked to see you."

Hannah jumped up from the bed. "Catherine, I'm going to be punished. Maybe I'll be flogged!" She flew to the door. "I'm going to run away!"

Catherine reached out and caught Hannah by her sleeve. "Oh, Hannah, you'll surely be pursued if you run away. I was there when Mrs. Gage asked for you. She didn't seem angry. She just asked where you were."

"You don't understand. I disobeyed Miss Lydia. I went to visit Gabriel—General Gage's horse. General Gage himself discovered me there."

"We'll go to Mrs. Gage together." Catherine held up Hannah's work dress and apron. "You must get dressed first. Hurry now." She pulled Hannah's pinafore and nightdress over her head and handed her her clothes.

Hannah dressed and continued to pray in an undertone. "Please, God, don't let them whip me. I will be obedient—until I can run away."

"Whist!" Catherine warned. "Better to purge those thoughts out of your head, Hannah."

Once Hannah was clothed and her clout set on her tangled hair, she nervously followed Catherine down the steps to Mrs. Gage's chamber on the second floor.

Miss Lydia, who stood by the door, glared at Hannah. "Get in there!" She spoke in a hushed yet threatening voice. "You've kept Mrs. Gage waiting long enough. She's no doubt heard from the general how you've been lurking about in the stable." Hannah cringed as she passed the woman.

"Excuse me, Miss Lydia," Catherine said, following Hannah.

Miss Lydia frowned at Catherine. "Mrs. Gage did not summon *you*."

"I promised Hannah I'd stay with her," Catherine objected.

Hannah turned to see Miss Lydia's face tighten into a threatening glare. "Never mind, Catherine," Hannah said. "I'll be all right." She held her head high and entered the room. Mrs. Gage was seated at a table, writing on a sheet of fine stationery.

"Here you are, Hannah," Mrs. Gage said, setting down her plumed pen. Hannah curtsied. "It seems you've been quite busy this morning."

Hannah nodded and looked down, waiting to hear her punishment. It didn't matter much anymore. She would still run away as soon as she had the chance.

"Miss Meg has requested to have you become her personal maid," Mrs. Gage explained. "My husband and I have decided that this might be appropriate. How would you feel about that, Hannah?"

Hannah was so taken by surprise that she couldn't speak.

A smile played on Mrs. Gage's lips. "General Gage thinks you will be happier waiting upon Miss Meg than working for Miss Lydia."

"Oh, yes, madam! I mean, I would be very happy to work for Miss Meg," Hannah sputtered.

Mrs. Gage leaned forward in the chair. "Miss Meg is a dear child, almost like my own daughter. She has been through much pain this year. We trust that you will help her in every way you can—with the hope of her becoming a happy child again."

"I'll try my best, madam." Meg certainly seemed happy as she flirted and pranced around the mansion giving orders and making plans, Hannah thought. But when she wanted something from the Gages, Hannah could see how Meg played on their sympathy to get what she wanted.

Mrs. Gage smiled. "Indeed. I will have Mrs. Dudley find suitable frocks for you." She eyed Hannah's work clothes. "When you have changed, you may go upstairs to Miss Meg's room. She'll be waiting for you."

"Thank you, madam."

Mrs. Gage turned back to her writing, shielding the words with her hand. "Oh, and Hannah," she added, setting her pen down again, "there may be times when I shall talk with you privately about Miss Meg's needs and her ... er ... state of mind."

Hannah was about to leave, when Mrs. Gage continued. "It will be best if Miss Meg is unaware of our concern. Do you understand?"

"Yes, madam. I understand." Hannah didn't really understand, but it didn't matter to her as long as she wouldn't be working for Miss Lydia anymore.

Hannah curtsied and turned to leave the room, when she suddenly noticed a tall chest-on-chest of fine mahogany, with drawer pulls of burnished brass, standing against the wall. There was something familiar about the piece.

"Is there something else, Hannah?" Mrs. Gage asked, looking up from her writing.

"No, madam." Hannah answered. "It's just this chest. I think it was built by my father."

"General Gage brought that tallboy from Danvers. It's a favorite of his."

"My father sold many fine pieces of his work in Danvers."

"Is there some way to tell if this is his work?" Mrs. Gage asked.

"If this is my father's, there should be a secret drawer."

"A secret drawer?" Mrs. Gage stood up and walked to the chest. "Show me."

Hannah opened one of the top drawers and placed her hand inside. She felt a latch. "It *is* my father's work!" she exclaimed, pushing the latch. "See?"

Mrs. Gage peered into the drawer. "There's a false back to this drawer," she said. "And a secret cache! How clever! Your father was a gifted craftsman."

"He was that, madam," Hannah answered. "A truly remarkable craftsman."

"Thank you for showing me this, Hannah," Mrs. Gage said with a smile.

Hannah was relieved and happy as she headed back to the kitchen. Seeing her father's tallboy chest made her feel as if Papa were nearby, watching over her. And she wasn't going to be punished for being with Gabriel and speaking out of turn. Best of all, she would never have to answer to Miss Lydia again! God had heard her prayers!

m eg was waving to someone from her window, and she looked up in alarm when Hannah entered the room. Then she clapped her hands in delight. "I knew Uncle Thomas would let me have you for my chambermaid!"

Hannah stood before Meg in her new striped dress and heavily starched apron. She smiled weakly, unsure how to behave with Meg, who was now her mistress.

Meg looked Hannah over, turning her around by the shoulder. "I see they have given you presentable clothes," she said approvingly.

Hannah was delighted with the four new dresses Mrs. Dudley had given her. They were far more fashionable than her own homespun clothes. Her apron and cap still indicated her position as a maid in the household, however. Even with her new clothes, Hannah felt plain in comparison to Meg, who wore a soft white cotton dress dotted with pink rosebuds. Her tiny waist was pulled in tight by a corset, as was the style of the day. The bodice had sleeves that came below the elbows and were trimmed in lace. A rose-colored satin ribbon at her waist matched the one that was woven into her blond curls. Hannah blushed at the startlingly low neckline. Having been brought up a Puritan, she would never wear anything so revealing, herself. Meg was beautiful, Hannah thought, absently pulling the lock of hair that covered her pockmark.

"Now that you're my chambermaid, Hannah, you'll help me dress, and you'll clean my rooms." She gestured at the small drawing room and bedroom that made up her suite. "And you'll bathe me and fix my hair." Meg pointed to the washbowl and pitcher on the washstand. "I do need this water removed and replaced. Right away."

Dutifully, Hannah emptied the washbowl into the pitcher. The water sloshed on her shoes and apron.

"Be careful!" Meg exclaimed. "You're spilling it!"

Hannah carried the heavy pitcher downstairs and into the courtyard. She emptied it into a trough that carried away wastewater into an underground cistern. She was rinsing the pitcher at the well when Caleb came out of the stable and approached her. He looked cautiously around the courtyard. "Are you still going with me tonight? There's going to be a shadow play." He leaned closer and whispered, "But there's more to it than just amusement."

"I'm now Miss Meg's chambermaid. I don't know if I can get away."

Caleb looked disappointed. "If you can, meet me here just after candlelighting."

"How can we leave? There are guards every-where."

"We're not prisoners," Caleb answered. "Many servants go out in the evening." He took the pitcher from Hannah and began pumping the handle of the well.

"I'm not sure if Miss Meg will . . ."

Caleb laughed, then said in a whisper, "Miss Meg has her own engagements in the evening, as you'll soon find out." The water began gushing out from the well, and Caleb filled the pitcher, then handed it to Hannah. "Remember," he said as he headed back to the stable, "right after candle-lighting."

Hannah carried the pitcher back to Meg's room, wondering what Caleb meant about her "engagements."

"Good!" Meg said with a dazzling smile when Hannah returned. "What a fine time we will have together." She patted the chair next to her. "Sit here and I will tell you about my plans."

Hannah placed the water on the stand, then sat down while Meg chatted.

"We will go out on carriage rides through the town. Uncle Thomas doesn't like the idea of my riding alone, even though there's a footman and a driver. He worries because the local 'factions,' as he calls the rabble-rousers here in Boston, often throw stones at carriages that have the royal crest. You know that the common folk are stirring up trouble, don't you?"

"I've heard about it," Hannah said.

"They don't want to recognize the authority of King George. There's talk about rebellion."

"Will it be safe to go out in the carriage?" Hannah asked.

"We'll use a smaller carriage that has no emblem." Meg stood up. "We can dine out on the Common."

"I've heard the Common is full of soldiers."

"Of course! That will make it all the more enjoyable." Meg beamed. "You'll be more than my chambermaid, Hannah: You'll be my lady-in-waiting, and I'll be just like the queen! However, I need to be sure that you will respect my wishes—and my privacy."

Hannah suddenly remembered her promise to inform Mrs. Gage about Meg. She looked away. "I . . . I shall do my best."

Meg didn't notice Hannah's hesitancy. "Are you sad about leaving Miss Lydia?" she asked.

Hannah was uncertain how to answer until she saw the merriment in Meg's green eyes. "I will miss her greatly, especially her beautiful voice."

"Her beautiful voice?"

"'You little wretch!'" Hannah squealed in a high-pitched nasal tone. "'I'll fix you. You'll work in the scullery and do the pans with Annie!'"

Meg looked stunned, then burst out laughing so hard she flopped back into her chair. "That's a perfect imitation!" she gasped.

Hannah smiled. "It's the one talent I have."

"You do have an unusual ability," she agreed. "Perhaps we will use your gift for our own ... er ... *amusement* sometime."

H annah was busy that afternoon, helping Meg in and out of several lovely gowns, some of which belonged to Mrs. Gage herself.

"Aunt Margaret is planning a ball this weekend, and I must choose what to wear," she explained to Hannah. "I have no new gowns, and there's nowhere to buy a decent one here in Boston. I'd have a gown made, but fabrics aren't being shipped in because of the embargo. Aunt Margaret has loaned me some of her ball gowns, although they may need minor alterations."

"This green silk looks best on you. The color matches your eyes," Hannah said, wishing Meg would be satisfied with the choice.

"It does," Meg agreed, turning around and around before the mirror.

"I've been told that General and Mrs. Gage have many balls and entertainments," Hannah said.

"That's true. Uncle Thomas arranges entertainments to keep our officers occupied and away from the commoners."

By candlelighting, Hannah's hope to go to the shadow play with Caleb had almost vanished. But surprisingly, Meg suddenly dismissed her. "I won't need you any longer tonight," she said. "It's supper time and I shall be busy all evening. You can sup with the servants and then do whatever you wish."

"Thank you, Miss Meg," Hannah said with a curtsy. Perhaps it wasn't too late to meet Caleb.

Hannah scurried down to the courtyard, where Caleb was sitting on the edge of the well wall. "Ah, Hannah, I was just about to go by myself. Come on," he said, getting up. He led her toward the guardhouse at the entrance to the Province House.

"I haven't had time to eat," Hannah complained.

"I took this from the kitchen." Caleb handed her a cloth packet.

Hannah opened it to find a slice of ham and bread, which she ate greedily.

When they approached the guardhouse, a red-coat soldier was standing on watch. "Where are you going, Caleb?" he asked.

"To visit friends," Caleb answered. "Hannah here is going with me tonight."

"Hannah? I've never met this girl."

"I work here at the Province House," Hannah explained.

"How old are you?" the soldier asked.

"She's Miss Meg Montcrieffe's chambermaid," Caleb said quickly.

"How old is she?" The soldier repeated. "I can tell she's too young to be leaving the Province House after candlelighting. I don't want to be responsible."

"Hannah's sixteen," Caleb argued.

"If she's sixteen, I'm Methuselah." The soldier turned to Hannah. "Go back, miss. I'll not be the one to let you out in a town that's closed down because of possible riots."

"You go on anyway, Caleb," Hannah suggested, turning back.

"No," Caleb whispered, following her. "If you were a boy, you'd be allowed to leave." He pulled

Hannah by the hand and led her back toward the stable. "Come with me. We'll dress you like a boy."

"A boy! I don't look like a boy!" Hannah protested. "Besides, what if I get caught?"

"You'll be with me, and no one in Boston's going to bother *me*," Caleb bragged, lighting an oil lantern. "You'll be as safe as baby Moses in his basket." He led her to an empty stall. "Wait in here while I get some clothes."

Hannah huddled in the dark and waited. She held her breath as she heard a horse and carriage go by, heading to the carriage house at the back of the property. Perhaps she should go back up to her room. Besides, Catherine might get worried and set up an alarm.

But before she could move, Caleb was back with clothes and the lantern. "Here, put these on," he said, thrusting the clothing into her arms.

"I heard a carriage go by," she told him.

"Someone was returning to the mansion," he said. "They're near the alley, way down behind us. Trust me." Caleb placed the lantern on a shelf behind the door of the stall. "Hurry. I'll wait outside."

"What about my new dress and apron?"

"Hang them on the hook. You can change again when we get back."

Caleb waited outside the stall while Hannah struggled out of her apron and dress. She pulled on the rough pants, shirt, and waistcoat that Caleb brought, which smelled of horses and hay. She hung up her own clothes and covered them with a blanket to hide them.

This shadow play of Caleb's had better be worth the chance I'm taking, she thought. Still, the shiver of excitement she felt was similar to the sensation she always had when riding a horse full gallop and heading for a jump over a hedge or wall. "I'm ready," she whispered.

Caleb came into the stall and helped Hannah tie her shoulder-length hair into a pigtail with a piece of twine. Then he set a tricorn hat upon her head. He stood back and squinted in the light of the lantern. "You'll pass for a boy," he assured her. "Let's go." He spit into the lantern to extinguish the flame, then set the lamp on the blacksmith's bench.

"What if the soldier recognizes me?" Hannah asked.

"He won't. He has more important things on his mind than a couple of boys going out."

"Who goes there?" the soldier called out as the two friends walked by the guardhouse.

"Just going for a walk with my cousin . . . Hans," Caleb said. "We'll be back before curfew."

The young redcoat soldier peered out the door at Caleb and Hannah. He frowned. "Do I know Hans? Where are you from, lad?"

Hannah swallowed, took a breath, and answered in a deep voice. "I'm out of Salem, sir."

"Salem, is it? They're a bunch of rebels out in Salem," the soldier mumbled. "General Gage had to get out of there for fear of his life!"

"I resent that, sir," Hannah snapped in her male voice. "We're Loyalists to the grave."

"Go ahead," said the soldier waving them on. "But watch out for those troublemakers. And be back before curfew."

"Aye, we will," Caleb said, pulling Hannah by the sleeve.

Once they were out of earshot, Caleb burst out laughing. "Where did you find that voice, Cousin Hans?"

"I keep it in my pocket for such occasions," Hannah told him. "It comes in handy now and then. What time is the curfew?"

"Eleven o'clock for those who work here at the Province House."

"*Now* you tell me this? Caleb, it's bad enough that I've come out under the pretense of being a boy. What happens if we don't get back in time?"

"Don't worry so much. I promise we'll be fine."

Hannah was tempted to go back, but Caleb seemed cheerful and sure of himself, so she decided to trust him. They walked down King Street to North Square and stopped at a house that was dimly lit. "The shadow play may have already started," Caleb said. He knocked on the door, and it was opened by a stocky man who ushered them in. "We're just beginning, Caleb," he whispered. "Who's this lad?"

"My cousin Hans." Caleb nudged Hannah. "This is Mr. Paul Revere." Hannah nodded.

The man stepped aside. "Come in."

"Must I pretend to be a boy here?" Hannah whispered when they were out of Mr. Revere's hearing.

"Of course. Otherwise everyone will wonder why a girl is dressed like a boy," Caleb whispered. "We don't want to call attention to ourselves."

Men and women, seated on chairs and benches, filled the great room. Children knelt on the floor. A muslin sheet was stretched across one end of the room, lit from behind by several lanterns. Since all the seats were taken, Caleb and Hannah sat on the floor near the back. Hannah stole a quick look at the strangers that crowded the room.

"That's Sarah Revere," Caleb whispered, gesturing to a dark-haired girl who seemed a little older than Hannah. She was holding a child in her lap that Hannah suspected was her sister. "Their mother died a few months ago," Caleb explained. Next he pointed to a tall man with a high forehead and dark eyes, who stood near the window. "Over there's Dr. Joseph Warren. He's a wondrous speaker and patriot."

A man standing with Dr. Warren had a vacant expression, as if he were preoccupied. There was something familiar about him.

"Who's that?" Hannah asked.

"Dr. Benjamin Church. He's a patriot who also speaks up for the rights of colonists." Caleb leaned his face close to Hannah's. "He's one of the Sons of Liberty."

"How do you know that?" Hannah asked, knowing full well that the Sons of Liberty were a special association of patriots. Each member was given a silver medallion that had the words *Sons of Liberty* and the Liberty Tree engraved on it.

"I know," Caleb assured her.

Hannah peered over at the man again. Where had she seen him before? She tried to remember, but her thoughts were interrupted when Mr. Revere spoke up from the front of the room. "We are ready now!" he called out.

The lanterns in the room were dimmed, and the lights behind the muslin drape brightened. Shadows appeared on the sheet.

Two clear silhouettes pranced onto the white muslin. One puppet was obviously a British soldier, for although the distinctive red coat could not be seen in the shadow play, the familiar cocked hat perched high on his head was cleverly accentuated. He brandished a sword and called out, "Halt! Who goes there? Before you pass, you must pay a tax."

The other figure, wearing the tricornered hat of a colonist, answered, "Hi, ho, fiddle-dee-dee. No taxes will you get from me!"

Several people in the audience clapped their hands.

"You must take me home and keep me quartered," the soldier went on.

"Not around my wife and daughter!" exclaimed the colonist. Everyone roared with laughter.

Hannah recalled Will telling her about the quartering act. She was beginning to understand more clearly the demands and restrictions placed upon Bostonians by the king. She was American but she was also a British subject. Aunt Phoebe was a Loyalist and rigid in her beliefs. She wondered what her father and mother's allegiance would have been and where her own loyalties should lie.

The colonist puppet began to sing, and the audience joined in the popular street ballad "The Rallying of the Tea Party":

Rally, Mohawks—bring out your axes!
And tell King George we'll pay no taxes
On his foreign tea.
Our Warren's there, and bold Revere,
With hands to do and words to cheer
For liberty and laws!

Hannah's attention turned again to the gentle-man in the back of the room. She was positive she had seen him somewhere. Then her eyes fell upon a woman sitting not far from him.

Catherine!

H annah turned away. Had Catherine seen her?

When the shadow play was over, Hannah pulled Caleb to the door. "We'd better get back before curfew or we'll be in trouble," she warned him. She took a quick glance to where Catherine had been, but she was already gone.

"How did you like the shadow play?" Caleb asked her as they walked along the dark streets.

"It was amusing," Hannah said. "I didn't realize how much bitterness there is among American-born patriots."

"*America* is our country," Caleb said. "Not England."

"But George the Third is our king," Hannah protested. "He has the right to rule."

"Only because of his birth. Not by his heart or his deeds," Caleb argued.

Hannah didn't answer. Back in Salem it had never mattered to her who was king, or what England did, or where her own sense of duty lay.

Across the street they heard footsteps and low voices. Three men passed by and turned the corner onto Union Street. In the light of a street lantern Hannah recognized Paul Revere, Dr. Warren, and Dr. Church.

"They're heading for the Long Room Club in Dassett Alley. The most important members of the Whigs meet there to discuss—"

"Rebellion?" Hannah said.

"The rights of our people," he answered.

"How do you know?"

Caleb was silent for a moment and then answered. "I've been there. You must promise never to tell anyone." He touched her arm.

"I promise," she answered.

It was half past ten when Hannah and Caleb boldly passed the guard at the entrance of the mansion. Caleb swung his arm around Hannah's shoulder, and the two of them sang "God Save the King" in a loud, jolly manner, like two young men who had had a few too many beers. Then, after quickly changing her clothes in the stable, Hannah said good night to Caleb and raced across the courtyard to the kitchen door.

When Hannah reached her room, she noticed a crack of light from beneath the closed door. Quietly she turned the knob and tiptoed in. A candle cast a soft glow across Catherine's bed, where she appeared to be sleeping, although she was still dressed and on top of the quilt.

Suddenly Catherine sat up. "Hannah! Thank the dear Lord. I've been so worried! I tried to stay awake, waiting for you. But I must have fallen off to sleep."

Hannah felt she could trust Catherine, and she decided to confess where she had been. After all, Catherine had been at Mr. Revere's house too. "I'm sorry you were worried," she said. "I went out to the shadow play at a Mr. Revere's house. We just got back."

Catherine's face paled. "You were... where?"

Hannah reached out for Catherine's hand.

"I saw you there, Catherine. But you wouldn't have recognized me. I was in disguise. The guard wouldn't let me leave as a girl, so I dressed as a boy. I went with Caleb."

Catherine didn't speak for a long moment. Then she said, "No, I didn't see either of you. Of course, it was dark." She sighed. "I went to visit an old and dear friend. I haven't seen him in several years. Tonight we met at Mr. Revere's house for dinner. I stayed for a short while but left by the rear door before the shadow play was finished. I was fearful that I might be seen leaving there."

"It was a good thing to see your friend," Hannah said.

"Yes, it was. He is very dedicated to the cause of freedom, even though he is known as a Tory." She squeezed Hannah's hand. "I trust we will keep our mutual visit in confidence, my dear."

"Of course, Catherine," Hannah promised.

Catherine looked relieved. "I was worried about you when I came back and found you gone. You said that you were going to run away, and that's all I could think about—that you'd actually broken your bond! I didn't dare ask anyone if they'd seen you, for fear they'd send out an alarm." She shook her head. "Oh, my dear, you mustn't do this again. You could be punished severely if you don't keep the curfew or if you are found in the house of Paul Revere! Thank the Lord you were not discovered tonight."

Hannah pulled away. "You frighten me, Catherine."

"Boston is a dangerous place. Don't get involved with the political elements here and you'll be safe, Hannah. Remember, while you are a bound girl living here you *must* keep your opinions to yourself." Catherine lay back on her pillow. "Do you understand?"

"Yes, I understand."

When she finally climbed into bed, unfamiliar night sounds surrounded her: Catherine's even breathing, the scampering of a mouse within the walls, and the clatter of a horse's hooves on the cobbled street. Hannah wondered about Promise and Will. Were they well? Did they miss her as much as she missed them?

the next morning Catherine bent over Hannah's bed and shook her gently. "It's almost dawn, Hannah. I'm going to work now."

"I'm so tired," Hannah said.

"Don't fall back to sleep and be late," Catherine admonished. "You don't want Meg to become angry."

"I'll bring her breakfast to her room. She'll like that."

When Hannah arrived at Meg's room with a tray of fruit, rolls, and tea, she was surprised to see that her mistress was already up and dressed.

"Oh, how delightful!" Meg sat by the window and Hannah placed the tray in her lap. "I have plans for today. We're going to have that outing on the Common."

"An outing?"

"Yes. Go down to the kitchen right away and have them prepare a little feast for us." Meg put her finger to her cheek. "Let me see. We'll need meat, cheese, ale, bread . . . some sweet cakes . . ."

Hannah headed for the door when Meg called after her.

"Tell the cook to have it ready by ten—and to make enough for three."

"Three?"

"You heard me correctly," Meg said, biting into a roll.

"Miss Meg, what if someone asks who the lunch is for? What shall I say?"

"Simply say I'm ravenously hungry! Oh, and tell Caleb to have an unmarked carriage and driver ready by ten as well."

Downstairs, Mrs. Dudley was drinking tea at the servants' table. "Sit down, Hannah. You haven't eaten yet, have you?"

Hannah slipped onto the bench and poured herself a cup of tea. "Miss Meg is planning a little feast on the Common today." She listed the food that Meg had ordered.

Mrs. Dudley frowned. "Does Mrs. Gage know about this 'little feast'?"

"I don't know," Hannah answered truthfully.

"Are you going with her? The Gages have been concerned about her safety, what with the anti-British feelings here in Boston."

"Yes, I'll be with her." Hannah took a sweet roll from a dish and bit into it.

"Well, maybe it will be all right, then. Miss Meg has complained that she feels like a prisoner in this place. Now that you're with her, perhaps some of the rules have been lifted."

"Oh, and Miss Meg requested enough food for three people." A flash of suspicion came over the housekeeper's face. "She said she's ravenously hungry," Hannah added quickly. She stuffed the remainder of the roll in her mouth, grabbed two apples from a bowl, and left. "We'll be leaving around ten," she called behind her.

Caleb was cautiously cleaning out Gabriel's stall when Hannah peeked in. Caleb had placed a bale of hay between him and the golden horse.

"Hello, Gabriel," Hannah said, holding out one of the apples. "Come see what I've brought you." The horse looked at her and nickered softly. Hannah clicked her tongue several times and then sang as she did for Promise: "La, la la, pretty horse. Come have an apple, sweet boy."

Caleb watched nervously as Gabriel went to Hannah and took the apple gently from her open hand. Hannah petted the horse's muzzle as he chewed the fruit.

"You have a special way with horses," Caleb told her. "No one else, not even the general, can stroke his nose like that."

Hannah turned to Caleb. "Miss Meg needs a chaise by ten o'clock."

"I need to ask Mrs. Gage's permission," Caleb answered. "She doesn't want Miss Meg going off without a guard."

"Well, the driver and I will be there." Hannah hadn't realized so many questions would be asked about a simple jaunt to the Common.

"I'll have it ready, but only with Mrs. Gage's approval." Caleb came out of the stall and closed the door behind him.

"She doesn't want a carriage with a crest," Hannah said, leaving the barn.

. . .

Meg was brushing her hair when Hannah returned. "Did you give everyone my orders?"

"I did. Caleb wanted to get Mrs. Gage's approval for the carriage."

Meg whirled around from the mirror, her face flushed. "How dare he? I'm not going off alone! Did you tell him not to report to Aunt Margaret?"

"I said the driver and I would be there."

Meg rolled her eyes and heaved a disgusted sigh. She pointed toward a cage by the window in which a tiny yellow bird perched. "I feel like that bird. I have no freedom."

"I'm sure everything will be fine," Hannah said soothingly.

By ten o'clock a carriage with two horses had pulled up to the rear door of the mansion. "Aunt Margaret must have given her approval." Meg smiled in satisfaction as she climbed into the enclosed chaise. The front of the passenger seat was open, but the sides shielded their faces from any curious eyes.

"Joseph is driving," Hannah observed. Perhaps Mrs. Gage was keeping an eye on Meg after all.

"So I notice," said Meg coolly.

Joseph placed the food basket on the back of the chaise while Hannah petted the two horses. "What are their names?" Hannah asked as she fed one horse the other apple from her pocket.

"Mary and Martha," Joseph answered. "Martha is a busybody. The one you're feeding is Mary, and she's a bit lazy. But when they're hitched up together, they get along just fine."

"Come on, Hannah!" Meg called impatiently. "I don't want to be late."

Late for what? Hannah wondered. She scratched Martha's head, then climbed into the carriage. Joseph clicked the reins, and the horses clomped down the brick driveway and into the street. Hannah could see Caleb watching from the stable, shaking his head. What was the problem? Why was everyone concerned that they were going out?

The grasses of the Common were turning a russet gold in the late summer weather. In the distance Hannah could see tents; General Gage had ordered troops to be camped on the field to establish a strong British military presence in Boston. The waters of the Charles River sparkled under the blue sky.

"It's a right glorious day," Hannah said as they neared a grove of large shady trees.

"Stop here!" Meg called out to Joseph. "This is a perfect little place."

Soon Meg and Hannah were sitting on a rug that Joseph had spread out for them. He set the food basket down and then climbed back into the chaise again.

"Come back in an hour or two," Meg told him.

Joseph looked unsure. "Mrs. Gage doesn't want you to be alone, Miss Meg."

"I'm not alone. Hannah is with me. Besides, soldiers are all around us. They'll protect us."

"And who's to protect you from the soldiers?" Joseph retorted.

Meg stood up, "I said, come back later!"

"I shall water the horses and then be back," he told them as he turned the horses away. Hannah felt sorry for him. She knew he could be in trouble with the Gages for leaving them alone.

Meg looked around as if searching for someone. Then she sat down on the rug. "Open the basket, Hannah, and spread out the food."

Hannah was laying out the small china plates

when a tall British officer appeared from the elm
trees. He was leading an unusual, rust-colored
horse with a perfect white crescent on its forehead. "Ah, you came as you promised." He tied the
horse to a tree, and then sat down next to Meg.

Although he whispered, Hannah could hear
every word. She felt her face redden as the officer
held Meg's hand to his cheek. "My Meg," he said.
He kissed her hand.

The soldier took off his hat, and his straight
brown hair slipped over his forehead. He looked
over at Hannah with icy blue eyes. "Who is this?"

"This is Hannah, my chambermaid," Meg
answered. "I rescued her from Miss Lydia."

Hannah recognized the soldier as the handsome young Lieutenant Pratt whom Meg had been
flirting with at dinner on Hannah's first night at
the Province House. "Good morning, sir." She busied herself dividing the bread, cheese, and thick
hunks of ham into lunches for three.

"Hannah has a talent that amuses me," Meg
said. "She can mimic anyone."

Hannah shrugged and continued sorting the
food onto china plates.

"Let her amuse me, then," said Lieutenant Pratt. "Show me your unusual talent, miss."

Hannah could feel her anger rise. Was she to perform like a trained monkey? Without looking up she aped the officer's haughty British accent. "'Let her amuse me, then. Show me your unusual talent, miss!'"

For a moment there was silence. Then the lieutenant said scathingly, "How *dare* you insult me."

"'How *dare* you insult me!'" Hannah exclaimed in a perfect imitation of the officer.

The lieutenant jumped up, grasped Hannah's collar, and pulled her to her feet. She faced his angry eyes. Alarmed, Meg yanked his hand away from Hannah and began to laugh. "Chester! She's only doing what we asked. You must admit she captured your resonant and commanding voice perfectly. Surely you can see the humor. She's a delightful and amusing servant."

"Certainly I see the humor," Lieutenant Pratt said with a forced smile. "And now perhaps your 'amusing servant' will take her food elsewhere. We have things to discuss that servants should not hear."

Hannah did not like this man's cold arrogance, and it was all she could do to refrain from imitating him again. She gathered her skirt around her and walked away, leaving her uneaten food behind.

So this is what Meg had in mind—a tryst with that British officer. Meg was only fifteen. How could she steal off like this? And how could she make Hannah perform like a household pet? She had a mind to stomp all the way back to the Province House, but that would cause more talk, and Meg would certainly send her back to work for Miss Lydia. No, she'd wait a while and then go back to Meg. Hopefully Lieutenant Pratt would be gone by then.

She crossed the field, where horses, cows, and sheep were grazing together. She climbed onto a large boulder and leaned back. The sun had warmed the stone, making it a peaceful place. She closed her eyes and listened to the distant beating of a drum—a signal to the troops on the Common, no doubt.

She realized she had dozed off for a while when she heard voices and the clomping of

horses' hooves. Looking up, she saw two horsemen galloping toward her. One of the riders
looked like Caleb. She squinted against the sun. It
was Caleb. The other rider was on a sleek horse, as
black as pitch, its coat shining. Was she still
dreaming?

The rider's sun-streaked hair flew back from
his face. Why . . . could it be?

Yes! It was Will—and her Promise!

"Will! Caleb!" Hannah stood on the boulder, waving her hands. "Promise!" The black horse came to a stop, and then reared. As Hannah raced toward them, Promise pulled against the reins, snorted, then trotted to Hannah.

"There she is!" Will yelled with a laugh. "Promise recognized your voice!"

Promise stopped next to Hannah and was nudging her arm and nickering. "There's my beauty," Hannah whispered as she threw her arms around the horse's neck.

"I went to the Province House to find you," Will said, dismounting. "I was sure you'd already be known at the stables, so that's where I went first. Your friend Caleb here said you were on the Common and that he'd take me to you."

Hannah turned to Will and was about to embrace him, but then pulled back, embarrassed. Instead she thrust her foot up into the stirrup and flung herself astride the saddle. "I've been waiting for this day to come so I could ride my Promise again."

Will laughed. "It's been less than a week since you left Salem, Hannah."

"It feels like a hundred years!" Hannah flipped the reins and Promise picked up his ears. He trotted into the field, then hesitated, waiting for Hannah's directions. When they approached a wide clearing of grass that led to the river, she tucked her skirt around her legs as well as she could and called, "Giddap, Promise!" The horse leaped forward, his legs stretching into a long gait as if his hooves were not touching the ground at all.

Hannah's clout flew off and her hair swept back like Promise's dark mane. A redcoat backed away in alarm as they galloped by him and then down to the riverside. It was as if Promise remembered their days running with Papa along the Merrimack River—or through the willows by the sea in Salem. Hannah's view became blurred as tears welled up in her eyes. "Take me up to the clouds, Promise!" she called. "Let's leap right off the earth!"

Once they had splashed for a while in the water, Hannah turned the horse back. Will was waiting, and she needed to talk to him to find out how long he'd be staying in Boston. As they drew near to the boys, she pulled on the reins and Promise slipped into a smooth trot.

"You ride like a man!" Caleb said, his voice full of admiration.

Hannah looked at him scornfully. "Is that a compliment? Not all men ride well."

Caleb corrected himself. "You ride better than most men."

Hannah smiled and slid off Promise's back. "How long will you be in Boston, Will?" she asked as she stroked the horse's long sweaty neck.

"I came as a courier for the Whigs in Salem." Will had retrieved Hannah's clout and handed it to her.

She set it atop her wind-blown hair, then put her arm around Promise, who leaned against her. "Why? What is happening in Salem?"

Will looked uncomfortable and his eyes went to Caleb. "You know how things are nowadays with the trouble between the British and Americans." He shifted from one foot to the other.

Caleb frowned. "If you are a friend of the Crown, say so. If you are striving for liberty, then say so."

"I . . . I'm . . ." Will looked at Hannah uncertainly. Then he said, "I am American-born, and I long for liberty."

"As do I," Caleb said, putting out his hand. Will grasped it firmly.

Will turned back to Hannah and said apologetically, "I can only stay a few days, Hannah, unless I find employment."

"Say no more," Caleb told him. "You can stay with me at the stables until you find work. If anyone asks, I'll say you are my cousin." He looked at Hannah and laughed.

"Caleb has another cousin named Hans," Hannah said in her male voice.

"Oh, I can see that Hannah has been up to her tricks!" Will said, grinning.

Hannah shielded the sun from her face and peered toward the grove of elm trees. "I must get back to my royal mistress. She may be looking for me."

"We passed poor Joseph up the street," Caleb told her. "He was watering the horses and worrying about Miss Meg. Mrs. Gage ordered him to stay nearby."

"She's being well attended by a tall, sniggering, simpleton lieutenant." Hannah mimicked the lieutenant's high-pitched British accent: "'We have things to say that *servants* should not hear.'" The boys laughed. Even Promise whinnied and tossed his head.

"Come into the stable later tonight, Hannah," Caleb said, still laughing. "We'll meet there."

Hannah kissed her horse's cheek. "I cannot wait to ride him again," she said as Promise nestled against her shoulder. "I want him to take me far away from here."

"They'd find you if you ran away," Caleb reminded her.

"Aye, perhaps. Good-bye for now, my Promise," Hannah said. "You've been good to him, Will, and I thank you for that."

Will and Caleb mounted the horses and headed away.

Hannah walked toward the elm grove where she had last seen Meg and her lieutenant. "Miss Meg?" she called hesitantly.

"Over here," Meg answered. She and Lieutenant Pratt were reclining on the rug. Meg leaned against the officer, who was whispering in her ear. He gave Hannah a scornful look when she approached. He said something again to Meg, who laughed and pushed him away playfully.

Hannah felt a rush of anger and was about to stomp off, but then decided to take the food she'd left behind earlier.

"What are you doing?" Lieutenant Pratt asked as Hannah bundled up the meat and cheese in a napkin.

"I haven't eaten, and this is mine."

"Your chambermaid doesn't know her place," the young man complained to Meg.

"It's quite all right, Chester," Meg said. "Hannah, do stay and eat, for Joseph will be here soon." She patted the lieutenant's arm. "I prefer to give Joseph very little to report about me to Aunt Margaret. I don't want a long list of questions from her when I return."

Chester Pratt pursed his mouth into a pout. "Very well, I'll leave, but sadly." He stood up. "I'll see you again..."

Meg put a finger to her lips. "Whist." A look passed between Meg and Chester that was not lost on Hannah.

The lieutenant untied his horse and hoisted himself into the saddle. Hannah looked again at his unusual mount. The horse's rusty coat was almost blood-red in the afternoon sun. Its only other color was the white of the "stockings" on its hind legs and the half-moon on its forehead. Hannah could not help but admire the horse's smooth, high-stepped gait as Lieutenant Pratt clicked the reins and the horse trotted away.

In the carriage on the way back to the Province House, Meg asked quietly, "Who were the young horsemen I saw you with?"

"I beg your pardon?"

"Chester and I took a walk along the promenade, and we saw you with two young men," Meg said in a teasing tone. "We all have little secrets, don't we?"

"I don't have any little secrets, Miss Meg,"

Hannah retorted hotly. "The young men you saw were only Caleb and his cousin."

Meg put her fingers up to her mouth concealing a coquettish smile. "Oh, Hannah, you don't fool me."

Hannah could feel her face flush. Evidently, Meg had not seen her riding Promise. "Truly, Miss Meg. Caleb was only taking a jaunt through the park and happened to see me there."

"No need to make excuses, Hannah. I won't tell a soul." She folded her hands and said sweetly. "Aunt Margaret wouldn't like it one little bit if she knew you had left me all alone on the Common while you dallied about with the stable boys."

"You and your friend ordered me to leave!" Hannah retorted.

"I'm willing to forget the whole incident. We don't want Aunt Margaret to be upset, do we?"

Hannah closed her eyes and turned away. Now she understood! She was not to tell Mrs. Gage about Meg's meeting with Lieutenant Pratt. If she did, Meg would turn everything around and blame it all on Hannah.

fortunately for both Hannah and Meg there were no questions when they returned to the Province House. Hannah told Catherine what had transpired on the Common. "Be on guard with that devious girl," Catherine warned. "She'd stop at nothing to have her own way, including lying about you."

At candlelighting Hannah was relieved to be dismissed by Meg, who said, "Aunt Margaret and I will be dining at Mrs. Wheatley's this evening." As soon as their carriage left, Hannah rushed to Catherine.

"I'm going with the boys to ride Promise," she said.

"Be careful, Hannah," Catherine replied with a worried frown.

Caleb was waiting with a lantern. "Will is upstairs," he told her.

"Where is Promise?" Hannah asked, looking around.

"In a stable in Valley Acres, this side of Beacon Hill." He led Hannah through the corridor of stalls. "As winter approaches, these stalls will soon be full," Caleb explained.

Gabriel peered out at them suspiciously and snorted at the shadows the lantern created as they walked by.

"It's all right, boy," Hannah told the horse. Several other horses were now housed in the large barn, and they whinnied in response to Hannah's voice. Caleb held the light high as they climbed the rough wooden steps to his quarters. At the top was a narrow room the length of the barn. Will, who had been lying on a cot, jumped up. "Hannah!" he exclaimed. "Tell me about Boston! How fortunate you are to be living here!"

"I'd rather be anywhere else," Hannah said, "and be free."

Will sank back onto the cot. "I spoke without thinking."

Caleb pulled a chair up for Hannah and then sat on a pile of hay. In the lantern light Hannah told Will about her servitude to Miss Lydia.

"She sounds like your aunt Phoebe!" Will exclaimed.

"And now I'm serving Miss Meg, who warned me she might tell Mrs. Gage that I was dallying with the stable boys."

"That Meg is a minx," Caleb said.

"I feel I'm stuck in a pickle barrel!" Hannah said. "But tell me why you're here, Will."

"I'm working for the Committees of Correspondence of Salem and Boston," Will explained. "We're keeping close watch on the movements of British officers and troops, and on their dealings with American Whigs."

"The British want us to stay dependent on them by punishing us with their Coercive Acts," Caleb added. "We call them the Intolerable Acts, 'cause we ain't gonna tolerate them!"

"What are the Intolerable Acts about?" asked Hannah.

"They're new rules that were put in place after

the Tea Party to bully Americans into submission," Will said.

"They closed the Port of Boston," Caleb interrupted. "They locked us up in our own town!"

"All thanks to your General Gage, I might add," said Will.

"*My* General Gage?" Hannah responded. "He's no friend of mine."

"He did save your neck from Miss Lydia," Caleb reminded her.

"That's true," Hannah admitted.

"He wants to keep the 'inferior people'—as he calls us ordinary folk—from meeting together and making our own laws," Will said belligerently. "According to the king and his Parliament way off in London, we 'inferiors' aren't allowed to have any say in the government.

"So we can no longer have town meetings, except by permission from General Gage. Town meetings are important because that's where anyone can speak his mind. When Gage heard that we had a town meeting planned in Salem this week, he sent soldiers to close it down." Will laughed.

"But we just locked them out and ignored all their hollering and banging at the doors."

"What did the troops do?" Hannah asked, thinking of all the families she knew in Salem that might have been in danger.

"They scratched their heads and marched away!" Will said, still laughing.

"From what I've heard around the stables, the general feels the real problem ain't the common folk," Caleb objected, "but the colonial bigwigs, like John Hancock and Sam Adams and Dr. Warren. Gage would love to get his hands on *them,* 'cause they stir up the common folk with their speeches."

"Most of the folks back in Salem want the British to leave so we can have our town meetings and make our own rules," Will said.

"I don't know why the British treat us like this," Hannah said. "We're British too."

"They're afraid we Americans will rebel," Caleb answered. "England had no concern for us until their treasury got low. Then they taxed us unfairly and put us under laws that take away our freedom."

Hannah bristled. "Then Americans are indentured servants, just as I am."

Caleb nodded. "Aye, we're all indentured to England."

The three friends were silent for several moments, their faces illuminated by the flickering lantern.

Then Will continued. "Once I turned sixteen this week, the Patriots in Salem asked me to become a courier between Salem and Danvers and the Sons of Liberty in Boston. If I can get work here in Boston, I'll find out a lot that's going on."

"Will, do you have other references from Salem that could get you a trade here in town?" Caleb asked. "Something from a merchant that can show you're a good worker? Then I'm sure I can get you employment somewhere."

"I have papers to get me engaged by Tories if need be. I can work for either side, and you can be sure my ears and eyes will be open to everything."

Hannah held out apples that she had brought from the kitchen on her way, and she bit into one. "Enough talk about Tories and Whigs. I want to ride Promise."

"Now?" Will asked.

"Please? Just a little ride along the streets where there's lamplight."

"It's getting late," Caleb said, "and you know the trouble you had going out the other night."

Hannah eyed some familiar clothes hanging on a peg. "Yes, I know. But no one will pay a bit of attention to Cousin Hans."

Disguised once again as Cousin Hans, Hannah accompanied Caleb and Will through the gate with only a brief check by the guard. As horsemen and pedestrians passed by, Hannah asked Will, "Do I look like a boy?"

"Not to me," he answered. "I know you too well."

Hannah felt a rush of relief. She didn't want Will to see her as a boy.

Caleb pointed to the lanterns that lined the street. "Mr. Revere was in charge of getting these lights put up in town," he told them.

"Makes a person feel safer to see who might be coming after him," Will said with a laugh.

They headed up Marlborough Street to

Cornhill and then over to Valley Acres, where Promise was stabled.

When they entered the barn, a stable boy who had been sleeping on a bed of hay jumped up and raised the wick on the dim lantern. "Will you be riding?"

"Go back to sleep. We'll saddle the horse ourselves," Will told him, taking the lantern. The boy gratefully climbed onto the hay again and pulled a blanket over himself.

Upon seeing Hannah, Promise neighed and circled his stall several times. "He's not sure it's me in this disguise," Hannah said. "Here my boy," Hannah said, offering him the last apple from her pocket. "I saved this for you." Promise put his head through the top half of the door and took the apple. "Ah, now you know me," Hannah said. Once inside the stall she rubbed the horse's muzzle and ears.

Will and Hannah saddled the horse quickly, and Hannah's heart beat fast as she mounted him.

"Don't get lost!" Caleb called out.

"And don't take long!" Will shouted after her. "I'm tired after this long day."

"We'll be back soon," Hannah assured him. "Within the hour."

Promise's ears went back as Hannah guided him onto the pasture and over the hill, past the beacon. A windmill turned in the breeze, and Promise skittered nervously. "It's all right, Promise," Hannah said soothingly. "We're together again, and everything will be fine."

They ambled down a street where a band of men were gathered under a streetlamp, speaking in low, angry voices.

"Now Gage has replaced all our judges with his own," one man was saying. "And rather than have a trial here in Boston, he's sending those he calls guilty to Britain for judgment."

"How can we get fair trials with this kind of nonsense?"

"I'm a lawyer and a Whig. I'm not representing anyone in front of Gage's judges. That's my stand!" the third man said irately, pounding his fist into his other hand with a *smack*.

Promise sidestepped and then began to run. "Whoa!" Hannah cried out.

"Slow down!" one of the men called out to her.

"Is that a girl riding that horse?" another man asked.

Hannah gasped. She had spoken in her own voice. "Giddap!" she called, this time as a boy. Promise leaped from a canter into a gallop.

"Hey, you. Stop!" yelled the lawyer. "Don't run a horse in the street like that! Someone could get hurt!"

Hannah headed Promise down a side street toward the harbor and pulled the reins until he slowed to a walk. Promise seemed calmer now and content to be with Hannah again. "Such a good boy," she said. "You know it's me on your back, don't you? She changed to her masculine voice and spoke softly. "You'll need to be familiar with this voice too, if we're going to ride together when I'm disguised."

An easterly breeze carried the sound of splashing waves. "Hear the sea?" she asked. "Just like Salem." They had approached a wharf that extended far out into the harbor. "This must be Long Wharf," Hannah said to Promise. "Shall we go have a look?"

Promise pulled his head forward, tugging at

the reins, and headed down the thick wooden planks. After passing rows of sheds and buildings, they came to a length of wharf where she could see soldiers standing in groups, talking quietly. Dozens of longboats silhouetted on the water were being maneuvered up to the dock and secured to its massive posts.

This is a strange time of night for so much activity on the waterfront, Hannah thought. Caleb had told her that the Boston waterfront was guarded now; no one could come or leave without permission of the governor.

Suddenly a soldier looked up. "Who goes there?" he yelled.

Hannah was startled, and Promise, who sensed her alarm, whinnied and lurched uncertainly. "Friend!" Hannah answered in her male voice.

"A messenger?" The soldier came closer.

"No."

"Who are you? You are not allowed here."

When Hannah didn't answer, another soldier approached. "Someone should be posted at the head of the wharf. No one is permitted down here tonight."

As the soldiers came closer, Hannah felt trapped and instinctively snapped the reins. With a sudden bound and a loud clattering of his hooves, Promise darted back to the street.

"Stop that rider!"

But Promise, with Hannah bent low over his neck, was already galloping down a dark road, away from the streetlights. Though the way was unfamiliar, in a short while they were back on Cornhill. "We escaped!" Hannah exclaimed as they headed slowly and cautiously toward the stable at Valley Acres.

"I saw a dozen or more longboats lined up at Long Wharf," Hannah told the boys as she removed Promise's saddle. "It must be a secret mission, because the soldiers took after me and then posted guards at the head of the wharf."

"I wonder what they're up to," Will said.

"Whatever it is, we'll find out soon," Caleb answered. "Nothing is a secret for long in this town."

Hannah rubbed the sweat from her horse with

a fleece. "Thank you for whisking me away from those soldiers, Promise. What a fine, clever horse to take me into a dark street where we could disappear from their sight!" Promise nickered at her shoulder. "You love me, don't you, my sweet boy." She patted his neck. "I will see you again soon."

When Hannah and the boys returned to the Province House, the soldier peered out from the guardhouse. "Who goes?" he called.

"Just me, Caleb, and my cousins," Caleb answered.

"You'll need to get back here earlier from now on," the soldier said, "and your cousins may need permission to be inside the gates at all. General Gage is becoming more concerned about spies. There will soon be even more precautions taken as to who's coming and going."

"Something big is going on," Caleb whispered when they were inside the stable.

Catherine was in her bed, her breathing even, when Hannah returned to their room. She slipped quietly into bed and was soon asleep herself. But her slumber was disturbed by many dreams. She was on

Promise and racing . . . somewhere. Suddenly Promise turned into a bird, and they were flying over the river and into the clouds. One white cloud turned into a beautiful golden horse: Gabriel!

There were soldiers marching with rhythmic footsteps in her dream. Or was it a dream? Hannah sat up in bed suddenly, then climbed on her knees to peer out the open window. She could see nothing in the darkness, but the sounds of marching troops indicated soldiers were nearby. She could tell they were coming down School Street behind the Province House and heading up Cornhill.

"What's happening?" Catherine asked sleepily. "Are you all right, Hannah?"

"I hear soldiers marching," Hannah answered.

"They may be on maneuvers." Catherine yawned. "Did you visit Promise?"

"Yes. I was able to ride him again. I'm glad you didn't wait up for me." Hannah fluffed her pillow and settled herself once more. "I wonder if those troops are heading to Long Wharf. There were soldiers and longboats out there when I passed by on horseback."

"General Gage seemed preoccupied tonight at supper. And his staff were unusually quiet and tense."

Hannah closed her eyes and listened to the sound of marching feet.

t he next morning Hannah helped Meg dress. "I was so disappointed at Mrs. Wheatley's last night. It was utterly boring listening to those long, arduous poems by Miss Phillis. She's always asked to perform—like a trained puppy," Meg said with a pout. "I was hoping my lieutenant would be invited—and perhaps he was—but he never showed up. There seems to be some military action afoot."

"We'll soon find out," Hannah said. Then, quoting Caleb, she added, "Nothing is a secret for long in this town."

Meg gave Hannah a warning look. "I do hope that's not true. *We* have a few secrets we want kept, don't we?" She began brushing her hair.

Hannah opened the curtains. Then she took

Meg's water pitcher down the stairs and out to the trough, where she emptied it and rinsed it in the water from the well. There was more than the usual activity in the stables. A few soldiers were saddling their mounts and talking to one another. She recalled her own joyful ride on Promise the night before. Maybe she'd ride again tonight!

Her thoughts were cut short as a horse and chaise came rattling around to the back of the house. The driver, in British uniform, jumped off. "Caleb!" he called as the boy came out of the stable. "Come tend to this horse. Colonel Maddison is meeting with General Gage and it may be some time before he leaves." The driver removed his gloves and went into the mansion.

Caleb beckoned to Hannah with a quick tilt of his head, then led the horse to a hitching post. Hannah went over to him. "I've been hearing the reg'lars talking," he told her in a quiet voice. "Some Tory reported to General Gage that the local folks beyond Charlestown have been stealing the gunpowder from the powder house over on Quarry Hill and hiding it." Caleb pulled a rag from his pocket and began wiping down the horse.

"So before dawn this morning Colonel Maddison's troops rowed up the Mystic River in those long-boats you saw last night at Long Wharf. They raided the powder house and took two hundred and fifty half barrels along with cannons out to Castle William in the harbor!"

Hannah gasped. "Why? That powder belongs to the people, doesn't it?"

"It's all in how you look at it, I reckon," Caleb said. "The local towns and the British stored munitions in there. Lately the townspeople were pulling out their own munitions, but they never touched what belonged to the British. However, the British weren't so decent. They took everything."

Hannah was beginning to understand why the American Whigs were concerned about ways to defend themselves while people loyal to the king, the Tories, conspired against them.

Hannah and Caleb were interrupted by a group of soldiers. "Who's this lassie?" a redcoat with a Scottish accent asked. "Your sweetheart, Caleb?"

Another young soldier took Hannah's left hand and pointed to her mother's wedding ring. "No, it's his wife!"

Hannah blushed. "That's my mother's ring!" She raced back to the well, gathered the pitcher into her arms, and ran back to Meg's room.

Meg had gone down to breakfast, so Hannah straightened the bed and dusted. When she finished with her morning duties, she wandered out into the hall, where the rest of the family's sleeping quarters were situated. Meg had to be finished eating by now, but she was nowhere in sight. As Hannah approached General Gage's private office near the head of the grand stairway, she could hear laughter and loud voices coming from inside. Curious, she moved closer to the door.

"A perfect maneuver." General Gage was speaking. "We removed the powder and the cannons right from under their noses. Congratulations, Colonel Maddison, on a mission well done."

"Thank you, sir. To think the Yankees slept through the whole thing!" A loud guffaw. Hannah assumed it was the Colonel.

A third man piped up. "The disappearance of the powder and artillery pieces should add a new verse to 'Yankee Doodle.'"

Again General Gage spoke. "Serves them right

for pilfering the powder. King George should be happy that we outwitted them. Our next move will be the reserves in Worcester."

Suddenly, to Hannah's horror, she heard soldiers' heavy footsteps racing up the stairs from the lower floor. If she attempted to run back to Meg's room, she would be seen in the hall. She slipped into the reception hall across from the general's office and tried to disappear into the shadows.

But the two uniformed men who dashed up the stairs never cast a glance in her direction. Instead they pounded on the office door. "General Gage, sir!" one of them called. "We have urgent news!"

"Enter!"

The soldiers went in, leaving the door ajar. "There are twenty thousand men marching on Boston. The Americans are outraged that we've emptied the powder house, sir," one of the men said breathlessly. "They're saying you've robbed the province."

"Those bushmen!" General Gage snapped. "They're too daft to realize my concern is to keep the peace!"

The second soldier spoke. "Rumors are

spreading, sir, that war has begun and that six people have already been killed! They believe that King George's ships are bombing Boston!"

"That kind of dangerous talk must be stopped before there *is* a war," General Gage exclaimed. "Get my staff in here! I'm closing this town. Order all Boston inhabitants to surrender their weapons!"

The two officers raced out of the office and down the stairs. The door slammed behind them. Hannah emerged cautiously from the reception room. Seeing no one, she darted back down the main corridor that led to Meg's chamber.

Meg was standing by the window with her little bird perched on her finger. "Where have you been?" she asked.

Hannah gestured to the neat room. "After I finished here I went ... out to the privy," she lied.

"Something very strange is going on," Meg said. "There are many soldiers about. And lots of whispering."

"Really?" Hannah asked innocently.

"Church bells are tolling constantly. Don't you hear them?" Meg petted the bird as it pecked lightly on her lip.

"I didn't notice," Hannah answered. She was sweeping up seeds from under the birdcage when Miss Lydia knocked on the open door. "Miss Meg, you must go to Mrs. Gage's room right away. It's urgent."

"What is so urgent?" Meg asked.

"There's trouble brewing with the Massachusetts people, and Mrs. Gage is quite concerned. She'll tell you about it." Miss Lydia walked away with a swish of her skirts.

Meg placed the bird back in its cage, and then turned to Hannah. "Didn't I say something strange was going on? Come with me."

Hannah followed Meg to Mrs. Gage's chambers. When Meg entered the large sumptuous room, Mrs. Gage was at her desk. Hannah waited in the doorway.

"Come in, Meg," Margaret Gage said, standing up. "You, too, Hannah. You both need to hear this." The expression on her face was anxious and a little sad. "There's been a disturbance in the province. The people are . . . displeased . . . that the British soldiers have taken the powder and artillery at the Quarry Hill powder house. General Gage was trying to prevent any dangerous uprising by removing the weapons this morning. Apparently, it has only made the situation worse. The general has surrounded the town and waterfront with cannons and soldiers. No one can come or go without passing through guards on the Neck, which is the only entrance by land."

Meg's face paled. "Are we being attacked?"

"No. At least not yet. The Whigs have tried to calm the people, but the country folk have already mustered an enormous army. We have only a few thousand British regulars stationed here in the town to protect us." Mrs. Gage sighed. "Boston is a dangerous place for you to be, Meg. We may need to send you to England for your own safety."

"To England?" Meg frowned. "When?"

"I don't know yet. But until this rebellion has subsided, you and Hannah must not leave the Province House." Mrs. Gage went to the window and looked out. "It hurts me to know how much the Americans hate the British." When she turned back to the girls, Hannah could see tears in her eyes. "I am an American. But I'm British, too. I seem to be caught between two fires."

Meg and Hannah went back to Meg's room. "I wish I had never left New York, where I lived with my family. Life was pleasant there . . . until I lost my mother."

"My mother died this past spring," Hannah said quietly.

"Oh . . . I didn't realize that." Meg went to the bird and tapped the cage with her fingers. "Poor little bird," she purred. "You and I are prisoners here, aren't we?" Meg watched Hannah for a long moment. "We are each prisoners in our own way, Hannah," she said.

Hannah was taken aback by Meg's show of empathy. Was she sincere? It was hard to tell. But despite herself, Hannah did feel a surge of warmth toward Meg.

Meg took the bird out of the cage again and set it on her arm. She looked at Hannah. "It seems now that I won't be able to see Lieutenant Pratt."

"You see Lieutenant Pratt right here in the Province House when the Gages entertain."

"Yes, but that's only on occasion," Meg answered. "Besides, it's not the same with people all around. If only there were a way to get out of here."

"That would be far too dangerous, wouldn't it?" Hannah asked, although she was already wondering the same thing.

"I'll find a way," Meg said.

And so will I, thought Hannah.

"I have good news," Will told Hannah in the barn that night. "Caleb found me work with Mr. Hubbard, the cooper."

"What do you know about making barrels?" Hannah asked.

"You don't understand, Hannah," Will said. "Mr. Hubbard is a member of the Boston Committee of Correspondence. I'll be free to come and go to Salem and the other towns by working as his apprentice."

"How? The town is closed," Hannah said.

"Mr. Hubbard is a prominent and necessary merchant. He and those who work for him are sure to have permission to come and go. General Gage knows he can't keep *everyone* from selling or buying products out of town. We'd all starve without farm products and other supplies. And barrels are needed by every merchant and farm."

"Mr. Hubbard is on the side of liberty," Caleb agreed.

"Excellent! And what about Promise?" Hannah asked. "Will he stay at Valley Acres?"

"Yes. I can pay for Promise's keep there," Will said. "Father gave me a goodly amount of money for room and board, but since I've been staying here at no cost, I have enough to take care of Promise's keep. And the Whigs back in Salem will help me with expenses too."

"Where will you be staying now, Will?" Hannah asked.

"At Mr. Hubbard's, but I'll come here whenever I can."

"How, now that we're all being watched so carefully?"

"I don't know yet," Will admitted.

"Between the Intolerable Acts and the powder house being robbed, the whole of Massachusetts is ready to explode. Things are going to get worse and it's going to be harder to move around," Caleb said. "And I have an important message to get out to old Boston Town."

"What kind of message?" Hannah asked.

"A warning to lawyers who work with biased Tory judges." He pulled out a bundle of handbills and handed them to Hannah. "Read these."

Hannah read aloud:

Thursday, September 1, 1774
Any One and every One of the Bar that shall presume, after this Day, to appeal in Court or otherwise to do any Business with the Judges, shall assuredly suffer the Pains of Death.

"Pains of death!" Hannah exclaimed.

"No lawyer is going to risk death by doing business with the king's judges," Will responded.

Hannah gave the handbills back to Caleb. "What are you going to do with these?"

"Post them at every lawyer's place of business, and on the courthouse itself," Caleb said.

"When?" Hannah asked. "It's dated today."

"These were printed downstreet just hours ago. I was hoping to get them out tonight," Caleb said.

"How did you dare bring them onto the grounds here?"

"No one's gonna search me. They all know and trust me," Caleb said.

"With things as they are, you may get searched next time," Hannah warned. "Caleb, if they find you with these handbills, you could be shot!"

"Hannah's right," said Will. "The regulars will be on a tight guard after today's raid on the powder house. The colonists are up in arms. I could hear the church bells tolling from over the river. And there are fire beacons lighting up the sky tonight all across the countryside. These are warnings of possible war! The regulars will be right nervous and watching like crows over a cornfield. You've been lucky so far, but it's more dangerous now. You'd better not bring those handbills out through the guardhouse."

Hannah sank back on her chair. Caleb and Will were willing to risk their lives for freedom. Freedom! Wasn't that what Hannah wanted too? "I would like to help you with the handbills," she said, "but there's no way out of here now."

Caleb leaned forward and whispered. "There might be."

Hannah sat up. "Do you know of a way out?"

"I have something to tell you, but you must swear by all that's holy that you will never tell."

"I swear," Will said.

"I swear!" Hannah said solemnly, raising her right hand.

"I'll show you. But first Hannah must become Cousin Hans." He lit another candle and handed it to Hannah.

Hannah went down the stairway to an empty stall where she had hidden "Hans's" garments under a stack of blankets. She placed the candlestick on a bench, took off her frock, and changed into Hans's clothing. After braiding her hair in the back, she put on the tricornered hat, retrieved the candlestick, and found the boys waiting for her by the stairway.

"Follow me," Caleb said, lighting the way to the rear door behind the stairs. "By using this back way we won't be seen by anyone, and we won't have to pass Joseph's living quarters. Once we leave the stable, I'm snuffing the candle, so stay close."

"Where are we going?" Hannah whispered.

"To the old woodshed," Caleb answered. "I

found a tunnel there. It's just a short one, but it will take us outside the walls." He opened the rear door and extinguished the candle.

"How did you find it?" Hannah blew out the flame on her candle.

"About a year ago, when I first came to work here, I was cleaning the stalls. I piled the manure over near the rear gate where it's taken away. One day Jim, the Negro gardener, told me to put some aside for the flower beds, so I decided to dump it near the old shed. There was nothing out there but leaves that had gathered. Well, I had just dumped a third or fourth barrow full, and I was about to head back to the stable, when I heard a noise. I peered around the far corner of the woodshed where I had dumped the manure, and I saw the whole pile rising up in the air!" Caleb chuckled. "It was a trapdoor opening up! Out stumbled a shadow of a man. He was cursing and smelling to high heaven of manure."

"Did he see you?" Will asked.

"No! I ducked around the shed. I could hear him brushing himself off and swearing. I watched him head into the mansion by the back entrance. He was tall and thin, but I couldn't see who it was, and I never saw him again. Later, I explored the tunnel and found that it leads to Baker's Alley on the other side of the wall. I've used it a few times, but it's not something you want to use if you can come and go the normal way. It's filthy down there."

"And you never told anyone?" Hannah asked.

"I figured I'd keep it a secret." Caleb put his finger alongside his nose. "Don't forget you swore by Heaven never to tell anyone."

"We won't," Hannah promised, "but I hope we never meet that person, whoever he was, in the passageway."

"I've never seen anyone come or go through it since that one time," said Caleb.

They walked quietly through tall weeds and thistle. When they approached the shed, Caleb led them around to the back, near the brick wall that surrounded the Province House. "The entrance to the tunnel is under here," he said. "We can light a taper now. No one can see us."

Caleb pulled a flint box from his pocket and struck the flint and steel. After a moment a spark ignited the scrap of dried linen he kept in the box.

Will lit the candle from the flame and Caleb blew out the linen. Then he carefully replaced the tools in the box. "This is the best strike-a-light I've ever had," he said as he put the flint box in his pocket again.

Will held the candle while Caleb cleared away brush and last year's dead leaves. Hannah joined him in wiping away debris. Suddenly she realized that there was wood beneath her hands. Caleb found the handle and pulled.

With a creak the trapdoor opened up, revealing stone steps that descended into a dark passageway. "Here it is," Caleb said. "Our escape route."

Caleb took the candle and descended the four stone steps that led down into the darkness. "I'll lead the way. The ceiling is low, so you have to stoop."

Hannah followed into the musty and damp passageway. "It's so dark in here. Light our candles, Caleb. We can't see a thing." Caleb held his candle flame to Hannah's and Will's, then began creeping ahead of them.

"That's better, except that now I can see what an ugly place this is," Hannah said, looking at the dirt walls that surrounded them. "What if it caves in?"

"The tunnel is safe. It's propped up with huge timbers." Caleb paused and held the candle high so she could see the wide planks. "This tunnel must have been built with the mansion a hundred years ago."

"Who built it?" Hannah wondered. "And why?"

"We may never know," said Will.

"Well, as long as this is a way to get out and see Promise, I don't care how old or ugly it is, or how it got here," Hannah said.

"We're almost there," Caleb told them, and soon he was climbing granite stairs leading to another wooden trapdoor.

Hannah heard the squeaking of a hatch, then leaves and sticks falling as the door rose. Caleb clambered up the steps, then took her hand to pull her out.

Will came out of the passageway. "I'm glad to be out of that stinking hole!" he exclaimed.

"We should douse the candles and leave them here with the flint box," Caleb said.

Hannah brushed her clothes off and looked around. They were on a wooded lot near a small alleyway. Lights from the street failed to illuminate this out-of-the-way plot of land, and a large boulder obscured the entrance to the tunnel.

Hannah and Will covered the hatch with leaves while Caleb divided up the handbills. "Now

we're ready to deliver our messages," he said,
pulling a cloth packet from his pocket and unfold-
ing it. "Here are tacks to mount them. You'll need a
stone to hammer them in."

Hannah found three stout rocks, and the trio
walked out onto School Street. It was late now; the
streets would be empty except for any soldiers who
might pass by on patrol. There were none in sight.

"Will I have time to see Promise?" Hannah
asked.

"Not tonight," Caleb said. "We had a late start,
and we've got to post these leaflets."

Hannah took off her hat and held it against the
tack to muffle the sound as she pounded the first
handbill on the main door of the courthouse on
Queen Street. Will used the same method to post
the second notice on the front door of the Old
South Meeting House.

Under Caleb's direction the small group moved
quickly around the town, posting the warnings on
the doors of buildings most likely to be used by
lawyers and judges. Several times they crouched in
shadows or alleys while redcoats on duty walked

the streets. "They have no idea we've defied the British, right under their noses!" Will whispered.

By the time they finished, a few early risers were opening stores. The first pale light of morning lit their way back to School Street.

"Look, someone has already torn down the leaflet I put on the meetinghouse door." Will reached into the packet, pulled out his last copy, and pounded it into place just as a soldier turned a corner farther down the road and saw them.

"Who goes there?" he yelled. "Stop in the name of the king!"

The trio turned onto School Street and raced into the alley where the entrance to the tunnel was located. They could hear the running foot-steps of the soldier close behind them. As they crouched behind the huge boulder that shielded the hatch from view, Caleb grabbed the handle and pulled open the trapdoor. "Get down there, quick!"

Hannah leaped into the opening. Will seized the candles and flint box and jumped in after her, with Caleb right behind. They were silent for a moment, listening for the soldier, but there was no sound above them. "He didn't see us," Caleb finally whispered.

"Go, Hannah," Will whispered. "Move!"

First in line this time, and without light, Hannah scrambled and groped in the darkness. The smell of damp earth and rotting wood made her feel sick. Still, knowing that she could get out of the Province House whenever she needed to gave her a sense of freedom.

"Light a candle, Will," she said, pausing. "We must be near the end by now."

Will obliged, and Hannah could see the stone steps in front of her.

"Push the door," Caleb told her. "It's not latched."

Hannah lifted up the heavy door, letting in the morning light and the smell of the stable. Relieved, she climbed out, and the boys followed her.

"It's daylight now, and soldiers will be coming soon," she said. "I've got to fly!" She dashed through the rear door of the barn and grabbed her clothes from the peg. She slipped into yesterday's uniform, dropping Hans's clothing onto the floor. "Will you pick up after me, Caleb?" she asked. "I must never be this late again!"

Hannah went to the well, pumped icy water into her hands, and splashed it onto her face. She smoothed her hair, then dashed by the kitchen and the nearby scullery, where Annie was already boiling water in big tubs on the fires. "May I have hot water for Miss Meg?" she asked. Annie obliged by filling a pitcher for her. Hot water for washing would be a treat for Meg and a good excuse for being late.

Meg was in her dressing gown when Hannah entered the room. "You're late, and you look like a ragamuffin," she began. But she stopped and smiled when she saw the steaming pitcher in Hannah's hands.

Meg washed blissfully, but eyed Hannah from the mirror. "You need a clean smock, Hannah. And where's your clout?"

"I'm sorry, Miss Meg," Hannah stammered. "I wasn't feeling well . . . and I fell asleep in my clothes last night. And when I awoke it was rather late . . ." She could feel her face redden, as it always did when she lied.

Meg looked at Hannah with an amused smile. "That's strange. I was looking for you late last night, and Catherine said you hadn't come to bed."

When Hannah didn't reply, Meg continued. "Well, go change, and I'll eat breakfast in the dining room this morning."

As Hannah left the room, Meg added, "I'll have to keep my eye on you, Hannah."

During the next few weeks Hannah—as Hans the stable boy—was able to get away through the tunnel and have her midnight rides with Promise. She became familiar with every street and alley and knew the routes of the redcoats who patrolled the town. Although the "boy" was questioned twice, the soldiers paid little attention. "Hans" answered respectfully and rode carefully through the streets. Only at the Common or at pasturages did Hannah give Promise his head and let him gallop over the open fields.

Since the powder house incident, dangerous and alarming confrontations were occurring every day in Massachusetts, and the Province House was charged with tension. There was talk of groups of minutemen—a militia that would be ready to march and fight at a moment's notice—being formed throughout Massachusetts. The staff whispered and trod softly around the huge halls as solemn-faced officers came and went.

One morning in the middle of September, Hannah, curious about the loud voices coming from General Gage's private office, tiptoed to the reception room and listened as the officers spoke angrily about the Continental Congress being held in Philadelphia.

"I'm hoping that the twelve colonies represented there will reconcile the differences between America and England," General Gage said.

"I've heard Dr. Warren has drawn up resolutions right here in Suffolk County!" another man exclaimed. "They call the Coercive Acts illegal."

"They're even recommending sanctions against England!" an officer added.

General Gage sounded weary. "My sources tell me that someone is taking those resolutions to Philadelphia—probably that courier, Paul Revere. With rabble-rousers like Sam Adams at the Congress, it's hard to know which way the tide will turn."

· · ·

Late one morning when the stable was quiet, Hannah met Caleb by the well. "Things are really moving now," he told her. "Someone's racing to Philadelphia with resolutions from the nearby towns."

"Is it Paul Revere?" Hannah asked.

Caleb looked surprised. "How did you know?"

"General Gage already knows from some source that Paul Revere is taking Dr. Warren's papers to the Continental Congress."

Caleb pounded his fist into his hand. "I'd love to know who his 'source' is. It's got to be someone close to the Sons of Liberty. Gage always knows what's going on." He smiled. "Well, the Committees of Correspondence are keeping our folks aware of what's going on too. Will is riding Promise to Salem and Danvers right now to report to the Committees of Correspondence there. He'll be back in a day or two."

Suddenly the shrieks of a horse sounded from the stable. Caleb and Hannah raced into the barn.

"It's Gabriel!" Caleb yelled. As they ran through the building, the other horses began to whinny nervously at the commotion.

Hannah and Caleb approached Gabriel's stall to see the horse pacing and kicking furiously. "Gabriel!" Hannah called as she drew near the terrified horse. "Quiet, boy!" she commanded in a gentle voice. "Everything's fine, sweet boy."

"Whist, whist, Gabriel," Caleb said.

Suddenly General Gage came into the stable. "What's going on?" he asked with a frown.

"Something scared him," Caleb said.

"There, there! Quiet down!" General Gage spoke sharply to the stallion. When he brandished his whip, the horse made a fierce kick.

"If you please, wait, sir," Hannah pleaded. "You're only making him more afraid." General Gage stepped forward angrily, but stopped as Hannah made a clicking sound with her tongue and sang, "La, la, la, Gabriel, my love."

The stallion responded to the gentle sound. "Come, boy," she murmured, holding out her hand.

Gabriel paused on the far side of the stall and watched Hannah defiantly. "Hush, hush, la, la, la," she continued singing. Gabriel snorted and pawed the floor again, but he didn't rear or kick.

General Gage was about to speak, then stopped.

Slowly the horse made his way to the open stall door where Hannah stood. "Sweet boy," Hannah crooned. "What frightened you so?"

The horse nuzzled her hand, and General Gage took a deep breath. "This horse responds to you very well indeed."

"If you'll excuse me, sir, my father always told me that whipping a horse isn't the way to win its loyalty," Hannah said.

General Gage frowned thoughtfully. Then he glanced down at Caleb, who was on his knees in the stall. "Did you find what frightened the horse?"

Caleb stood up with an orange kitten in his arms. "Yes, Your Excellency."

"A cat! Get it out of here. Drown it!" the general demanded.

"No!" exclaimed Hannah, taking the kitten from Caleb's arms. As she cuddled it, the kitten began to purr and paw at her smock. "Please, sir . . . Your Excellency . . . er, General . . . I'll find a home for her."

General Gage looked incensed at Hannah's boldness. Then . . . did Hannah see his face soften with the faint glimmer of a smile? Before she could decide, the general turned on his heel and headed for the door. "Very well," he said. "But I never want to lay eyes on it again. And don't let it back in the stable."

"Thank you! Thank you, sir," Hannah exclaimed.

General Gage left the stable, muttering, "I have enough to contend with these days without distractions such as this!"

Hannah stroked the kitten. "You are a naughty little thing, frightening Gabriel as you did." She held the kitten up to the horse. "What a silly horse you are to be terrified of this tiny pussycat." Gabriel, who was calmer now, stretched his head closer and eyed the kitten curiously.

"Where are you going to keep a cat?" Caleb asked.

"In my room. Oh, I hope Catherine won't mind!"

"General Gage has taken to you, Hannah," Caleb said. "He was right angry when he came into the barn, but as he watched you calm Gabriel, his expression changed. I saw him smile. I've never seen the likes."

Hannah named the kitten Gypsy. Catherine was agreeable to keeping her in their room with the door shut at all times. "Gypsy must not wander through the house," Hannah cautioned. "General Gage warned me that he doesn't want to see her ever again!"

It was only a matter of hours before Gypsy had taken over the bedchamber, sleeping contentedly under the quilt in a little heap or sitting with her nose pressed to the window, watching the birds. Hannah fixed a box of sand and brought scraps of meat from the kitchen, which the cat ate daintily. At night Gypsy curled up at Hannah's feet and purred loudly.

One October morning Mrs. Gage called the servants together in the dining room. "Our officers are in need of entertainment and relaxation.

Therefore General Gage has ordered that we open the Province House for small gatherings and dancing several evenings each week. You will be requested to assist with these occasions, to make them as pleasant as possible."

Hannah helped Meg choose dresses for each event, did her laundry, and ironed her clothes and hair ribbons. Mrs. Dudley asked Hannah to help the rest of the staff by ironing linens, trimming candles and lantern wicks, and polishing silver.

During the parties, Hannah peeked into the drawing room, where there was dancing, music, and card playing. She could see Meg's delight as she danced the nights away with several young men, including Lieutenant Pratt, who watched Meg possessively.

Hannah missed seeing Will and Promise. Caleb, who often met with Will at the meetings of the Sons of Liberty, kept Hannah abreast of Will's journeys. One afternoon Caleb approached her as she hung clothes at the rear of the mansion.

"Will wants you to know he will be at Valley Acres tonight," he said. "Can you get away after the party?"

Hannah nodded eagerly. "I'll be there."

She tried not to show her excitement as she helped Mrs. Dudley prepare for the officers' party that night. As she was placing a tray of delicate teacups in the drawing room for the evening affair, Meg appeared with Lieutenant Pratt at her side.

"Oh, Hannah," she said. "I do wish you would entertain tonight by doing imitations for us."

"Oh no, Miss Meg, I couldn't do that," Hannah said, her face flushing. "It might be misunderstood."

"How dare you disagree with your mistress," Lieutenant Pratt exclaimed, scowling at Hannah. "Such impertinence. You need to be put in your place!"

Hannah's temper was rising. She turned to Meg. "Please forgive me, Miss Meg. I'd be only too happy to imitate Lieutenant Pratt for tonight's entertainment." She cleared her throat and drawled in a haughty English accent, "'How dare you disagree with your mistress. Such impertinence! You need to be put in your place!'"

The officer's face turned purple with rage, but Meg burst into laughter. "You must admit that Hannah has a rare talent, Chester." She patted his arm. "However, she was absolutely right in refusing. Why, she'd make you the laughingstock of the evening." Meg put her hand over her mouth to stifle her mirth. "You don't want that, now do you, Chester?"

Lieutenant Pratt drew himself up tall and tried to mask his annoyance. "Whatever you say, my dear." He took Meg's arm, and as the couple walked away, Hannah heard him mutter, "You're much too permissive with that chambermaid!"

You're much too permissive with that chambermaid! Hannah had to bite her tongue not to spit the words out after that arrogant simpleton. How could Meg be so besotted by him? At least she had taken Hannah's side.

Hannah was kept busy serving and cleaning for the party that night, but as soon as the group of officers had left and Meg had retired, Hannah went to her room to tell Catherine she was going to ride Promise.

"Hannah, I don't want to know how you get away from the Province House—"

"You know I'm sworn to secrecy, Catherine," Hannah interrupted.

"I understand, and I would never tell anyone you've left the grounds, but I am worried about you. Sooner or later someone is sure to find out." Catherine leaned closer. "Let me ask you this. Are you helping the Patriots?"

"Yes, I am. Catherine, we Americans are all indentured servants to England—just as I am indentured to the Gages. England wants our taxes and loyalty, but they've taken away our town meetings and fair trials. They've blocked our harbor . . ."

"And they will severely punish anyone they find who may be a rebel. Please be careful, Hannah."

Hannah hugged Catherine. "Don't worry about me, Catherine. What can a girl like me do to the British in any case? All I care about is riding my horse. It's the only freedom I have." She picked up her kitten and kissed its head. "Keep my bed warm, Gypsy."

When Hannah arrived at Valley Acres, Will was there. "All sorts of things are happening," he told her. "Did you hear about the riots in Cambridge? They're running Tory lawyers and judges right out of town. The governor had to give them refuge at

Castle William in the harbor, or they might have been killed!"

"I've heard all about it, Will. Are you forgetting I live in the governor's mansion? I hear more than I should." Hannah began brushing Promise. "Tell me what's happening in Salem, Will."

"The Salemites have strong sympathy for the Bostonians." Will grinned. "Except for your aunt Phoebe, of course. I heard she's been seeing that Tory lawyer, Mr. Parley."

"If he has money and he's a Tory, she'll hook her claws into him if she can. She's probably used up all my inheritance." Hannah put a saddle blanket on Promise, and Will threw on the saddle and buckled it.

"He'll soon be hard-pressed for money. He's sure to have heard the threat of pains of death to Tory lawyers by now." Will hoisted Hannah into the saddle. "Be careful out there, Hannah. I won't be here when you get back."

"We'll be fine, Will," Hannah assured him. She clicked her tongue, and Promise headed out into the night.

Hannah guided Promise over the pasture and

Beacon Hill to the Common, where the soldiers and officers were camped in their white tents. In the moonlight the park reminded her of a sea of ships in full sail. There were lights in the tents, and campfires crackled throughout the area.

"Let's ride over there," Hannah said to Promise. "The Common is for everyone—not just British soldiers." She touched her finger lightly on the reins and Promise trotted across the cobblestone street to a hill leading down to a small pond. The moon reflected on the water, and the night was still. Hannah gave Promise his head, and the horse ambled across the field toward the army camp.

Some of the soldiers' horses were tied to hitching posts or trees near the tents. In the glow of a campfire Hannah recognized Lieutenant Pratt's horse, rust-colored with the white crescent on its forehead. The saddle had been removed, but the horse was tethered tightly to a post.

"What a way to leave that beautiful horse," Hannah muttered, pulling Promise to a stop. "He can hardly move, the way he's tied up. And now that the nights are getting cold, he should have a blanket and be kept in a paddock."

Although Hannah could hear men laughing by the fire, there was no one close by. It was compulsory for soldiers to care for their horses as they would their own lives. But Lieutenant Pratt was nowhere to be seen.

What would happen if Lieutenant Pratt's horse got loose? Hannah wondered. *It would serve him right for leaving him like this.* Hannah dismounted Promise. "Stay here!" she told him.

Hannah ran to the red horse and unhitched him from the post. She slapped his flank, and the horse whinnied, turned, and raced off into the darkness.

Hannah darted back to Promise, hopped into the saddle, and galloped away.

although she was late returning from her midnight ride, Hannah found that the excitement of releasing Chester Pratt's horse made it difficult for her to sleep. She envisioned his expression when he discovered his mount had disappeared, and she wondered how far away the horse might have wandered. The thought of it made her laugh, and she had to cover her face with a pillow for fear of waking Catherine.

Meg was still sleeping when Hannah peered into her room the next morning. Rather than awaken her, Hannah joined Catherine and the other servants for breakfast at the big table in the kitchen.

"So much partying!" Sally complained. "The kitchen is busy constantly."

"It's as if we're working for two households instead of one," Catherine agreed.

"There's enough to do here without adding the entire British army!" Sally grumbled.

Caleb arrived and sat on the bench with them. "Soldiers who came in from the Common this morning to groom and shoe their horses said there was a bit of activity out at the camp last night." He looked at Hannah, then down at his oatmeal. Hannah could tell he was trying not to laugh.

"Well, then, tell us what happened," Edward, the butler, said.

"One of the officers lost his horse!" Caleb sputtered oatmeal, then wiped his mouth with a handkerchief. "I know it ain't funny, but . . ."

Hannah concentrated on her applesauce, not meeting Caleb's eyes for fear of laughing herself. She managed a quick glance at Catherine, who looked away.

"An officer? Whose horse was it?" asked Edward.

"Lieutenant Pratt's big red stallion," Caleb answered. "They found him clear down by Frog Lane."

Edward clucked his tongue. "Oh my, that's a serious offense. Lieutenant Pratt will be disciplined. He's responsible for the care of his mount, and he may be punished for an example, poor man."

"That Lieutenant Pratt is an earl or some such nobility," Sally said. "And from what I've seen at the parties, he's sweet on Miss Meg. Those facts may keep him from getting what he deserves."

"You don't believe that General Gage would show favoritism, do you?" Edward looked shocked. "Why, he's known for his honesty and impartiality."

"Right," Caleb interjected. "That's why his troops call him Honest Tom."

"The general has been fair and kind to me," Hannah said to everyone at the table.

She had not seen Miss Lydia enter the kitchen and was surprised when she spoke. "Well, Hannah, I can see that you have learned a good deal since you came here, including loyalty to General Gage and to your king."

Hannah didn't want to acknowledge the commendation since it was not true. However, she felt obliged to say, "Thank you, Miss Lydia." Hannah had meant what she said about General Gage, but it had become clear to her that her own loyalty would have to be neither to General Gage nor to King George, but to her countrymen.

Later that day, Hannah was fetching fresh water from the courtyard well when she saw Caleb combing Gabriel.

She ran to the elegant horse. "Hello, my beauty!" Gabriel nudged her and nuzzled the pocket where she always kept an apple for him. "Here you are, Gabriel. You do love me, don't you? Maybe someday you'll let me ride you."

"Don't get that idea in your head, Hannah," Caleb warned. "You're going to be in trouble sooner or later. It was you, wasn't it, who unhitched Red Roy?"

"What a fine name for Lieutenant Pratt's horse," she said innocently as she stroked Gabriel's long neck. "It is a red horse, isn't it?"

"As if you didn't know!" Caleb stopped combing Gabriel.

"Is Lieutenant Pratt in trouble?" Hannah asked hopefully.

"Colonel Maddison chastised him in front of

all his men. That haughty know-it-all Pratt deserved to be taken down a peg or two. But he's furious, from what I heard, and he swore he'll find out who's to blame."

"There was no one around who could have seen me. They were all by the campfire—probably drinking ale."

"Hannah, don't endanger yourself—and all of us—by letting your hatred for Lieutenant Pratt dim your common sense!"

Hannah threw back her head and laughed. "I wish I could have seen his face. He'd be even more humiliated if he knew a servant girl was responsible."

"Just be careful, Hannah," Caleb repeated, "for all our sakes. You said yourself that General Gage has his sources. We don't know who's watching."

"Don't the Sons of Liberty have their sources too?"

Caleb moved closer to Hannah, brushing the horse again. "The Massachusetts legislature met this week, against General Gage's orders, and they've organized a Committee of Safety. They'll watch every movement of the British officers and

Tories. We're turning the tables on the British. Mr. Revere says that the spirit of liberty never was higher."

The spirit of liberty. It sounded wonderful. Hannah suddenly remembered a scripture she had read with her mother: *Proclaim liberty throughout the land and to all the inhabitants thereof.* Would there ever be a day when Americans would be free?

"Will I be able to ride Promise tonight?" she asked Caleb.

"Will has been away to New York for Mr. Revere, but he's using one of Mr. Hubbard's steeds, so Promise is still at Valley Acres," Caleb answered. "Will is now part of Boston's Committee of Safety as well as Salem's Committee of Correspondence."

"I hope he's careful," Hannah said. "It sounds dangerous to me."

"A fine one you are to talk! Look at you running through the streets at night playing pranks! That's right dangerous too, Hannah." Caleb warned her in a stern voice.

Hannah mimicked Caleb's expression and voice. "But I must say Cousin Hans did right well giving Chester Pratt his comeuppance!"

Caleb looked startled. "Hannah!" he scolded. But after a few seconds the two of them burst into laughter.

That night Meg retired early—something she didn't do often. Hannah decided that the evening entertainments had become too tiring even for Meg!

As Cousin Hans, Hannah made her way through the tunnel and into the streets. With a slight swagger similar to that of other boys she'd seen in the town, Hannah strolled casually up the back lanes and alleys to Valley Acres.

Upon entering the stable, she nodded briefly to the stable hand. As usual he seemed pleased that "Hans" didn't request him to saddle Promise, but preferred to do it "himself."

Hannah and Promise ambled through the pastures around Beacon Hill, where the windmills turned slowly in the soft autumn breeze. They walked by the dark burying ground and the silent and solemn King's Chapel. The town was quiet, and only a few soldiers were on patrol in the streets Hannah chose to ride.

"Let's go to the Common, Promise. Then you can have a run."

The tents were alight with the flickering of lanterns, and fires sparked and glowed. Between the campfires and the streetlamps along Beacon Street, Hannah could see soldiers on horseback lined up and riding in an uneven row back and forth from the river. The string of redcoats was irregular, with large spaces between the mounts.

"They're practicing night maneuvers," Hannah told Promise, "and not doing too well, at that."

Hannah and Promise stayed in the shadow of the elm trees on the slope of the hill. When the line of horses had turned to head in the opposite direction, Hannah whispered, "Shall we break up their formation? Do we dare?" Promise seemed to understand and moved about restlessly.

"Fly, Promise!" Hannah tapped her horse lightly with a stirrup. Promise bounded into the clearing behind the row of cavalry. "Yah!" Hannah yelled in her male voice.

The horses in front of her shied fearfully, breaking the formation and scattering in various directions. Hannah and Promise galloped through the procession as the surprised soldiers tried to control their mounts.

The clamor of oaths and outcries thundered on the night air. "Get that rider!" several officers shouted. "Stop that horseman!"

Hannah and Promise flew into the trees near Frog Lane. From there they backtracked behind the hill. Hannah smiled as she watched the soldiers race across the field in the opposite direction. Below, near the river, she could see a paddock with a dozen or more of the soldiers' horses. What if she set them free?

"Fly!" Promise bolted down the west side of the hill to the enclosure. Without dismounting, Hannah brought her horse up to the fence, reached over and unlatched the gate, which swung open wide. For a moment the horses inside were oblivious to the freedom that waited beyond the fence.

"Yah!" Hannah shouted. Promise neighed and darted away as the herd whinnied and stampeded out onto the open pasture area of the Common. Hannah urged Promise into a fast gallop through a pasture between two homes on Beacon Street.

"Who's there?" someone called.

She continued through the alleys around George Street to Cambridge Street, then eastward through winding back lanes to the waterfront. In a narrow passageway by the wood yard, she led Promise behind a pile of white-pine lumber. "We'll hide here," Hannah whispered, rubbing Promise's sweaty neck. "Good boy."

As she clung to Promise, she heard the sound of hoofbeats and men's voices. The soldiers were coming closer! The clank of horses' hooves on the cobblestone was louder now. "When we find that Yankee rebel, we'll take him down to the river and shoot him!"

The sounds faded as the pursuers went off in another direction, but still Hannah waited in the narrow passageway behind the lumber. After several minutes had passed, she peered out onto the street. It was empty.

Hannah climbed onto Promise and guided him cautiously through the back lanes to Valley Acres. Promise seemed to understand the need for caution. Even without Hannah's guidance he walked quietly and kept in the shadows. His jet-black coat blended into the darkness.

The stable hand was asleep and only one lantern lit the barn when Hannah arrived at Valley Acres. She dismounted, took the lantern, and led Promise to his enclosure. After removing the saddle and bridle, she pulled a pile of hay into the stall.

Then she leaned her face into the horse's smooth neck. "We had excitement tonight, didn't we?" she whispered. "But we must not take chances like this again—for a while."

As she left Valley Acres and headed through the town, she saw that soldiers had gathered in a small group near the corner of King Street. She had to pass them to get to Baker's Alley and the tunnel entrance.

"Who goes there?" a soldier called.

Hannah wanted to hide, but it was too late. A mounted officer from the group was heading toward her.

"Who are you and where are you going?" he asked. As he passed under the gas streetlight, Hannah recognized the horse. Red Roy and Lieutenant Pratt! Surely he would recognize her, even in men's clothing. She lowered her gaze and shrugged her neck deep into the collar of her coat. She would need a different voice, one that didn't sound a bit strained or unusual. And perhaps a strong British accent. That would sound friendlier to him than an American voice.

"It is only I, sir," Hannah said, remembering

the way those soldiers who had come directly from England would speak. "A bit late, I fear, after a good time down at the pub."

"Your name?"

"Hans Gibbs, m'lord."

At that moment two men walked up the street. In the lamplight Hannah recognized the short, stocky figure as Paul Revere—and the other as Will!

Lieutenant Pratt's attention was diverted. He knew Paul Revere. "Ah, Mr. Revere," he said. "I suppose you are returning from one of your clandestine meetings?"

"If they are clandestine, their secrecy seems to have failed," Mr. Revere said with a smile. "To be more precise, my friend here and I just finished a bite to eat and a beer at the tavern."

Will smiled at Hannah. "Well, we meet again. I thought you would have been back to your loft by now!" He turned to the lieutenant. "This young fellow just took leave of us a few moments ago."

"Is there a problem on the streets tonight?" Mr. Revere asked the lieutenant.

"Some bloody wild rider has been disturbing the troops and horses at the Common. Once we find him, tar and feathers will be too good for him." Lieutenant Pratt turned his horse back to the other soldiers.

"Aren't you Caleb's cousin Hans?" Mr. Revere asked once the redcoats were down the street and out of hearing.

"Yes, sir," Hannah answered in her male voice. She cast a quick glance at Will, who looked about ready to explode with annoyance.

"And you are the bloody wild rider that's causing so much trouble, I'm sure," Will said in an angry whisper. "Caleb said it was you who set Pratt's horse free."

Hannah nodded. "I cannot abide that pompous fool! Nor any of those soldiers who are keeping us prisoners here in Boston."

Mr. Revere looked up the street to be sure the soldiers could not hear. The lieutenant had ridden down Marlborough Street, and the other men had resumed their patrol and were out of sight. Mr. Revere grasped her shoulder. "Young man," he said, "when General Gage closed the city and made us prisoners, he also imprisoned himself and his troops. Outside the city the people are organized and ready for any attack." He shook Hannah slightly. "It is well and good if you want to work with us toward the goal of freedom, but pranks like yours only inflame the British against us even more." He let go of Hannah with a shove. "Dr. Warren and Mr. Hancock and the Whigs here in town are trying to keep the peace by dealing with General Gage with deep respect. It's rowdies like you who are causing nothing but trouble for everyone!"

Hannah shrunk deep into Caleb's jacket. She was so stunned and ashamed that she couldn't speak. She had never thought of herself as a rowdy! She turned helplessly to Will, who stood by with his arms crossed over his chest. "I'm sorry, Mr. Revere," she finally said, forgetting to speak in her male voice.

Mr. Revere looked startled. "You're so young. Why, your voice hasn't even changed yet."

"He probably feels he's doing his part against the redcoats," Will put in, struggling to hide Hannah's identity.

"Remember what happened to Christopher Seider at the Boston Massacre," Mr. Revere warned. "He thought he was helping the cause, but the redcoats killed him. He was only eleven years old." Mr. Revere studied Hannah's face, then noticed Hannah's small hand and the ring on her finger. "You're no boy at all. You're a girl!"

Hannah had not given thought to her mother's ring and how it might identify her. She looked into Mr. Revere's eyes. "Yes, sir. And I am not really a rowdy. I don't want to cause trouble, but I do want to help the cause for freedom—"

Paul Revere interrupted. "You must stay out of mischief, my child, for your own safety!"

"I'm a chambermaid at the Province House, sir, and I am . . . privy to information. I mean, I over-hear . . ."

"You can help us simply by being discreet and keeping your eyes and ears open," Mr. Revere said kindly. "I have daughters, and I know you want to be of help. But you're just a girl."

"I may be 'just a girl,' but I'm the best horseman in Boston!"

"If you are the Midnight Rider, you do have that reputation," Mr. Revere agreed with a chuckle. "You have been able to outwit the soldiers so far," he added, patting her arm, "but you came close to being discovered tonight. That would never do!"

"I'll take her back," Will broke in. "Good night, Mr. Revere."

Hannah pulled away. "I can go myself! Don't treat me like a ... girl!"

"Good night, Will. Good night—Hans." Mr. Revere laughed as he headed up the street.

Once the sentries were out of sight, Will and Hannah walked quickly toward Baker's Alley and the tunnel. "Lucky for you that Mr. Revere and I happened to come along when we did," Will scolded. "You might have been searched. Or worse."

"Where were you coming from so late at night?" asked Hannah in an equally scolding tone. "I heard you were in New York."

"I was in New York for several days, but I came back today. And if you must know why I was out here with Mr. Revere, it was our turn to patrol. We go through the town two by two, keeping watch on the soldiers and all their movements. You know we now have a Committee of Safety."

"And the soldiers keep their eyes on you as you

keep your eyes on them," Hannah said. "An around-about that goes nowhere." Hannah stopped walking and crossed her arms. "Now tell me how Lieutenant Pratt knew that you're having secret meetings. Someone must have told him."

Will shook his head. "General Gage has an agent who is close to us. Some of our words have been told verbatim to General Gage and then used against us. We have our own spies among the Tories who have reported as much. In fact, Dr. Warren has an informant high among the British officials, though he is sworn to silence never to tell who it is." Will took Hannah's hand. "You must swear to keep everything you've heard about meetings, or anything, a secret."

"Surely you must know that I'd never betray you or Caleb . . . or anyone!"

Hannah and Will began walking again. "What do you think is going to happen, Will?"

"As Mr. Revere said, when General Gage blocked off the town, he walled himself inside as well. The British are more fearful than we are! That's why they want all the cannon and ammunition. They know it's only a matter of time before the guns will turn on them."

"Do the people want war?" Hannah asked.

"No one wants war. We had hoped England would hear our complaints and pleas. As Mr. Revere explained, the Whigs have tried to be fair and respectful, but the British have punished us with soldiers, taxes, and those damnable Coercive Acts. And now the siege of Boston has made us all prisoners—Tories and Whigs alike." They reached the tunnel entrance. "Tensions are worse than ever, so remember, Hannah," Will said as he quietly raised the secret doorway, "no more pranks in the parks. There's more important work at hand."

"I'm sorry, Will. It seems my dislike of that arrogant Chester Pratt got in the way of my good sense," Hannah whispered as she climbed into the tunnel opening. "The Midnight Rider won't be troubling anyone anymore."

"Ah, but Hannah, everything that goes wrong for the redcoats, from sick horses to fallen tents, is now blamed on the Midnight Rider. If you are ever connected to even one prank, you will be held responsible for all."

"I only wanted to help the cause of liberty, Will."

"As Mr. Revere said, keep your eyes and ears

open in the Province House. Let us know what's going on. And don't ride Promise for a while. Soldiers are on the watch for a black horse."

"All right, Will."

"Godspeed, Hannah." Will shut the door behind her.

Eerie shadows trembled on the earthen walls as Hannah lit her candle and shuffled through the passageway. Each time she made her way through the dark tunnel, she feared she might come face to face with the man Caleb had once seen emerge from the passage. Or, even worse, that the ancient timbers might give way and she'd be trapped.

Hannah was relieved when she reached the end. She climbed up the stone steps, pushed open the trapdoor, and blew out the candle. After removing Hans's scratchy garb and slipping into her own clothing, she headed to the Province House and made her way up the stairway to her room.

Catherine stirred as Hannah entered, then sat up. "Hannah, oh Hannah," she said in an anxious voice, "you have been found out! Miss Meg was looking for you, and she wants you to go to her room right away."

"What do you mean? Does she know I left the Province House?"

"I think so. She barged into this room and said, 'Tell Hannah to come to my room as soon as she returns—no matter what the hour.'"

Hannah felt as if she would throw up her stomach. Her hands trembled as she lit a candle from the oil lantern in the hallway and headed back down the stairs again.

Meg reached out, grabbed Hannah's arm, and pulled her into the bedchamber. "I know how you get out!" she whispered. "I followed you tonight and saw you go into the stable, change your clothes, and head down into that tunnel behind the carriage house." Meg took the candle from Hannah and placed it into a holder. "Now, sit down. We have much to talk about."

Hannah's worst fears had come true. Meg knew everything. Had she told the Gages? What would happen to her? Her knees were weak and she sank into a chair.

"You have a sweetheart, don't you?" Meg demanded. "You're leaving the Province House at night to meet with your . . . what, Hannah? With your stable boy?"

Hannah was taken by surprise. So *this* is what Meg thought she was doing at night. Meg didn't realize that Hannah was the Midnight Rider who had been plaguing the soldiers. She had no idea that Hannah had posted warnings to Tory lawyers or that she was meeting with members of the Committees of Correspondence and Safety. "Oh, my. You've found me out," Hannah said, trying to look guilty.

"You can't believe I'm so daft that I didn't know you had a secret. Hannah, you disappear at night so quickly. It's obvious you've been meeting someone."

"I'm sorry, Miss Meg. I shan't do it ever again. Please forgive me." Hannah tried to sound contrite.

"How did you discover that tunnel?" Meg asked.

"I saw someone come up through it one night when I was . . . at the privy," Hannah replied, remembering Caleb's story. "I don't know who it was; I could only see his outline in the dark."

"Did you report him?"

"Oh, no. I was afraid."

In the dim light Hannah could see that Meg was pleased. "Good!" she said. "Then no one else knows except you and me."

"I don't know if anyone else is aware of the tunnel."

Meg was smiling. "Now I can make a visit to *my* sweetheart. But you must never tell."

"Oh, Miss Meg, it's dangerous for you of all people to be out on the streets at night."

"You're a fine one to talk! If I told Aunt Margaret what you've been doing, she'd probably have you flogged."

Hannah felt ill at the thought. "Please don't tell!" she begged.

"I don't intend to—under one condition: that *you* do not tell on *me*."

"What if Mrs. Gage comes looking for you and you're not here," Hannah asked.

"That's where you come in. You will be in my bed, and if Aunt Margaret comes knocking on this door, you are to call out—*in my voice*—'I'm so tired, Aunt Margaret. Please let me sleep.' She won't disturb you. She's happy when I'm tucked away in bed and not bothering her. Now, do we have a pact?"

Hannah hesitated. She was relieved that Meg had not discovered her real escapades outside the

Province House. Still, suppose Meg told everyone about the tunnel! "There's one thing *you* must promise."

"You have no right to ask promises from *me*!"

"A request, then. Please don't tell Lieutenant Pratt how you got out."

"Why not?"

Hannah had to think quickly. "What if General Gage is aware of the tunnel and has kept it a secret? It could be an escape route for him at some point. The general would be furious with you if he found out you've uncovered the secret passageway and told Lieutenant Pratt."

Meg was quiet.

Hannah went on. "The general would probably close up the tunnel or post guards. Then neither of us could leave."

"All right," Meg answered, "I won't reveal how I get away. Now tell me where the tunnel leads."

"It will take you to Baker's Alley, just beyond the north wall. You must be careful not to be seen."

"I'm not stupid, Hannah."

"How often will you be meeting your lieu-tenant?" Hannah asked.

"It won't be often. Maybe once or twice. Aunt Margaret's been talking about sending me back to England. She's already written to my father. All I want to do is say good-bye to Chester."

"He's here three or four times a week. Can't you say good-bye right here in the mansion?"

"No! I want to see him alone." Meg scowled. "You meet your sweetheart alone, don't you?"

"I'm sorry, Miss Meg." Hannah said. She'd almost forgotten she'd let Meg believe she was having a tryst with a sweetheart.

"All right," Meg said. "I will not tell anyone that you've been leaving the grounds, and you must promise the same. Silence is golden. Do we have a pact?"

"Yes, we have a pact."

Several days passed, and Meg had not yet made plans to use the tunnel. Hannah lived in hope that the girl would be sent to England before her plan could be carried out. When Catherine asked Hannah why Miss Meg had wanted her so late that night, Hannah simply said Miss Meg had given her a dressing-down for not being available when she was needed.

The following Sabbath arrived, and several of the servants were allowed to go to church "to pray for the king and his general." Catherine asked Hannah to accompany her to Christ Church on North Street, near the Reveres' home.

Hannah wore her one Sunday-go-meeting dress, and since it had turned cold with the onset of fall, she put on her mother's red woolen cape. When

Hannah complained that her clouts were not fit to wear to church, Catherine loaned her a pleated bonnet with a red ribbon to match her cape.

As they passed the Old South Meeting House, Catherine said, "I was told this is the place where the signal was given for the Tea Party to commence."

"What was the signal?" Hannah asked.

"'Let every man do his duty, and be true to his country.' At those words the Sons of Liberty, dressed as Mohawk Indians, headed for Griffin's Wharf to dump the tea into the harbor."

"I'm surprised the soldiers have left the Old South standing," Hannah said.

"The British would like to rip it apart and use it for a stable. But that would infuriate the Bostonians. And they don't dare do that, let me tell."

"The British soldiers and officers need to be reminded that we're just as British as they are," Hannah said. "They taunt us and ridicule us and keep us prisoners here. Why should we consider ourselves British any longer, Catherine? I feel more American than British."

"For now we are British," Catherine said. "We

have to keep the peace and protest under law. The real patriots have been patient with England. They are not rioters."

"For how long will they be patient?" Hannah asked.

"As long as it takes, I suppose," Catherine said with a sigh.

They walked to Salem Street along the shore, where ships were tied to the wharves, their rigging clanking in the rough sea. The Royal Navy's ships, with cannon pointed from their hulls, encircled the town with silent threats.

It was a beautiful, clear morning. The leaves on the trees that lined the streets were bright orange and scarlet, and the deep blue of the sky seemed to join the sea at the horizon.

Catherine and Hannah sat near the back of the church with the other women. The front pews and the balconies were filled with men who spoke loudly with one another until a hymn brought solemnity to the gathering.

When the minister spoke, everyone listened attentively. But Hannah wasn't sure what the message was. He talked about slavery and servitude to the king. He quoted scriptures about freedom and used them in ways Hannah didn't understand. His voice droned in a monotone and Hannah's eyes began to close. She was relieved when the sermons were over and the final hymn was sung:

> *Let tyrants shake their iron rods,*
> *And Slav'ry clank her galling chains.*
> *We fear them not, we trust in God.*
> *New England's God forever reigns.*

Several people were gathered outside the church. "I want you to meet a friend of mine," Catherine said, taking Hannah by the arm. She led her to a well dressed gentleman who had merry eyes and a gentle smile. She recognized him as the man Catherine had been sitting with at Mr. Revere's house the night of the shadow play.

"This is Joseph Greenleaf," she told Hannah. Turning to the fine-looking gentleman she added, "And this sweet child, Hannah, is my good friend."

The man smiled and nodded with a slight bow.

Hannah curtsied and said, "A pleasure, sir."

"Joseph and his partner are publishing a new periodical called *The Royal American*," Catherine said as they began their walk back to the Province House.

"*The Royal American?*" So-called Royal Americans were Loyalists—Tories. Certainly Catherine was not a Loyalist. And hadn't Joseph Greenleaf attended dinner and the shadow play at Mr. Revere's house?

"*The Royal American* is really a Whig publication," Catherine explained in a low voice, "under the guise of being Tory."

As they strolled along Middle Street, Hannah said, "The minister quoted a scripture that said, 'A slave cannot serve two masters.' Does this mean you can only work for one master or mistress? I've been working for Miss Meg. But I've also been asked to help Mrs. Gage and Mrs. Dudley."

"The scripture means that you can't give all your strength and support to more than one cause," Catherine explained. "Sooner or later your love and devotion will become divided and you must make a choice."

"I see," Hannah said, realizing that the sermon

had been more about choosing sides between the American and British causes than her work as a chambermaid.

They approached a group of rowdy young men who had gathered on a corner. One dark-haired fellow in tattered clothes seemed to be the leader of the mob and was singing loudly:

> *In truth it's judged by men of thinking*
> *That Gage will kill himself by drinking . . .*

Before he could sing the next verse, Catherine put her hands over Hannah's ears. "Stop singing those vile words. Stop right now!" she yelled at the men.

"Oh, the ladies are offended," a man mocked.

"Do you love General Gage, the swine?" the singer sneered. "Do you love him?"

Hannah and Catherine walked by them without another word. Hannah heard one of them say, "Old General Gage will get his one of these days."

"Those are the kind of people General Gage refers to when he calls Bostonians the worst of all bullies and rabble-rousers," Catherine said.

. . .

For the next two weeks Hannah stayed within the walls of the Province House. She did not see Promise or Will in all that time. However, the commotion "Hans" had caused out on the Common had not faded. Caleb related new stories about the Midnight Rider that were being told everywhere. Soldiers wagered with each other as to who would be the one to catch the daring horseman, who was now being blamed for every problem that arose among the troops.

One morning Miss Lydia stopped Hannah in the hallway. "Mrs. Gage wants to see you in her chamber right away."

When Hannah arrived, the door was open and Mrs. Gage was removing paper from the secret drawer of the tallboy. Mrs. Gage looked up, and upon seeing Hannah she flushed, darted to the door, and shut it.

Hannah stood at the closed door, perplexed. But in a moment Mrs. Gage opened it and called her into the room.

"I have an errand for you, Hannah," she said.

"Please deliver this letter to Miss Phillis Wheatley for me."

"I will need permission to leave the grounds."

"Of course. I shall give you permission." She dipped her quill into the inkstand and scratched out a brief message granting Hannah leave. "Miss Wheatley lives near the Old South Meeting House at the corner of Milk Street."

"I know the way," Hannah said.

"Oh, really?" Mrs. Gage looked surprised. "You know your way around Boston Town?"

"To some degree, madam," Hannah answered. In truth, since her night rides with Promise, she had learned almost every lane and street in the town.

Mrs. Gage looked thoughtful as she put a wax seal on the letter for Miss Wheatley. Then she handed the two papers to Hannah. "Please take the letter to Miss Phillis Wheatley right away. And Hannah, don't give it to anyone else, including Mrs. Wheatley."

Hannah headed out the door and down the brick pathway to the sentry. She handed him the unsealed paper. "Mrs. Gage has given me permission to leave."

The sentry opened the paper. "There's nothing on here," he said, handing it back to her.

Hannah looked at the paper. There were no words on the page, only a decorative flower—a lavender iris. "Mrs. Gage must have sealed the wrong letter," she said to the sentry.

"I cannot unseal the other one," the guard said. "You'll have to go back and straighten this out with Mrs. Gage."

"I shall," said Hannah. She turned back to the mansion. This was strange. Why would Mrs. Gage send her out to deliver a letter that had nothing on it?

When Hannah returned, Mrs. Gage looked startled. "What are you doing here?"

"I'm sorry, madam," Hannah said, holding out the papers. "It seems you put the seal on the wrong letter."

Mrs. Gage, a slight frown on her face, snatched the messages from Hannah's hand and examined the open letter. She laughed nervously. "I was so concerned about using the correct words for Miss Wheatley's invitation that I must have neglected to write the message at all!" Shaking her head, she ripped up the sealed letter and quickly penned another note on plain paper. She handed the note to Hannah. "Here is your permission to leave the grounds. I wish to write my message in private. Please wait in the hall,

Hannah." She stood up and indicated the door with her hand.

When Hannah stepped into the hallway, Mrs. Gage closed the door. Hannah looked down at her feet and waited, and in a short while Mrs. Gage opened the door and thrust the new sealed note at Hannah.

"Here, take this and go. And Hannah, remember to give it directly to Miss Phillis."

Hannah took the invitation and curtsied. She was about to walk away when she caught a glimpse of Mrs. Gage through the open door. The lady had returned to her writing table, slumped into the chair, and put her hands to her head as if in pain.

How distressed she looks, Hannah thought. *The situation in Boston must be troubling her more than anyone realizes.*

Hannah returned to the sentry and handed him the new letter giving her permission to leave. She walked along the street, enjoying being outside the fortified mansion. The weather was cool but still pleasant, and winter seemed far away.

She walked up the granite steps of the Wheatleys' house and knocked loudly on the heavily paneled door. Mr. Wheatley was the best tailor in the colonies and was in great demand by the elite of Boston. They were well-to-do, and their house stood on the main street of the town.

Miss Phillis opened the door and smiled. "Good morning," she said. She was dressed in the garb of a servant, but the clothes were colorful and beautifully made.

"Good morning, Miss Phillis. Mrs. Gage requested that I deliver this to you in person." She held out the sealed invitation.

To Hannah's surprise, the young poet slipped outside the door, closed it behind her, and then reached for the letter. "Thank you," she said.

"Is there a reply that I might give to Mrs. Gage?" Hannah asked.

"No." Phillis quickly slipped the envelope in the pocket of her dress. Then the young woman went back into the house, closing the door quietly behind her.

Puzzled by Miss Phillis's odd behavior, Hannah started to head back toward the Province House, then changed her mind. While she was outside the mansion, shouldn't she make the most of it and go see Promise? She turned on her heel and walked swiftly toward Valley Acres. It had been so long since she'd seen her horse! She wished she could take the time to ride, but she didn't dare spend too much time away.

She wondered if Will had taken a trip to Salem with Promise in the last couple of weeks. "We've gone to Salem so many times that Promise knows the way by himself!" Will had told her.

I hope Promise is there, Hannah thought as she turned the corner into Valley Acres. She smiled as she spotted him in the field with two other horses and a cow. The three horses were huddled together, as if discussing a secret. Suddenly Promise trotted over to the cow and nudged her with his rear flank. He then trotted back merrily to the other stallions.

Hannah bent over laughing. "You naughty boy," she yelled, "teasing that poor cow!"

At the sound of her voice, Promise's ears twitched and he looked her way.

"Here I am, my beauty!" she called. The horse neighed and trotted to her.

Hannah climbed over the rail and threw her

arms around him. "I've missed you so much," she whispered, stroking his glossy neck. Promise nickered and nuzzled her, pushing his head under her arm. "You haven't forgotten me, even though you're having such a good time here with your wayward friends, my sweet boy."

"Who's there?" the stable hand shouted from the barn.

Hannah froze. Would he recognize her as the boy who often came to ride Promise? She fluffed her hair around her face and waved. "Just passing by," she called. "Such a pretty horse!"

The stable hand headed toward her. "Stay outside the fence. We don't want to be responsible for anyone to get hurt if the horses act up."

"I'm leaving," Hannah said climbing out of the pasture.

"Have I met you before?" the stable hand asked.

"Oh, no," Hannah said, looking down and shrugging the scarf around her face. "I've never been here." She made her voice soft and low, like Catherine's.

"People keep asking questions about that horse. An army officer was watching him this morning."

"What did he want?"

"He was very interested in him. Asked who owned him."

"And what did you tell him?" Hannah asked. "Who does own this horse?"

"A lad who works for Mr. Hubbard."

Hannah turned to leave. "Well, perhaps the soldier wants to buy him. He's such a beautiful animal."

"Maybe he does," the stable hand said.

Hannah walked swiftly along Treamount Street to School Street, then down the hill to the Province House. An officer was asking the stable hand who owned Promise. Did this man recognize the jet-black horse? If so, would Will be charged as the Midnight Rider?

The governor decided that the American Thanksgiving should be celebrated at the Province House. "We should recognize and respect the customs of the people here," General Gage said. "Otherwise it will be another complaint against us." So the household staff began the huge task of preparing a banquet.

The ovens in the kitchen began burning at dawn on Thanksgiving morning, when Catherine and the other cooks began their work making pies and breads. Vegetables from the root cellar were washed, pared, and put to boil in the huge kettles. Hams and venison had been turning on spits all night, and their aroma filled the mansion and the grounds. Smoke curled and sparks sputtered from the chimneys. There was a sense of tranquility and camaraderie, even with sentries posted at every gateway.

Outside, the trees were now bare, and the wind sang eerily as it howled through the branches. Gulls soared inland—a sign of an oncoming storm. By noonday icy snow whirled in the wind gusts and then pattered as it settled on the dry leaves and walkways.

Hannah was put to work cleaning chambers, polishing silver, and ironing linens. As she unfolded the huge damask tablecloth over the dining table with Mrs. Dudley, she asked, "How many guests have been invited to the feast?"

"At least forty."

"I don't know why we are celebrating an American holiday," Miss Lydia complained as she scurried through the dining room. "We bend over backward to appease these American bumpkins!"

Mrs. Gage had entered the room from the front hallway, and she gave Miss Lydia an icy stare. "I happen to be an American!" Hannah held back a powerful urge to burst into laughter as Miss Lydia paled and immediately began prattling excuses.

"Of—of course, madam," Lydia stammered. "I was speaking of the ruffians, the common ... inferiors ... the, er ... ah ... 'Yankee Doodles' ... certainly not people of your ... breeding ..." Mrs. Gage stood tall and commanding as she watched Lydia with narrowed eyes. "Please excuse . . . you misunderstood ..." Miss Lydia rambled on, her lips stretched into a mollifying smile. "Certainly Thanksgiving is a time for giving thanks ... and ..."

"Enough!" Mrs. Gage snapped. "I do not need you to tell me what Thanksgiving is about. *I am American.* Remember that!" Mrs. Gage's voice echoed through the massive rooms. And then there was silence. Even the clattering of pans and murmuring of voices in the kitchen had stopped.

Mrs. Gage turned on her heel and marched out of the dining hall. Miss Lydia, head bowed and eyes lowered, walked briskly into the kitchen.

The hush that fell over the rooms gave way to whispers. Hannah didn't speak as she smoothed the shiny damask cloth over the table. Mrs. Dudley filled the brass candelabras with tall white candles and said nothing.

Before the banquet, Hannah and Catherine

went to their room to change into their best aprons and lacy mobcaps. Gypsy greeted them at the door, purring and rubbing against their legs.

Hannah picked up the kitten and kissed the top of its head. "You are such a goody."

Catherine was quick to disagree. "Not a goody at all! Gypsy is anxious to get out of this room. She waits by the door, and as soon as it opens, she'd be out of here lickety-cut if she could."

"You cannot go outside, Gypsy. General Gage warned us that you must never leave this room!" Hannah pulled some scraps of chicken from her pocket and placed them in the kitten's dish. Gypsy sniffed at the food and began nibbling eagerly.

"Mrs. Gage was especially huffed with Miss Lydia for belittling the Americans, wasn't she?" Hannah said as she washed her face and changed her apron.

"It's only natural for Mrs. Gage to defend the country of her birth."

"What was it the pastor said last Sabbath? 'You cannot serve two masters,'" Hannah quoted. She fastened the mobcap under her chin.

"Poor Mrs. Gage," Catherine said. "The time is coming when she must choose which master she will serve."

Hannah left the room and hurried to Meg's chamber, where she helped Meg into a rose velvet dress that had been Mrs. Gage's. The neckline was trimmed with French lace tied with rose satin ribbons. She wore white stockings and soft, ivory-colored leather dancing shoes.

Hannah took out the curl papers she had put in Meg's hair hours before. "You don't need these," Hannah said as she arranged Meg's hair into ringlets. "Your hair always waves prettily at the touch of the brush."

"Chester will be here for the banquet tonight," Meg told Hannah. "But I'm planning to meet him later by the Old South Meeting House. I shall be using the tunnel, so I want you to take my place in my bedchamber tonight, Hannah."

Hannah sighed. Meg had not mentioned the tunnel since they had made their pact, and she had hoped Meg had decided not to take the chance of meeting Chester outside the Province House. "It is cold and icy, Miss Meg."

But Meg would not be discouraged. "I will be gone only a short while. It's a perfect time to leave. No one will suspect I've gone anywhere on this cold, miserable night." She stood up. "You stay nearby. I will leave shortly after the entertainment has begun. I'll tell Aunt Margaret that I'm very tired and I'm going to bed. You will come up the back stairway and I shall slip out when everyone is enjoying the entertainment."

"Miss Meg, I don't understand. Why do you need to take such a chance? Lieutenant Pratt will be here tonight."

"I never see him alone. We are always in the company of other people. We have plans to make."

"Plans? What are you planning?"

"That is none of your business, Hannah."

"If I'm to take your place, it is my business. I hope you're not running away or—"

Meg put up her hand. "Of course not! How could I run away with thousands of soldiers packed into this town?'" She stood in front of her mirror and primped her hair. "You worry too much. Don't forget our pact: Silence is golden." When Hannah turned to leave, Meg added, "And remember your place, Hannah. You are my chambermaid, not my guardian."

When Hannah opened the door to the stairway, Catherine was on the landing. "Hannah! When you left our room, Gypsy slipped out. I can't find her anywhere."

"Oh no! Not now! Not with all the guests coming."

"I've searched every room in the servants' quarters upstairs. I was going to look on this floor next, but you must do it, Hannah. I'm needed downstairs. Go find that cat!"

Hannah turned back to search the second floor. "Gypsy! Gypsy!" she called softly. "Cat, cat, cat!" But there was no sign of Gypsy. Could she have slipped into Meg's room?

Hannah knocked on the door and Meg answered. "What do you want?"

"I've lost my kitten. Is she in here?"

"I hope not! She'd go after my little bird!" Meg opened the door wider and the two girls looked under the bed and in the adjoining dressing room. Gypsy was not there.

The door to Mrs. Gage's chamber was closed.

Hannah didn't dare try the door; Mrs. Gage might be in there. Then what about General Gage's office? If Gypsy had wandered into that room, it would be dreadful! But that door was shut too. Hannah searched under the chairs and tables in the reception room, calling, "Gypsy! Gypsy!"

What if the cat had wandered down into the banquet room? If General Gage discovered Gypsy, he'd be sure to drown her. Why hadn't she been more careful? She must find Gypsy!

Carriages and chaises arrived at dusk and pulled up to the lantern-lit entry. Officers in their red and gold uniforms escorted ladies dressed in fashionable gowns that had probably been sent from England or France. Although fabrics could not be brought into the port of Boston because of the embargo, the wives and daughters of British officers often received gifts from abroad.

The evening went by quickly as Hannah helped serve the dinner, carried out Mrs. Dudley's orders, made coffee, and cleaned dishes. All the while she watched for a sign of Gypsy. Had she slipped out the door and into the cold night? Hannah was distracted all evening. Even Miss Lydia seemed concerned. "Are you ill? If so you should not be serving food."

"No, Miss Lydia, I'm not ill."

"You're acting as if you're in another world. Pay attention to your duties."

Meanwhile, Meg was as charming as ever, and she stood out from everyone in Mrs. Gage's soft velvet gown. While many young officers flirted and surrounded her, a stern Lieutenant Pratt stayed close by her side.

Mrs. Gage herself was stunningly attractive in an amber and rust Turkish-style dress and turban—the latest trend in Europe. She was a beautifully exotic woman. Her dark eyes and hair captivated everyone. Hannah assumed she had inherited her striking coloring; it was rumored that she was of English, Greek, and Portuguese descent. Yet she was still American, Hannah thought, remembering Mrs. Gage's declaration to Miss Lydia earlier that day.

When Madeira wine from Spain and entertainment were announced, everyone withdrew to the drawing room. Hannah, still on the lookout for Gypsy, carried a tray of French pastries, which she offered to the people who milled about.

One woman sat demurely in a large cushioned chair, sipping wine. She was stylishly dressed in a blue and white striped dress with blue tassels around the hem. Suddenly Hannah caught a glimpse of a tiny paw that reached out from beneath the chair and snatched at a tassel. Gypsy!

Hannah plunked the tray of pastries into the nearest gentleman's lap, dived toward the woman in the tasseled dress, and thrust both hands under the chair, causing it to teeter. The woman screamed as she slid to the floor and the kitten skittered out.

Hannah raced after Gypsy, who darted among the startled guests, then hid from Hannah under another woman's skirt. The lady shrieked and stamped her feet, frightening the kitten, who scampered out, tangling one paw in the lady's petticoat. As Hannah reached for Gypsy, she tripped on the leg of a chair. *Slam!* Down she fell! But this time she was able to snatch Gypsy just as the kitten was about to pounce away.

When Hannah looked up, people were standing around her, aghast. General and Mrs. Gage watched in astonished silence. "Excuse me, please.

I . . . I didn't want anyone to fall . . . on the kitten."
Hannah could feel tears forming. Would General
Gage take Gypsy away to be drowned?

Hannah could see Lieutenant Pratt looking on
with disgust. "I'd throw that animal into the river,"
he announced, "and the girl with it!"

eg frowned at Chester Pratt and made her way over to Hannah. "No! I won't let you drown it." She took Gypsy from Hannah's arms and petted her. "It's a darling kitten, and I would like to keep it. I promise it won't escape from my chambers, Uncle Thomas."

"Very well, but be sure you keep *your* door shut," General Gage said with a cold glare at Hannah.

There was an awkward silence among the guests as Mrs. Gage headed furiously toward Hannah. To Hannah's relief, Colonel Leslie interrupted what was surely to be an unpleasant encounter. "That was an exciting entertainment you arranged, Your Excellency," he said with a smile. "The trained lion was most charming."

The gentleman with the tray of pastries stood up. "Cake, anyone?"

Mrs. Gage seized the tray from his hands and with a dazzling smile began offering the pastries to her guests. Everyone laughed, and the tension abated.

General Gage took a sip of wine. "Let the second act begin." He waved his hand to the string quartet that waited nearby. The music began, and Hannah's incident with Gypsy was soon forgotten.

"Oh, thank you, Miss Meg," Hannah whispered. "I'm so sorry this happened."

Meg thrust the kitten at Hannah. "Keep the kitten locked up, Hannah. I'm not sure I could save it from Uncle Thomas a second time."

"I will," Hannah promised as she gathered Gypsy into her arms and headed to the rear stairway. As she passed through the kitchen, she noticed that the servants were already buzzing with laughter at what had happened. Catherine shook her head and rolled her eyes at Hannah.

As Hannah raced by, Miss Lydia grabbed her arm. "What cheek! Imagine, sneaking a cat into the Province House."

Hannah was about to retort that General Gage had given her permission when Catherine spoke up. "Oh, the cat belongs to Miss Meg now. Hannah's been punished enough. Leave her alone."

"But Gypsy will be back in our room," Hannah said, taking Catherine aside and out of Miss Lydia's hearing. "Miss Meg has a bird, and she's afraid Gypsy might go after it. I hope you don't mind."

"You must be more careful coming and going," Catherine warned.

After depositing the kitten in their chamber, Hannah closed the door tightly. Then she tiptoed to the third-floor landing of the grand staircase, where she watched nervously for Meg. It wasn't long before Meg ascended the steps, smiling and waving to the guests, as she made a grand departure from the party.

Hannah immediately scurried to the floor below, and they met at Meg's room.

"Good!" Meg exclaimed, opening the door and pulling Hannah inside. "Light the lamps and get my wrap. Quickly!"

Hannah fired up the oil lamps that hung on the wall while Meg lit a candle on the dresser.

"You're going out in that dress?" Hannah exclaimed as she pulled a white fox wrap from the chest at the foot of the bed. "You'll turn into an icicle."

"I'll be warm enough in this," Meg said, tossing the fur around her shoulders. "Now remember, lock the door when I leave, and if anyone comes by, simply call out, 'I'm tired and do not wish to be disturbed.' Let me hear you say it in my voice, Hannah."

Hannah closed her eyes and concentrated on Meg's soft voice and British accent. "'I'm tired and do not wish to be disturbed.'"

"Wonderful!" Meg said with a laugh. "You sound exactly like me."

"What if Mrs. Gage or someone insists on coming into the room?"

"Stay under the covers and draw the bed hangings around you when you lie down—they will block any view of your face." Meg peeked out of the door cautiously. "Everyone is at the entertainment. Then they'll be dancing all evening."

"Your shoes!" Hannah exclaimed, looking at Miss Meg's frail dancing slippers. "You can't wear those out in the cold and through that dirty tunnel."

"It's all right," Meg insisted. "I won't be walking far. Chester will meet me with his carriage on Marlborough Street. We will be going to a secluded tavern for mugs of chocolate. No one will be there at this hour."

"Someone in the kitchen may see you leave."

"Whist!" Meg put her finger to her lips.

"Don't forget there are candles at each end of the tunnel."

But Meg had already disappeared down the back stairway.

Hannah locked the door to Meg's room and went to the window. The snow had stopped, but there was frost on the glass, and she could feel the cold air creeping in around the panes. She wondered if Lieutenant Pratt had left the banquet yet, and if anyone suspected he was meeting Meg.

The sounds of music and laughter drifted through the mansion pleasantly. Hannah tapped the birdcage, and the little yellow bird, which had been sleeping with its head under its wing, responded with fluttering and peeping. "You are sweet," Hannah told the bird, "and you are warm and safe, which is more than I can say for your mistress."

The tall clock on the stairway landing struck nine times. There was nothing to do, so Hannah drew the woolen bed curtains around the canopy, pulled the coverlet down, and lay on the bed. Occasionally she heard footsteps and men's voices. "It's probably General Gage and his staff meeting in the office. Or perhaps he's meeting with his informant!" she told herself. Caleb had said there were several informants, but one had to be close to the Sons of Liberty, since the general knew every word spoken at their secret meetings. Hannah wondered if that person had come through the tunnel to speak to General Gage. *After all, someone else knows about the passageway.* Could that dark shadowy figure Caleb had seen on the night when he first discovered the tunnel be the informant?

Hannah yawned. She yanked the coverlet over her and sank into the pillow, pretending for a moment that the bed was hers, along with all of the pretty clothes and fine jewels that filled the room.

She had had a sweet bed and her own room before Papa died. Sadness flowed over her. Would she ever have a home of her own and someone to love her again?

Hannah thought about Caleb and Will. They seemed to be fond of her. They confided in her and were concerned for her welfare. Still, they probably liked her in the same way they enjoyed each other's company—as if she were only their daring friend Hans instead of the girl she really was.

Caleb was strong and hardworking. He loved horses like she did. He was not handsome, with his wayward brown hair and freckles, but he was true to his convictions and faithful to his friends. He'd make someone a good husband, though he was surely not interested in Hannah except as a friend.

Will was handsome. Hannah noticed how girls watched him when he rode by. He could have his choice of girls. He had a fine home in Salem with parents who provided for him. And he didn't mind sharing Promise with Hannah. He understood how much she loved the horse. Perhaps he did care for Hannah.

No, she told herself. Will will never love me the way young men love beautiful women. Hannah rolled over, clutched the pillow, and fell into an empty and dreamless sleep.

A knocking on the door awakened her. "Are you all right, Meg?" It was Mrs. Gage.

Hannah instantly sat up and took a breath. The sounds of music and voices had stopped, so the entertainment must be over. She needed to concentrate and give the answer Meg had ordered. Her heart was pounding. "I'm fine, Aunt Margaret," Hannah said in Meg's voice. "I'm just tired and want to sleep."

"Very well, dear," Mrs. Gage said.

Mrs. Gage's footsteps pattered down the hall to her room, and Hannah sank back into the bed wondering what time it was and when Meg would be returning.

Before long the clock struck eleven. Where was Meg? She said she'd only be gone a short while. Hannah was becoming anxious. She got up and looked out the window, which faced the quiet street. It was snowing hard again. The large white flakes billowed in the light of the streetlamps.

The candle on the chest had burned out. Hannah adjusted the whale-oil lamps to make them brighter. Shadows leaped across the paneled walls.

What if Meg *had* run away with Lieutenant Pratt? Mrs. Gage had asked Hannah to keep her informed. Surely Hannah would be blamed if Meg didn't return. She decided that if Meg didn't come back by dawn, she would go back to her own room and pretend she knew nothing of Meg's actions.

She lay on the bed listening to every sound, real and imagined, when quite suddenly she heard a soft knock. Hannah jumped out of bed and tip-toed to the locked door. "Who is it?" she whispered in Meg's voice.

"Meg!"

Relief flooded over Hannah and she unlocked the door and gasped. There stood Meg, her shoes in her hand, Mrs. Gage's velvet dress in tatters, the fox wrap falling off her arms, and her hair wet and matted with snow.

"What happened?" Hannah asked.

"I shall tell you," Meg said tossing the fox cape onto the bed, "once my tongue thaws and my bones stop shaking. I'm nearly frozen to death. The tunnel was slippery and I fell. See?" She showed Hannah a cut on her arm. "I stumbled through that awful place, and the candle went out when I was halfway through. So I had to grope my way to the end." Meg gestured to the buttons on the back of her dress, and Hannah began undoing them. "I wish you had warned me! I wish you'd told me how dirty and dark and *cold* the tunnel is."

"I did warn you," Hannah protested.

Meg ignored her. "When I was finally able to open the heavy trapdoor on the other end, I made my way to the Old South." Her voice became muffled as Hannah pulled the dress over her head. "That simpleton Chester wasn't even there! After all I went through to meet him!" Meg climbed into the bed and shivered in her chemise. She pulled the covers around herself. "Oh good, you've warmed the bed for me."

Hannah would have laughed had she not felt so sorry for Meg. At last Meg had discovered that Chester was a simpleton. Hannah had known it all along.

Meg's teeth stopped chattering. "He finally came, all apologies and sweetness. It seems he had to take another lady home first, while I stood there in the cold waiting for him! Never again will I speak to him!"

"He was terribly cruel to keep you waiting like that," Hannah said consolingly.

"He wanted to escort me home the way I came—"

Hannah put her hand to her mouth. "You didn't tell him about the tunnel, did you?"

"Of course not. I kept my word of silence. I would not allow him to escort me anywhere. I stomped off by myself and left him by the Old South watching after me. He probably saw me go up School Street, but he never knew a thing about the tunnel.

"I must admit I was tempted to come back here through the gates on Marlborough Street rather than go through that hellhole again. However, if I did, I knew I'd be questioned by Uncle Thomas." Meg looked as if she were ready to throw something. "When I finally made my way back, the guests were all leaving in their carriages, and the snow was coming down like a blizzard! I had to wait for everyone to go. I couldn't let anyone see me looking like this as I headed across the courtyard. That's what took me so long. Sitting there inside that tunnel, popping open the trapdoor now and then—which sent a flood of snow over me. I'll probably expire from the cold."

"May I get you a cup of hot tea, Miss Meg?" Hannah asked.

"Yes, yes, tea would be good." Meg pulled the quilt around her and shivered again. As Hannah started for the door, Meg grabbed her arm. "Hannah, I cannot believe how much love you must have for whomever it is you meet, to escape through that dark and dirty place."

Hannah pulled away gently, not ready to tell Meg that it wasn't for the love of a man that she took those chances, but the love of a horse.

Over the next several days Meg was bombarded with love notes from Lieutenant Pratt. In one letter the Lieutenant had written a poem, which Meg read aloud to Hannah.

Alas, I die in heartsick pain
Because my heart is broke in twain.

Hannah envisioned Chester Pratt in lovesick pain and wanted to laugh. But she had no right to make a comment, so she took a deep breath and concentrated on her shoes.

"This is a lot of drivel," Meg exclaimed. "I hope Chester's heart *is* broken. I never want to see him again." She tossed the poem into the fire.

· · ·

One morning Hannah was called into Mrs. Gage's chamber. Mrs. Dudley was there, arranging teacups on a sideboard.

"I will be serving a ladies' tea in my chambers today," Mrs. Gage said. "I'd like this to be a cozy fireside gathering. I'll need you to help with the service."

Mrs. Gage and Meg greeted the women who arrived. Among the twelve guests were Mrs. Wheatley and her protégé, Phillis. Hannah took their cloaks into another room. While Mrs. Gage poured tea, Hannah served pretty pastries, colorful marzipan, and delicate tarts. For an hour or so the women chatted idly about their families. Hannah glanced at Meg, who looked bored as she sipped her tea. Hannah noticed that Miss Meg was not as vivacious and dazzling as she was when young officers were present.

Gradually the topic changed to the city and how difficult it was being unable to travel freely or acquire fabrics or other imported materials.

"At least we are still drinking our tea," said Mrs. Wheatley. "Most Bostonians won't buy it or drink it since the taxation and the Tea Party."

"The ordinary folks here in Boston don't seem to be suffering much," one officer's wife replied. "The merchants and farmers outside of Boston have some way of smuggling food, clothing, shoes, and other necessities into the town for their own people."

"It's a strange turnabout," another woman commented, "for we Loyalists to be the ones going without!"

"You must realize, though, that the Whigs themselves have kept the peace. They've presented their protests and requests courteously and in proper order to the governor," Mrs. Gage said. "It's the *factions*, as my husband calls them, that cause most of the trouble here."

Phillis Wheatley spoke up softly. "I understand that the Whigs—Dr. Warren and John Hancock— were able to calm and turn back the twenty thousand men who marched to the aid of Boston during the powder house incident."

"Thank goodness," a guest said, and everyone nodded in agreement.

As they continued to chat, Hannah tidied up the tea service and brushed crumbs from the sideboard, wishing she could speak up and tell these women how difficult and hopeless it was to be in slavery to any person or nation. *Miss Phillis must understand,* she thought, *having once been a slave.* Some of her poetry dealt with the subject of freedom.

Hannah wondered if any of these women had an inkling of the organized preparation of the minutemen, the Committees of Correspondence and Safety, and what was going on at the clandestine meetings at the Green Dragon Tavern. They seemed oblivious to the measures being taken by the Patriots.

"I don't like to ask," said the officer's wife, "but do you think there will be . . . war?"

Several women put their hands over their mouths in shock.

Margaret Gage quoted Shakespeare in a low voice: "'Upon my knee I beg, go not to arms.'" A long silence fell on the room. Then Mrs. Gage spoke again. "I pray my husband will never be the instrument that sacrifices the lives of my countrymen." She stood up and walked to the window. Outside, the snow whirled in the rising wind. "The snow is becoming heavy."

Taking this to be a sign of dismissal, Meg stood up, and most of the other women followed. Hannah helped them into their capes, and they paid their respects to Mrs. Gage, who remained standing by the window watching the snow. She nodded absently to her guests as they left. Hannah busied herself collecting the cups and saucers onto a tray, but she could see pain in Mrs. Gage's face.

Mrs. Wheatley and Phillis were the last to leave. Mrs. Wheatley patted Mrs. Gage's hand. "It's a difficult time for you, I'm sure," she said kindly, "being both American and British."

General Gage's wife gave her a wan smile. "There is another passage from Shakespeare's *King John* that represents my feelings very well." She began to quote:

> *"Which is the side that I must go withal?*
> *I am with both. . . ."*

Mrs. Gage's voice broke and she turned to the window again. Phillis Wheatley continued the quotation.

"Whoever wins, on that side shall I lose
Assured loss, before the match be play'd."

"Ah, yes," Margaret Gage said. "Yes."

After the Wheatleys left, Hannah straightened the chairs. She was about to bring the trays of utensils to the scullery to be washed, when Mrs. Gage called to her.

"Hannah, please sit down for a moment. I have a question for you."

Hannah set the trays on the sideboard and took a seat in front of Mrs. Gage.

"Hannah, you have been Miss Meg's chambermaid for several weeks now."

"Yes, madam."

"Since Miss Meg is in our care, General Gage and I are naturally concerned about her welfare."

Hannah felt her face flush. What was she going to be asked about Meg's escapade on Thanksgiving night?

"Hannah, I would like to know if Miss Meg is meeting someone. A young man, perhaps?"

Hannah looked down at her lap and realized

she was clasping and unclasping her hands nervously. As far as she knew, Meg was no longer meeting Lieutenant Pratt.

"I don't believe Miss Meg is meeting any young man, madam," Hannah answered. She looked up and saw that Mrs. Gage was watching her with a penetrating gaze. Hannah quickly fixed her eyes on her hands again.

"Hannah, you must realize that you are indentured to *us*—not to Miss Meg. I am your mistress. You owe your loyalty to me, and I'm trusting you to be honest."

Hannah looked into Mrs. Gage's dark eyes. "I am being honest, madam. Miss Meg is beautiful, and many young officers admire her. But I can truthfully say that as far as I know, Miss Meg is not meeting any young men right now."

Mrs. Gage smiled faintly. "Right now?"

Hannah had promised not to betray Meg. And if she revealed everything she knew about Meg, then everyone would know about the secret tunnel, too. "As I said, Mrs. Gage, to the best of my knowledge, Miss Meg is not seeing any young man."

"Has she seen someone in the past?"

Now Hannah felt trapped.

"Hannah?"

Hannah swallowed. "I . . . I'm sure Miss Meg is so . . . charming . . . that it's impossible for her *not* to be pursued by men."

Mrs. Gage was silent for a while, and then she stood up. "Never mind, Hannah. You are quite right. It is impossible for her *not* to be pursued by young men. She is as adept at manipulating as she is at flirting. She's obviously manipulated you as well." Mrs. Gage gazed out the window once more. "Or perhaps you are unsure where your loyalties lie. I understand that only too well." She waved her hand, dismissing Hannah. "You can go."

Hannah curtsied and hastily left the chamber. She had to talk to Meg right away. Should she be questioned by Mrs. Gage, she needed to know that Hannah had not betrayed her. After depositing the trays in the scullery, Hannah darted down the hall to Meg's chambers and knocked hard on the door several times.

"Who is there?"

"It's Hannah. I need to see you, Miss Meg."

Meg opened the door and stood aside. "What

do you want? What's so urgent that you're banging on my door?"

"After you left the tea, Mrs. Gage asked me to stay in her chamber. She asked about you and whether you are meeting any young men."

Meg gasped. "What did you tell her?"

"I told her that as far I know you are not seeing anyone."

Meg's shoulders relaxed. "Thank you for lying for me, Hannah."

"I didn't lie! You told me you're through with Lieutenant Pratt."

"Did you tell her anything about my meetings with him?"

"Of course not. I kept my promise to you. I've told no one."

Meg paced the room. "She must know something. I wonder if Chester has betrayed me in some way."

"She may just be curious. But I swear that I was never disloyal to you. And you must remember your vow to me—that you will never inform anyone about the tunnel."

"I won't," Meg said. "I swear."

"Mrs. Gage reminded me that she is my mistress, not you." Hannah sighed.

"Aunt Margaret gave you to me, so you owe your loyalties to me!" Meg insisted.

Hannah bristled. "No one has the right to *give* me to anyone. I don't belong to anyone but myself."

Meg ignored Hannah's words. She sat on the bed and pounded the pillow with her fist. "I just want to leave this place. It's becoming a prison! I hope Uncle Thomas sends me to England! It would be far better than living here in the Province House." Meg's face lit up. She stood, held her skirt prettily, and whirled around. "If I were in England, I might be invited to the royal court. Perhaps I'd find another earl, or even better, a count. He would promise me anything! I could become a countess! Wouldn't that be elegant, Hannah?"

Hannah shrugged. "My dreams are far different from yours, Miss Meg."

"Oh? What do servants like you wish for?"

Hannah answered without an instant's hesitation. "Freedom."

two weeks had passed when Mrs. Gage sent Hannah to the Wheatley's residence to deliver another sealed letter to Miss Phillis. "This must be given only to Miss Phillis" were Mrs. Gage's explicit orders. "If someone else answers the door, don't deliver it at all." As if to quell Hannah's curiosity, Mrs. Gage added, "It's an invitation to tea. I'd like to visit with Miss Phillis on a more intimate basis, without Mrs. Wheatley, to discuss her poetry."

Hannah noticed that the envelope she delivered to Miss Wheatley was of the same stationery as the earlier one. She could see the outline of the flower inside. Hannah would not have been curious had she not seen the earlier letter that contained no words at all.

It also seemed peculiar that there had been no tea with Miss Phillis. Perhaps Miss Phillis couldn't find the time to visit with Mrs. Gage. However, an invitation by the governor's wife would hardly ever be refused. Why was Mrs. Gage so reticent? Why did she keep that stationery in the secret drawer Hannah had shown her?

One December morning, when Catherine was cleaning out the chest at the foot of her bed, she removed her treasured book on the language of flowers and placed it on her bedside table.

"May I look at the book?" Hannah asked.

Catherine handed it to her. "Turn the pages carefully, Hannah. It's so old, the paper crumbles."

Hannah turned each page slowly. After several pages she found what she was looking for: an iris. Her eyes fell upon the remains of a blossom and its meaning in the ancient language of flowers.

Iris: I have a message for you.

So that's what an iris meant. But now Hannah was even more confused. If Mrs. Gage was sending a blank page with an iris embossed on it to say, "I have a message for you," then where was the message? What was this peculiar correspondence all about? She placed Catherine's book back on the table.

One afternoon, when Meg had gone to an afternoon party with Mrs. Gage, Hannah was ordered to straighten and clean Meg's chamber. She carried Meg's bedsheets and towels to the scullery for Annie to wash, then returned to the chamber to make up the bed with fresh linen. As she was working, she heard angry voices coming from General Gage's private office. Cautiously, she tiptoed down the hallway and into the reception hall. Taking a cloth from her pocket, she dusted the rich mahogany furniture, all the while paying close attention to the conversation in the opposite room.

"I sent dispatches to His Majesty and to Parliament," General Gage stated to the staff who were congregated in his headquarters. "I demanded—I *begged*—for more troops to be sent to Boston. I promised they would save both blood and treasure if they would heed my needs." Hannah heard a *smack!* and imagined General Gage pounding his desk. "To think the king himself rejected my warning as 'absurd'! What does he or

Parliament know about America or Boston or what I am up against here?"

"But Your Excellency, you asked for twenty thousand men," one of the officers said. "The reply says that it is not possible to collect such a force unless we are in a state of war."

"We may well be in a state of war before long, and then it will be too late," General Gage replied. "The Americans have already gathered a militia that will march at a moment's notice! This whole country is in arms and in motion!"

"Where did you hear about the American militia?" an officer asked.

"I have an informant right in the midst of them. I know all about their Committees of Safety and Correspondence. I know every move and plan the Whigs are making during their secret meetings at the Green Dragon. Yet despite all this intelligence, the king calls my warnings 'absurd.'"

Hannah continued dusting with rapid, aimless strokes, all the while straining to hear more.

"King George might as well be on a distant star, Your Excellency," came another voice. "He cannot comprehend what a treasure this country is, nor how quickly he may be throwing it away."

"Very well, then we must move on as best we can." General Gage sounded resigned. "We have a law prohibiting the export or import of munitions from and into North America. What we need to do now is rid the provinces of the arms they already have. I understand there is a large supply of powder and arms at Fort William and Mary at Portsmouth in New Hampshire."

"Yes, Your Excellency," replied an officer. "And the fort is not well guarded. The people of New Hampshire could overpower that fortress easily and make off with the munitions."

The voices became muffled, and Hannah could only hear a few more words: "expedition" and "warships," "HMS *Somerset*" and "on their way."

Fort William and Mary. Portsmouth is only fifty or sixty miles away! That would be the next strike by the British to remove American powder and cannon. She had to get word to Will and Caleb!

Later that evening, recalling how Mr. Revere had noticed her mother's ring, she tucked it safely away in a drawer. Hannah slipped out to the stable, but neither boy was there. She had promised Will and Caleb that she would not take Promise on any more midnight rides, but she needed to warn someone. Mr. Revere! She'd go directly to him and tell him what she had overheard.

Hannah changed into Hans's clothes and added an old jacket of Caleb's that hung on a hook in the loft. The collar felt rough against her face, but it would protect her from the cold.

She made her way through the familiar tunnel and out into the alley. Should she walk to Mr. Revere's house? It wasn't that far away. But she wanted to see Promise and ride him. She wouldn't play any pranks, she promised herself. She'd just ride to Mr. Revere's house and back to the stable. This was an important message she had to get to the Sons of Liberty.

When she arrived at Valley Acres, the stable hand was nowhere to be seen. Promise whinnied when he saw her and rubbed his head against her shoulder. "No apples tonight, my love," she said, as he pushed his nose toward her pocket. "We will have a ride together, but we don't have time for a saddle."

Hannah led Promise outside by his bridle.

Then, using a mounting step, she climbed onto his bare back. "Come on, Promise, let's go to Mr. Revere's house," she whispered, tapping Promise's flank. Promise shook his head, snorted, and leaped forward eagerly. It felt good to Hannah to be riding bareback, the way she often rode back in Salem.

The snow was not deep, but it softened the sound of Promise's hooves. As they approached a tavern Hannah could hear men inside singing the familiar and taunting "Yankee Doodle." Three soldiers' mounts were tied in an empty yard adjoining the tavern.

"General Gage's men are probably full of Madeira wine and have forgotten their duties to patrol the streets," Hannah whispered.

Lights still glistened through Mr. Revere's windows. Hannah tied Promise to a hitching post and knocked at the door. After a few moments, Mr. Revere opened the door. "Oh, it's you—Hans."

"I have some important news for you," Hannah said in her own voice.

"It must be important, for you to take the chance of coming here so late at night. Come in."

"The Province House is full of activity, with

soldiers and officers coming and going. Today I heard General Gage talking about the arms at Fort William and Mary in Portsmouth."

Mr. Revere listened intently as Hannah told him about the plan to secure the fortress and take the arms before the New Hampshire Whigs plundered the munitions.

"When is this to happen?"

"I don't know, but soon," Hannah said. "Perhaps the HMS *Somerset* is already on its way."

"I know warships are all along the coast of New England," Mr. Revere said thoughtfully. "They may be preparing to head for Portsmouth Harbor."

"General Gage wrote to the king and requested twenty thousand foot soldiers, but he was refused. The king said it was absurd."

"Now that's powerful information," Mr. Revere said.

"And here's something else," Hannah continued. "I heard General Gage tell his officers that he has an informant inside the Committees of Correspondence and Safety. Whoever it is informs him of everything that is going on. He even mentioned the Green Dragon Tavern."

"Who could be the traitor in our midst? Our men at the Green Dragon and in the Committees all swear on the Bible to secrecy and loyalty."

"I heard it with my own ears," Hannah stated emphatically.

Mr. Revere shook his head. "We have long wondered how General Gage is so often one step ahead of the Whigs and the Sons of Liberty. But still . . . a turncoat? I cannot imagine who it could be."

Hannah was disappointed. Perhaps Mr. Revere didn't believe her stories. She suddenly felt foolish in having come to the Reveres' house at all.

Mr. Revere spoke up, as if reading her thoughts. "I do believe you about Portsmouth," he said. "And you've told me all you've heard, then?"

"Yes, sir."

"Thank you. This information about Fort William and Mary is important, and we will take care of it." Mr. Revere held the door open for her. "Good night, Hans."

"Good night, sir."

"One more thing," Mr. Revere said as Hannah turned to go. "You must not discuss this with anyone. Traitors are taken down by the river and shot.

Your own life may be in danger at this point. Do you understand?"

"Yes, sir. And please, sir, do not let anyone in the Committees know I was the one who gave you this information. Your traitor, whoever he might be, would expose me to General Gage."

"I swear you will remain anonymous," Mr. Revere promised.

Hannah unhitched Promise and tried to climb on his back, but the bulky clothes made it difficult, since this time she did not have a step. Three boys watched and crowed at her from the opposite side of the street. They were standing under a lamp, and she recognized them as the surly young men who had sung parodies about General Gage when she and Catherine walked home from church that Sunday morning.

"Can't mount your horse?" the leader of the group called out.

"Did you sell your saddle?" another hooted.

Hannah tapped Promise's knees and the horse knelt on his front legs. "Good boy," she said in Hans's voice as she climbed on his back. "You remember what Papa taught you so I could mount you when I was a child." She patted Promise's neck.

There were murmurs of awe from across the street. "Did you see that?"

"Must be a trained warhorse from England."

"Could that be the Midnight Rider?" the biggest youth asked. "The horse is as black as midnight!"

"Hey, you! Wait!" called one of the lads as the group started toward her.

Hannah urged Promise into a canter and away from the rowdy boys, thankful that they were not on horseback. But when she approached Marlborough Street and looked back, she could see them by the tavern, talking to soldiers and pointing her way. They would almost certainly betray her to the soldiers. Those troublemakers had no sense of loyalty to either the British or the Americans. More likely they were looking for a reward for turning in the Midnight Rider.

"Fly, Promise!" Hannah called in her male voice. The horse leaped forward in a gallop. Once out of sight she reined him in to an acceptable trot and headed back to Valley Acres.

Back at the barn, the stable boy was snoring on

a pile of hay. He opened his eyes briefly, then nodded back to sleep again. Hannah wiped Promise down and removed his bridle. "There, my good boy," she said. "Stay warm in here until we ride again."

Out on the streets once more, she pulled her hat over her forehead to shade her face. There was no commotion, so she assumed the soldiers were not looking for her. Nevertheless, she picked up her pace and hurried down Marlborough Street to School Street and the alley.

She walked slowly toward the tunnel entrance, staying in the shadows, hoping the soldiers would not come searching for her. The large boulder blocked her view of the trapdoor.

Hannah stopped suddenly. There were footprints on the fresh snow. Big footprints. They couldn't have been Will's or Caleb's. The tracks were clear, as if imprinted by well made leather shoes, not like something the boys wore. The prints headed to the hatch. She was relieved to see that drifting snow had covered her own earlier footprints. But had they been visible when the person entered the passageway? Did she dare go back through the tunnel?

She did not have time to decide what to do, for

at that very moment she heard the grating sound of the trapdoor opening. Quickly she ducked behind the boulder, brushing snow over her fresh footprints with her gloved hands.

Shivering, she crouched close to the ground, as far behind the rock as she could get, praying she would not be seen.

She heard the door close and then the soft sound of footsteps on the snow. She waited silently, listening. Then, cautiously, she peeked out around the boulder. A man was standing under a streetlamp. He was tall and gaunt, with graying hair gathered in a pigtail at the back of his neck. She watched as he straightened his coat, brushed it off, and then pulled on some gloves. The stranger walked up the street with long strides and disappeared down one of the narrow lanes.

Hannah had seen this man before. It was on her first day at the Province House, when he had gone into General Gage's private office. There was somewhere else that she had seen this person too. But where? In any case, this must have been the person that Caleb had seen emerge from the underground passage months ago.

Hannah realized with a shudder that if she had crept through the tunnel a moment earlier, she would have met the man face-on!

Suddenly, Hannah heard a commotion. Soldiers on horseback galloped onto Marlborough Street.

"Where is that Midnight Rider? Those boys said he couldn't be far from here."

"When we get him, we'll bathe him in tar and feathers!"

"Then we'll hang him from their damned Liberty Tree!"

In a panic, Hannah pulled open the hatch and hurled herself down the stone steps into the darkness of the tunnel.

early the next morning, Hannah raced to the stable to tell Caleb about the stranger in the tunnel. But the stable was filled with soldiers urgently coming and going, and with a harsh look and shake of his head, Caleb warned her to leave.

The Province House was also filled with officers. Hannah overheard talk that Paul Revere had rushed to Portsmouth and set the Whigs into turmoil. Actual fighting had occurred at Fort William and Mary as the few British officers on duty there bravely defended the fort.

Two days later, when an express rider from Governor Wentworth of New Hampshire arrived at the Province House begging for troops to be sent immediately to Portsmouth, General Gage ordered another ship, the HMS *Canceaux*, to head there.

"We may be at war!" Catherine whispered to Hannah.

Later that morning, when Hannah was filling pitchers at the well, Caleb joined her. "Your midnight visit to Paul Revere caused quite a stir, Hannah. He rode off the next morning to warn the Whigs in Portsmouth that ships were heading to Fort William and Mary." He poured himself a cup of icy water from the bucket. "But your report was a bit off."

"What do you mean?" Had she given false information to the Committee of Safety?

"The HMS *Somerset* wasn't heading to Portsmouth. It was returning from England with more troops. The *Canceaux* was the ship commissioned to Portsmouth."

Hannah was silent. She had only heard the name of the *Somerset* in garbled conversation. Had she sent Paul Revere on a useless race? "But I knew for certain that General Gage and his officers were planning to reinforce the fort. I heard it with my own ears."

"You heard right. But Gage's troops were to get there a few days later. Aw, don't worry. It's just as

well that Revere brought the news as early as he did.
The New Hampshire militia—more than a thousand strong—attacked the fort and took away all
the munitions. When the British marines finally
arrived, the gunpowder and cannon were already
hidden." Caleb chuckled. "And the latest news is
this: When General Gage sent Admiral Graves and
his marines out on the *Canceaux*, they got jammed
in shallow water. They're stuck aground, Hannah,
and totally helpless!"

Hannah shook her head in disbelief. Had her
message caused all this chaos?

"Did you hear they actually came to blows at
the Portsmouth fort?" Caleb asked. "You might
have started a war, Hannah!"

"No! Don't say such a thing!" Hannah had a
sick feeling in her stomach, and she recalled Mrs.
Gage's words: *I beg, go not to arms.* "The things that
are happening are not silly jokes, Caleb."

"It's all for freedom instead of tyranny," Caleb
said comfortingly. "You said yourself that freedom
is everything."

"It is," Hannah agreed with a nod. "Will Mr.
Revere be arrested?"

"Everyone knows it was Revere who warned the Whigs in Portsmouth. Loyalists are saying he should be hung from the Liberty Tree."

Hannah shivered. Then she told Caleb about the stranger in the tunnel. "I've seen him before, coming from General Gage's office, and somewhere else, too, but I can't recall where." She described the man as best she could, but Caleb was unable to identify him.

"We'd better not use the tunnel for a while," he said.

"Where is Will?" Hannah asked. "He should be warned."

"He left for Salem with Promise early this morning. He'll be back in a few days." Caleb stood up. "I'll tell Will about the tunnel when I see him."

Winter set in with snowdrifts and icy winds. Children played in the snow, sledding on every available slope, often barely missing being hit by oncoming sleighs.

The Province House was decorated with holly and boughs of evergreens. Candles gleamed in every window, day and night. But despite the preparations and forced joviality, everyone knew that the Portsmouth Alarm was a humiliation to General Gage and Admiral Graves. To make matters worse, other New England communities had followed suit and absconded with ammunition from their local forts and armories before Gage's men could secure them.

One morning Meg and Hannah were allowed to ride on a one-horse open sleigh around the town. Hannah, in her mother's red cape, and Meg, in dark-green velvet with an ermine collar, sat side by side, bundled in a rug. Joseph drove the horse through the mall of bare trees at the Common and then around Beacon Hill and down to the waterfront. Ships strained at the docks where they were tied, icicles hanging from their masts and spars.

On the return, Meg had Joseph stop at a clothing store, where she purchased a flowered reticule with a shiny, ruby-colored tassel. "This is the perfect Christmas gift for Aunt Margaret. The popular French Empire styles are slim and clinging," she explained to Hannah, "and pockets under dresses bulge and spoil the lines. So the French have created these pretty little bags to hold money, or combs, or whatever a woman needs to carry about."

"I'm sure Mrs. Gage will be delighted with her gift," Hannah said.

For General Gage, Meg purchased a tooled leather belt buckle with silver trim.

"Are you giving gifts for Christmas, Hannah?" Meg asked.

"No, Miss Meg. I come from a Puritan family. We have never celebrated the Christmas holidays."

"Oh, you poor thing! You've missed so much!" Meg exclaimed.

Hannah had been taught that the Christmas celebration was a substitute for the ancient Roman celebration of Saturnalia, a festival of wild revelry that took place at the winter solstice. At one time fines had been imposed in the Massachusetts Bay Colony upon families that celebrated Christmas. Hannah had never felt that she was missing anything at all.

"Hannah, I shall give you your first Christmas present," Meg told her.

"No, Miss Meg. Please don't."

"Do not say no to me," Meg ordered merrily. "I insist."

That evening Mrs. Gage called Hannah and Catherine to her chamber. "You have both been faithful and hardworking servants, and General Gage and I would like you to accept a small token of our appreciation." She handed an envelope to each of them.

"Thank you, madam," Catherine said with a deep curtsy.

Hannah wondered if this was a Christmas present. If so, she should not accept it. Still, Mrs. Gage had said it was for their hard work and faithfulness, so she also curtsied and said, "Thank you, madam."

Hannah and Catherine each found a ten-pound note inside the envelope.

"What shall you do with this money, Hannah?" Catherine asked. "I believe I shall buy a new dress."

"I'm not in need right now. I might waste the money if I spend it," Hannah answered, recalling the Puritan saying "Willful waste makes woeful want."

Meg was in a constant state of jubilation about the upcoming holidays. Hannah wondered if she had a new beau. If so, she had not said a word about him to Hannah.

On Christmas Day, Hannah found a basket outside her door that was filled with ribbons of satin, lace, and even shimmering gold. A card inside read, "Merry Christmas to Hannah from Miss Meg."

"I asked her not to give me a present," Hannah said to Catherine. "I should return it."

"I think she would be hurt if you returned it," Catherine said. "Or angry."

"I'm the one who should be angry. She wants everything her way." Hannah sighed. "But the ribbons are lovely, aren't they?"

"She thought about you and chose something special."

"Then she could give it to me on another day." Hannah fingered the bouquet of ribbons. "Even though I'm only a servant, she should respect my wishes. Otherwise the gift doesn't mean anything."

"I think it does mean something," Catherine said. "Something more than just a Christmas gift."

Hannah was silent for a long moment. Then she said, "What does it mean?"

"To Meg you are more than a servant, Hannah. Meg knows you are the best friend she's ever had."

January came and went with icy winds that froze muddy roadways into ruts. Hannah stayed inside the grounds of the Province House, wishing mightily that she could see Will and Promise. Caleb kept her informed about the goings-on. But none of them dared to use the tunnel.

Meg had hoped to go to England, but General Gage felt the Atlantic Ocean was too dangerous to cross in the winter. It was decided that Meg would leave for England in the spring. Meanwhile, she made the most of the dances and entertainments that were held at the Province House, flirting away the evenings as a diversion from the boring New England winter.

One Sabbath, Hannah dressed in her best gray woolen pinafore. Usually she pulled her brown ringlets over the pockmark on her cheek, but today she brushed her hair back and tied it with a rose-colored satin ribbon that Meg had given her. "You look lovely," said Catherine.

Hannah and Catherine walked across the cobblestone street to attend church at the Old South Meeting House. "This was built as a Puritan church," Catherine told her. But to Hannah it did not seem to be a true Puritan service. Instead of a minister, the distinguished Dr. Warren, one of the Sons of Liberty, was in the pulpit. Hannah recognized him from the shadow play at Paul Revere's home. Dr. Warren was an eloquent speaker, and he appealed to the citizens to maintain order in the town. At the same time, his sermon was fiery and emotional for the cause of liberty and freedom.

Hannah noticed several other men she had seen at Paul Revere's house. They sat in the pulpit along with several British soldiers. How strange that they should be together. But then this was a place of worship; surely no fighting would occur.

Hannah noticed Paul Revere whispering with another man in what looked like serious conversation. When the man looked up, Hannah gasped. It was the stranger from the tunnel! She suddenly remembered where she had seen him before. He had attended the shadow play at the Reveres' house, and Caleb had identified him as Dr. Benjamin Church! Hannah had heard Dr. Church's name mentioned many times since then. He was always spoken of with great respect as one of the most trusted of the Sons of Liberty.

But Hannah was certain that this man was the informant. She could hardly contain herself. She had to speak to Mr. Revere right away!

Hannah fidgeted as she waited for the service to be over. She watched Dr. Church nodding his head as if in agreement with Dr. Warren's words, occasionally breaking into a smile. Yet Hannah knew in her heart that this man was not as he seemed.

When the service ended and the congregation was milling about, she caught sight of Miss Phillis Wheatley conversing with Dr. Warren. As Dr. Warren nodded politely, Hannah saw Miss Phillis pull a small envelope from her pocket and slip it into his hand. He placed it immediately into his inner vest pocket and walked away. Although she only saw it for an instant, Hannah felt sure that the envelope was similar to those she had delivered to Miss Phillis for Mrs. Gage. Certainly Mrs. Gage was not writing letters without words to Dr. Warren. She shook her head and tried to put the thought out of her mind.

When Hannah turned to speak to Catherine, she was gone. As she made her way through the parishioners, she caught sight of Catherine talking intimately to her friend Mr. Greenleaf. Catherine looked radiant as they laughed together. And Mr. Greenleaf seemed oblivious to everyone else around them.

Many unusual events were taking place at the Old South on this Sabbath! But now she had to warn Mr. Revere about Dr. Church. She was searching through the crowd when someone caught her by the hand.

"Hannah, I've wanted to see you," Will said.

"Oh, Will, where have you been?"

"I was in Salem. Friends asked for you. Old Skid and his family, Sarah Tarrant, Parson Barnard..."

"Aunt Phoebe?"

"I didn't speak with her. She was no part of the town meetings, being a firm Tory and all. But I did hear she and her Loyalist lawyer may marry."

"Marry?" Hannah burst out laughing. "I have great pity for the poor man."

"He's not poor. He's quite wealthy."

"Therein lies the attraction," Hannah said with a sniff.

As they made their way through the crowd to the small garden in the back of the building, Hannah noticed that Will was limping. "What's wrong with your leg?" she asked him.

"When I was on the road I had to spend a night in a stable, and a mad stallion stomped on my foot. The toes have been abscessed for a long time, and now they're turning black. I'm going to Dr. Warren tomorrow. He may do some surgery on it."

"Oh, I am sorry."

They sat together on one of the granite benches. "You look very pretty with your hair tied back like that," Will said.

Instinctively Hannah reached to pull a strand of hair over her cheek, but Will took hold of her hand. "You don't need to hide one speck of your beautiful face, Hannah," he said gently. "I've missed you . . . and so has Promise."

Hannah felt her face flush, and she trembled. When Will finally let go of her hand, a wave of disappointment swept over her. "I did ride him one night," Hannah stammered, suddenly filled with unexpected emotions.

"So I heard. The last time I saw Caleb at a Sons of Liberty meeting, he told me all about the man in the tunnel."

"I know who it was, Will," she whispered, returning to her senses. "It was Dr. Church. I saw him shake hands with General Gage, and I'm positive he is the informant that tells General Gage everything that's going on with the Sons of Liberty."

"No!" said Will in a low voice. "In no way would he betray us! He swears on the Bible at every meeting that he will never reveal what's going on."

"Haven't you heard of Judas Iscariot? He was one of the trusted twelve disciples, yet he betrayed Jesus for thirty pieces of silver. If Judas could betray Christ, couldn't Dr. Church be disloyal?"

"I've heard Dr. Church speak powerfully for

liberty and freedom," Will objected. "He's not a Judas."

Hannah shook her head in frustration. "In the event that there is a traitor among you, I've asked Mr. Revere never to disclose that it was I who warned him about General Gage's plan to reinforce Fort William and Mary," Hannah said. "And I pray that you have not revealed me to anyone in the Sons of Liberty either. Mr. Revere says I am in great danger now."

"Neither Caleb nor I have mentioned you to anyone, Hannah. I swear I'd depart this life before I'd betray you."

"Oh, I do wish you would believe me," Hannah pleaded. "I saw Dr. Church come out of the tunnel."

"It just cannot be so! It was dark—you must have seen someone who resembled him. We can't afford to have disunity in our Committees, especially now, so you mustn't say anything to Mr. Revere."

Hannah didn't answer. She would make no promises.

"There are traitors—or friends of liberty, depending on how you want to look at it—within the royal government also," Will went on. "We are not without informants ourselves. Dr. Warren is privy to someone in the uppermost levels, high in the midst of Gage's people."

"Whoever that may be has not revealed *your* turncoat however," Hannah pointed out.

"There are spies everywhere, Hannah. I've heard that some redcoat discovered Promise at Valley Acres and believes he's the Midnight Rider's mount. So I've decided to bring Promise over the river to Charlestown and hide him. Mr. Hubbard will help me. Once Promise is hidden, we'll all be safe. In the meantime you won't be able to ride. I'm sorry, Hannah, but it's all for the best."

"I understand, Will. I pray you will get Promise safely to Charlestown. And Will"—this time *she* took *his* hand—"I pray Dr. Warren will heal your injured foot."

Catherine appeared at the entrance to the courtyard. "Shall we leave now, Hannah?"

Hannah stood up. "I'm coming, Catherine." She leaned over to Will and whispered, "Please beware of Dr. Church. Don't let him know that you are riding to Salem."

"I'll be careful, Hannah." He gave her a teasing smile. "And never fear, we shall not reveal that you are the infamous Midnight Rider, Hans."

Even Will's teasing couldn't draw a smile from Hannah. "God be with you, Will."

"And with you, Hannah."

a week or more passed, and Hannah had not heard how Will was faring after his visit with Dr. Warren. Caleb had had no word either. And what about Promise? Was he still in danger at Valley Acres? Or had Will and Mr. Hubbard transported him safely to Charlestown by now?

Around the Province House there was more and more activity in General Gage's office. His staff often looked anxious or angry. There was much whispering, closed doors, and secrecy.

Then sore-throat distemper, a strange epidemic, spread among the soldiers. General Gage's confidential secretary contracted the disease and died. All entertainment for officers at the Province House was canceled. Meg was sent away to stay with a friend in a private home on Common Street for quarantine.

Hannah, who had little to do with the officers who visited the Province House regularly, was spared the illness, as were most of the servants. On this bleak February Thursday, since Meg was gone, Miss Lydia put Hannah to work in other capacities around the house. "Open the windows and freshen the air in every room," she ordered. "And change the bed linens."

It was late afternoon by the time Hannah finished making up Meg's chamber and cleaning the guest rooms, but Miss Lydia assigned her to mop floors and wipe down windows in the reception room near General Gage's office. Hannah set to work with duster, mop, and pail. The large windows were wet with condensation, and she began her work by pulling back the draperies to wipe the glass panes—at least as far as she could reach.

Two officers came into the reception hall and sat near the fire. They paid no attention to the servant girl at the windows, but Hannah noticed there was a sense of urgency between them.

Something was going on. She moved to a window closer to the fireplace, wringing out the wet rags over the pail and polishing each pane with a dry chamois, acting totally unaware of the gentlemen yet straining to hear each word spoken by them.

One of the men leaned closer to his companion who was dressed in the uniform of a high-ranking officer. Hannah had often seen him at the Province House. "Colonel Leslie, I've heard there are large stores of arms in Salem."

Salem!

"Good sources of mine have related to me that the Salemites are taking old ships' cannon and forging them into new field pieces."

"Yes, I have heard this too," agreed Colonel Leslie. "They've also broken the law by importing guns."

"That must be the reason for this urgent meeting."

At that moment General Gage himself opened the office door. "Come in, gentlemen."

"Certainly, Your Excellency." The men entered the general's office and the door shut with a click. Hannah never looked up or paused in her work.

Hannah put aside her washrags and began mopping the bare areas of the polished floor. Gradually she made her way out of the reception room and into the hallway. Then she swiftly worked her way toward the office door, where she could hear the anxious tones of the men's muffled voices.

Seeing no one around, she tiptoed to the general's office and leaned toward the door.

"Very well, then, Colonel Leslie," General Gage was saying, "we agree that the next Sabbath will be the day of our mission. You will be in command of the Sixty-fourth Foot Regiment, which fortunately has stayed in good health despite this confounded throat distemper that has plagued us all."

"We'll leave by ship from Castle William to Marblehead as you ordered, Your Excellency," Colonel Leslie answered.

"And I will keep the men under cover until we are ready to march to Salem and collect the cannon and arms," the other officer said.

Hannah scurried away from the door. She was certain now that Salem was the target for this secret operation. The next Sabbath was only three days away. She had to find Caleb, or Paul Revere!

Hannah darted back to the reception room and snatched up the washrags and pail. She carried them down the back stairway and deposited them in the scullery. Then she hastened to the stable, ignoring the icy wind that blew her skirts and took her breath away.

"Caleb!" she called, but there was no answer. She had not seen him in several days. In fact, Joseph had been the one working with the horses in the stable this week. She hoped she wouldn't bump into Joseph and need to make up explanations as to why she was there.

She ran by the stalls, where horses looked out at her. When Gabriel saw her, he whinnied. "No apples today, my pet," she called to him.

At the top of the stairs she found Caleb asleep

on his straw mat. "Caleb!" she exclaimed, shaking him.

"Don't get near me, Hannah," he whispered. "I'm sick."

She drew away. "Oh no!"

He rolled over and looked at her with feverish eyes. "I have the throat distemper." His voice was hoarse and garbled. "There's a white membrane forming in my gullet."

"What can I do for you?" Hannah asked.

"Don't come near me. People are dying from this, Hannah."

"I know, Caleb. But you'll get better, I'm sure." Hannah moved farther away. "So this is why I haven't seen you."

Caleb nodded. "Will is sick too. Dr. Warren had to remove two of his toes that had become as black as the plague."

"Oh, poor Will! Where is he?"

"Up in Mr. Hubbard's attic. He's sleeping most of the time. Dr. Warren says it will take a while for him to get better."

"And what about Promise?"

"Will was able to get Promise over to Deacon

Larkin's place in Charlestown. He's not far away—just across the river. Promise is in good hands there, Hannah."

"Caleb, I have information for Mr. Revere. I was hoping you could tell him for me, but I'll have to go myself to warn him."

Caleb looked up at her with bleary eyes. "What's acting up?"

"They're making plans to get the arms in Salem on the next Sabbath," she told him.

"That is important. You've got to use the tunnel and get to Mr. Revere," Caleb said, struggling to sit up.

"Do you think Mr. Revere will believe me?"

"Of course he will. He listened to you when you told about the Portsmouth Alarm."

"Yes, but I didn't give all the correct information."

"It don't matter. He got there in plenty of time and the New Hampshire folk were able to remove the cannon long before the soldiers came."

"What if I come upon Dr. Church?"

"It wasn't Dr. Church in that tunnel! Go, Hannah. Put on my warm clothes that are down in the stable." He threw a pair of gloves at her.

"Wear these or your fingers might freeze." He pointed to the table by his bed. "And put on my jerkin and boots, too." He lay back onto the pillow.

"But . . ."

Caleb put both hands to his head. "You're giving me a headache. Just go!"

Hannah hid in the empty back stall and changed her clothes. This time she added Caleb's warm jerkin under the waistcoat. The boots were big, but fitted better once she added Caleb's knitted stockings, which she found stuffed inside. After tying her hair back with one of Caleb's ties, she pulled his tricorn hat low over her face.

Hannah made her way across the deep snow, struggling as she sank through the icy crust. The tunnel door was frozen shut by the glaze of ice. She kicked the ice into pieces and then tugged the hatch open.

The candles and flint box were in their usual place, and once she was inside, she lit a candle. The flame cast strange, flickering shadows across the dirt walls.

Hannah had not seen Dr. Church at the Province House since her first day last fall. She wondered if he was contacting the general at night by way of the secret tunnel. Despite Will's and Caleb's denial, she was certain that Benjamin Church was giving information about the Sons of Liberty to General Gage.

Please, dear God in Heaven, don't let me meet up with Dr. Church.

Hannah was relieved when she reached the stairs at the other end of the tunnel. The trapdoor there was also stuck with ice, and she heaved against it again and again with her shoulder. Finally it gave way, and she looked up into the darkening sky, where the evening star was already glimmering.

She walked casually down Marlborough Street with long strides, imitating the demeanor of the young men in the town. She passed several taverns and could hear the boisterous singing of soldiers. When she saw groups of men, she crossed to the other side of the street hoping they wouldn't speak to "Hans" and draw "him" into a controversial argument about the Whigs or the Tories.

As she neared the waterfront on Fish Street,

the raw wind stung her face, and she pulled the collar of Caleb's jacket high around her cheeks. The lanterns on the ships glowed across the harbor. The Long Wharf, which always seemed to be bustling with people, was quiet this night.

Hannah could see lights in the windows of Paul Revere's home, and shadows of people walking about the large kitchen. One was tall and slim, and Hannah cringed. Was it Dr. Church?

She did not have to wait long to find out, for the front door swung open almost immediately and Benjamin Church came out onto the street. Hannah reeled about and headed back toward the harbor, hoping he would be going in another direction. When she heard the man's footsteps behind her, she walked faster. She came upon a small tavern and slid into the shadow of the doorway, waiting for Dr. Church to pass. When he looked her way, she opened the door and stepped inside the tavern.

"Hey! You want a beer, me boy?" A man in a white shirt came toward her.

Hannah shook her head and fled outside again. Dr. Church's lanky figure was farther down the street, so she headed back to Paul Revere's house.

When Hannah knocked on the heavy oak door, Paul Revere himself opened it.

"Hans!" he said. "I haven't seen you for quite a while." He stood aside and motioned for Hannah to enter.

"Caleb is ill with the throat distemper," Hannah whispered. "So I came myself to tell you some important information."

Mr. Revere shook his head in alarm. "Oh dear, I hope the boy recovers. This is a bad illness." He pointed to a chair and asked, "Would you care for some mulled cider to warm you up? It's a mighty cold night out there." Mr. Revere went to the stove, poured a mug of steaming cider that smelled strongly of cloves, and handed it to her. "You were correct about Portsmouth back in December," he said, taking a seat, "although your timing was off. The British ship was not heading for Portsmouth, it was on its way to Boston."

"I'm sorry . . . I could only report on what I heard . . ."

Mr. Revere smiled. "Oh, it worked out for the

best," he said. "And you should feel satisfied that the arms were long gone when the redcoats finally showed up."

Hannah sat down and sipped the warm cider gratefully. She could hear the sound of children in the loft. "May I speak freely?"

"Yes, of course," he said. "What do you have to tell me?"

"I heard General Gage discussing the arms in the town of Salem. They are planning to send the entire Sixty-fourth Foot Regiment posted at Castle William to recover the cannon and field pieces from Salem."

"And when is this to take place?" Mr. Revere asked.

"The next Sabbath, sir. They will send a ship with soldiers in hiding to Marblehead and march on Salem from there."

Mr. Revere leaned back and smiled. "I heard about this plot," he said. "In fact, it was brought to my attention just before you arrived." Mr. Revere continued. "There is one inconsistency, however. My source tells me that it will take place on Saturday."

"I don't know who your source is, Mr. Revere,"

Hannah said, "but I know for a fact it will be on the Sabbath."

Mr. Revere looked at her kindly. "Thank you, Hans. I made plans a few moments ago to row to Castle William tomorrow—Friday—and see what's actin' up at the garrison there."

Dr. Church must have informed him, but how did he learn of this new plot? she wondered, remembering the secrecy of the meeting General Gage had with Colonel Leslie and the officer.

She still felt that she was right about Benjamin Church. But then why had he brought this message to Paul Revere? And why did he say the ship would sail to Marblehead on Saturday, one day earlier than Hannah had heard?

Suddenly Hannah realized why! General Gage feared that once Paul Revere knew about the mission, he would ride out to Salem and bring the warning as he had done in Portsmouth. But if Mr. Revere and his men went to Castle William beforehand, they would be captured by the British, arrested for trespassing, and kept on the island until after the Sabbath. He was heading straight into a trap!

"Please beware, Mr. Revere," Hannah said anxiously, "if you go to Castle William . . ."

But Paul Revere only smiled. "You're just a little girl and should not be fretting so much about things like this. Besides, I've already been informed that there's action taking place out in the harbor, and we'll investigate. Thank you for being so concerned."

Hannah sighed. Perhaps Mr. Revere was right. After all, she hadn't heard everything that was spoken in General Gage's office, and that had been the cause of her error before. "Very well, sir," she said.

She had a feeling of hopelessness as she headed to the door. No one would ever believe a "little girl." What if Mr. Revere was captured out at

Castle William? What if it really was a trap and her information about Salem was correct? What could she do? Will and Caleb were both unable to ride. How would her friends in Salem be warned?

On Friday Caleb did not show up at breakfast. When Joseph came in, Hannah asked about him.

"The boy is feelin' poorly." Then looking at Mrs. Dudley, he said, "I'll bring him some cider and a slab of meat, if that's all right."

"Of course," she agreed. "I'll fix him a plate."

"I'll be happy to bring it to him," Hannah offered. "Joseph hasn't eaten yet, and I've finished."

"Don't get near Caleb," Mrs. Dudley warned. "Just leave it on a table."

She carried the food and a mug of hot cider to Caleb's room over the stable. He did look poorly— not flushed with fever, as he had yesterday, but pale, with large dark circles under his eyes. He sat up and pointed to the chair by his bed. "Put the food there, Hannah. I'm not sure I can eat anything." He spoke with more strength in his voice, but his throat and neck looked swollen.

"You need to eat," she said, opening up the

basket of food. "Are you feeling better?" She stepped away from Caleb's bed.

"Somewhat." He sipped the cider and flinched as he swallowed. "My throat is mighty sore." He watched her painfully from over the rim of the mug. "What happened with Paul Revere?"

"Someone had already informed Mr. Revere about Salem and suggested he go to Castle William and see for himself how the ships and troops are preparing for Saturday."

"Saturday? I thought they were heading for Salem on the Sabbath."

"Someone told him differently. Caleb, if Mr. Revere goes out to the island today, I'm afraid he'll be taken prisoner."

"He'll do it secretly, Hannah. No one will be watching for him."

Hannah shook her head. "I have a feeling someone out there *will* be watching for him."

Caleb bit into a biscuit and chewed it slowly. "Everything is in good hands. Whoever informed Mr. Revere about the action wouldn't suggest that he go out to Castle William if there was a chance he'd be captured."

"It was Dr. Benjamin Church who informed him," Hannah said.

"Well, then, as I said, everything is in good hands."

Hannah headed for the stairs. "You'll eat those words when Mr. Revere is captured at the Castle William fort." She suddenly knew without a doubt what she must do. Turning to Caleb, she announced, "And when Mr. Revere is unable to ride to Salem, I will go."

As sick as he was, Caleb laughed and nearly choked on the biscuit. "You're daft, Hannah!"

"We'll soon find out who's daft!" Hannah sputtered as she stomped down the stairs and back to the kitchen.

It was early afternoon when Hannah, who was in the scullery ironing linens for Mrs. Dudley, heard the sound of horses and unrestrained laughter in the courtyard. Peering out the window, she saw a group of redcoats tying up their horses at the hitching posts. Two of them ran around to the front of the mansion and entered through the main door.

"Announce us to General Gage," they ordered

Edward as they stomped up the grand stairway. "He'll be happy with this news." Hannah set the flatiron on the fire to heat up again. Then she grabbed a tablecloth and went out the scullery door to shake the crumbs, all the while straining to hear what the other soldiers were joking about out in the courtyard.

"What a prize! Revere and his three men caught blatantly spying on Castle William!" one of the soldiers exclaimed.

"It's about time he was thrown in prison," another said. "Let's hope Tommy keeps him there a long time."

"Ah!" said a third officer scornfully. "Tommy is too soft on these Yankees. He'll let Revere go in a few days to make more trouble for us." "Tommy" was another one of the nicknames British soldiers used for General Gage, and it was usually spoken with contempt. Many of the soldiers thought he was too easy on the Americans; they would have preferred that he have a mass hanging for the Whigs and Patriots.

Hannah had been right! Mr. Revere's trip to Castle William *was* a trap. And now Mr. Revere was in prison. Would he believe her about Dr. Church now? Would Caleb? Even Dr. Warren, the leader of the Sons of Liberty, trusted Dr. Benjamin Church. None of the Sons of Liberty would believe the man was a traitor. If she related to them the British plans for Salem, Dr. Church would discredit her, and her own disloyalty to General Gage would be found out.

The arms must be hidden before the soldiers arrived on the Sabbath the day after tomorrow! Hannah thought about her friends and neighbors in Salem and how they would be spending a quiet, reverent Sabbath, unprepared for the soldiers who would arrive to take away their only means of protection. It was up to her to bring the warning to Salem.

Her mind began to spin with plans—and fears. She would go to Charlestown and find Promise. Paul Revere had made the ride to Portsmouth in one day, probably changing to a fresh mount somewhere along the route. However, Salem was less than half the distance it was to Portsmouth, so she could ride Promise all the way.

But while Meg was not around, Mrs. Dudley

might have work for her. What would they do if
they found her missing? If they thought she was
sick with the throat distemper, would they stay
away from her room?

"Hannah!" Annie called from the scullery.

Hannah gave the table covering a final shake.
"I'm coming."

Annie had a load of wet linen to be hung outside. Hannah took the basket of laundry to the
back of the mansion, where clotheslines had been
strung neatly between posts.

The sun was low in the west, and as quickly as
Hannah could stretch the sheets across the
clothesline, they became stiff and frozen in the
cold wind. It would be another day before they
would be dry enough to be brought into the house.
While she hung the laundry, her fingers stinging
from the cold, Hannah planned her trip to Salem.
She would ride as Hans. The people of Salem, like
those of Boston, would be more inclined to believe
a boy than a girl.

What about Catherine? She hated to ask
Catherine to lie for her, but perhaps she could help.

That evening at the servants' table, Hannah complained she was feeling ill, but would take food to her room for later. Mrs. Dudley wrapped up a plate of smoked turkey and cheese and set it on a tray along with an apple and a pudding. "I hope you haven't caught the throat distemper, dear," she said.

"I'll take care of her." A worried Catherine took the tray and followed Hannah upstairs.

Once inside their room Hannah confessed to her friend, "I'm not really sick. I lied."

Catherine set the tray on a table, sat on the bed, and listened in alarm to Hannah's plans. "Hannah, you can't go off to Salem like this. It's dangerous. What if General Gage discovers that you've been spying for the Whigs right here in the Province House? Why, you could be sent to the river!" Catherine's words ended in a sob.

Hannah put her arm around her friend. "I'll be back the next day, Catherine. If anyone asks for me tell them I'm sick abed."

"What if something happens to you? And what if they find that I've been lying for you? It's not just your life that's in danger. Caleb, Will . . . we're all involved. The more lies, the more danger for everyone."

"Catherine, someone must warn the people in Salem."

They were both silent for a while. Hannah hadn't considered how others would be endangered. "There's no one else who can go," she said quietly.

Catherine covered her face with her hands. Then to Hannah's surprise she said, "If you must go, then so be it, Hannah. I'll make excuses for you."

"I will come back Sunday night," Hannah vowed. "Promise will be too tired to return to Boston, but I'm sure someone will bring me." She tied the turkey, cheese, and an apple in a napkin for her ride and gobbled up the pudding. Then she pulled out the ten-pound note that Mrs. Gage had given her for Christmas. This would more than pay for any expenses along the way. How ironic that the governor and his wife would be paying for her betrayal of them!

it was before sunrise on Saturday when "Hans" crept through the tunnel. The streets were quiet as Hannah made her way through the lanes to Mr. Hubbard's house near the waterfront.

Elderly Mr. Hubbard, the cooper, lived above his shop. Hannah knocked loudly on the door and soon heard footsteps approaching. Mr. Hubbard opened the door in his nightclothes and looked at Hannah without recognition. She had only met him a few times at church, and he didn't identify her in the disguise of Hans.

"What is it?" he asked as he peered into the darkness.

"I'm Caleb's cousin, Hans," she answered with a boy's voice. "I've come to see Will, sir. It's urgent."

Mr. Hubbard stood aside and waved her in.

"He's in the garret, and sick he is with his bad foot. I'm not sure he's awake at this hour."

"Please come with me, Mr. Hubbard. I need to speak with both of you."

Mr. Hubbard carried a lantern in front of them as they climbed up the narrow stairway to the attic, where Will was lying on a straw mattress. The room had only one window, and bales of hay surrounded the walls to keep out the cold.

"Dear, dear Will," she whispered as she moved to his side. "It's me, Hannah."

Mr. Hubbard inhaled a sharp breath. "Hannah? You're a girl?"

"Yes, and quite a girl she is, sir," said Will.

Hannah hastily related her plans to Will and Mr. Hubbard. "Mr. Revere is in prison at Castle William. Caleb is ill, so there's no one to ride to Salem with the warning that the redcoats are coming to take the munitions."

"Surely you cannot go," Mr. Hubbard exclaimed. "It's dangerous for a girl in these times."

"Can *you* ride to Salem?" Hannah asked him.

"No, not at my age," he said with dismay. "I

wouldn't be able to make the ride—especially on these snow-packed roads."

"Who else is there?" Hannah asked. "Mr. Revere has been captured at Castle William along with three of his best men. I'm sure the Sons of Liberty are being watched, especially with this secret mission about to take place. Besides, we know that someone in that group is a traitor. If we ask anyone else, our plan may be exposed and the warning halted."

"Still, there must be someone other than you," Will said.

"No one would suspect me," Hannah said. "And Promise won't be seen in Boston. I'll be riding from Charlestown. He's not known as the Midnight Rider's horse over there."

"I can't think of anyone else who could get ready, especially on such short notice," Mr. Hubbard said with a frown.

"I know I can do it. Let's not waste time. I will need help to get to Charlestown and find Promise, though."

"I can get you across the river," Mr. Hubbard

told her. "In my trade I'm allowed to go back and forth to Charlestown. But if soldiers see me rowing you across at this hour, they'll be sure to question me," Mr. Hubbard explained, "so we must be cautious."

Will propped himself up on one elbow and reached for a sheaf of paper near his bed. "You'll need directions. And a note to Deacon Larkin in Charlestown."

After Will explained the route she should take, he took her hand. "The snow and ice will slow you down, and although Promise is sure-footed, the ride will be treacherous, Hannah. There are places along the way where you can stable Promise for a few hours' rest, and you can get sleep too. Be on guard. There are those who might help you, but there are also Tories and informers who may report you."

"I'll be careful, Will," Hannah promised, "and I'll see you when I return. But please tell no one about me. Not even the Sons of Liberty."

"I promise." Will lay back on his pillow. "Take my saddlebag for your belongings. I wish I were going in your stead."

Hannah tucked her food and money, along with Will's map, into the leather saddlebag. Then she bent over to kiss his cheek. "Stay well, Will."

"Didn't you realize you had no hat?" Will pointed to his own gold-braided tricorn hat hanging from a hook. "Take mine. You'll need it."

Hannah took the hat and pulled it over her brow. Then Will grasped her hand again. "Godspeed, Hannah."

Dawn was breaking as Mr. Hubbard furtively rowed Hannah across the mouth of the Charles River. It was high tide, and large pieces of ice floated toward them in the fast current. Seated in the bow, Hannah pushed them away from the boat with a paddle.

On the opposite shore, Hannah jumped onto a wharf that was hidden in the shoreline brush.

"I must get back before daylight, or the soldiers may see me," Mr. Hubbard whispered. He pointed to a steeple. "Parson Larkin lives in the house next to that church. He has stables in the back, and that's where you'll find Promise." Mr. Hubbard tossed her the saddlebag. "Be safe, child," he said as he rowed off.

Hannah made her way up the cobblestone street to the rear of the parson's house. She proceeded over the icy walkway to the back door and knocked.

A woman opened the door and peered out. "Who is calling this early in the morning? Why, it's not even light yet!"

Hannah spoke softly in Hans's voice. "I have an urgent letter from Will Samson requesting that you give me his horse for the next few days." She held out Will's letter.

The woman took it and closed the door. Soon a kindly looking gentleman opened it again. "Come with me, Hans," he said, leading her to the barn behind their home.

Snow reflected the rosy winter sky. The air was bitterly cold, and Hannah could see her breath rising in small white puffs. The parson pulled open the door, and Hannah felt the warmth from the barn and smelled horses. Promise was peering out from a nearby stall.

"Oh, my Promise!" she exclaimed, remembering to use her male voice.

"Will said in his letter that you are familiar with Promise and an expert horseman."

"Yes, sir. Promise used to be my horse." Hannah went to the stall, and Promise nuzzled her hand. "See? He knows me."

Deacon Larkin nodded. He put the blanket and saddle on the horse, buckled on the saddle-bag, and led Promise out of the barn.

Hannah mounted quickly, and the deacon watched as she rode out of the yard and up the road. "Godspeed on your journey, Hans!"

Promise pranced along the road with a carefree gait, delighted to be out of the closed barn in the fresh, cold morning. Hannah felt the same sense of exhilaration as her horse, free at long last from the confines of the Province House. Perhaps she and Promise would never go back!

But then she remembered Catherine, and Will, and Caleb. They would surely be questioned if she disappeared, especially if her warning to Salem was successful. She pushed those dangerous thoughts of escape from her mind.

The roadway narrowed as she left Charlestown and moved into the quiet of farms and small villages. Hannah paused at junctions to read the wooden arrows and carved granite markers that directed riders to towns. When carriages or shays passed by her, Hannah pulled Promise to the side of the road and with a tip of her hat waved them on.

Promise trotted along the dirt roads, but after an hour or two Hannah reined him to a stop, dismounted, and stretched. She had not ridden in several weeks and was becoming saddle-sore. She ate her meat and cheese, then half the apple. She gave the other half to Promise. "Good boy," she said, rubbing his neck.

Hannah had been concentrating on the landmarks Will had noted on the map, so she hadn't noticed the clouds gathering. She frowned as snowflakes spattered on her face. Was a storm brewing? She couldn't be even halfway to Salem yet. If she were held up by a storm, she might not get there in time.

She mounted Promise and clicked her tongue. "Giddap, Promise. We have to pick up our pace or we won't make it to Salem tonight."

The country roads were rutted from an earlier thaw that had later refrozen, and it was hard to see the uneven ground beneath the gathering snow. Promise, always sure-footed on even turf, stumbled several times during the next few miles. Hannah pulled on the reins and the horse slowed to a walk. "Whoa, boy. We must be more careful. No matter what happens, I don't want you to be hurt."

The snowfall became heavy. Snowflakes froze on Hannah's eyelashes, blocking her view. When they came to another fork in the road. Hannah unfolded the map, which had become damp. "Oh no!" she exclaimed in dismay. "The ink has run. I can't read Will's directions."

The granite signpost at the fork was blanketed with snow. Hannah climbed off her horse and brushed the icy sleet from the stone, revealing two arrows. The one pointing to the left read MALDEN, and the one to the right read SAUGUS.

"Which road do we take?" Hannah asked, trying to recall what Will had told her. She stayed there at the crossroads for several minutes while the snow beat down on them. The chilling wind cut through Caleb's heavy coat. Which way to go?

With a sigh Hannah mounted Promise and pulled the reins to the left, toward Malden. She tapped Promise lightly with her heel. To her surprise, Promise balked at her command and tossed his head, flinging a spray of snow from his mane onto Hannah's face.

"What's wrong, boy?" Hannah asked. "We've got to keep moving. Giddap, Promise."

But Promise tossed his head again and pawed the ground.

"Don't you want to go to Malden?" Hannah asked in a gentle voice. Promise stood as if frozen. Once again she tugged the reins to the left. This time Promise pulled to the right. "We should take the other road? Is that what you're trying to tell me?"

She pulled the reins to the right, and Promise obediently moved in that direction. "Oh, I see!" she exclaimed. "You know the road to Salem. What a clever horse you are!" She leaned over to pat the horse's neck. "Good boy!"

The snow was deeper now, and ice was hidden beneath it. "Easy, Promise. We must keep going. But slowly."

Promise seemed to sense the danger and hesitated from time to time. Sometimes he slipped on the ice under the snow, but he quickly regained his footing.

The wind gusted, blowing snow and snapping limbs from the trees that arched over the roadway. *Crash!* A large branch split off an oak tree and hurtled to the ground directly in front of them, blocking their path.

Promise reared and then stopped abruptly. Hannah dismounted. She grasped a branch and pulled the heavy bough off to the side of the road. Where were they? She hadn't seen a farmhouse or any signs of life for a long time. Had Promise chosen the right road?

Her whole body was cold and aching. There had to be a wayside inn somewhere nearby where they could find shelter and warmth, if just for a few hours.

She led Promise beyond the tree limbs scattered on the roadway and trudged beside him for a while. It was late afternoon now, and clouds darkened the twilight. Hannah longed to give in to her own weariness.

Finally, as they rounded a bend, she saw a large building with light in the windows and smoke rising from the chimneys. She prayed that this might be an inn. As she approached, she saw a sign above the door: GREAT ELM TAVERN.

"Thank you, kind Lord," she whispered.

Hannah left Promise with a cheery stable hand who immediately removed the saddle and saddle blanket, rubbed Promise down, and covered him with a dry mantle. "I'll give him some oats and a little water. He'll be fine for the night, sir."

"I won't be staying all night," Hannah said. "Just long enough to rest up a bit. We're heading for Salem. Is it much farther?"

"In good weather, an hour's ride, but with the snow . . ." He shrugged and checked Promise's shoes. "He's done all right considerin' the condition of the roads. Where'd you come from?"

"Charlestown."

"Long ride on a bad day."

"I'll get a bed and something to eat," she said. "Then we'll be off again." Hannah petted Promise, who rested his head on her shoulder.

She took the saddlebag and went into the inn. Groups of men sat by the fireside, smoking pipes and drinking from large mugs. They looked up as she entered, then went back to their conversations.

The innkeeper, a tall woman wearing an apron over her homespun dress, approached Hannah. "What can I get you?" she asked.

"Food," Hannah answered in her male voice.

"We have pork pie tonight," the woman said.

Hannah found a table and sat facing away from the men at the hearth. In a short while the innkeeper brought a hot pie with a thick, flaky crust. "Where were you brought up?" she said with a sniff as she poured cider into a mug and set it on the table. "Remove your hat like a proper gentleman."

"Sorry," Hannah responded, removing Will's hat but lowering her head. She prayed silently that the woman would not see she was a girl. The hot fire warmed the room so well that she wished to remove Caleb's topcoat, but she kept the collar turned up around her face.

Hannah hadn't realized how hungry she was, and she gobbled up the pie. She would have loved a pot of tea, but drank the hard mulled cider as a young man would.

She began to feel sleepy and wondered how

much a bed would cost. A sign on the wall read: ONE TO A BED—TWO SHILLINGS; TWO TO A BED—ONE SHILLING; THREE TO A BED—SIX PENCE.

Hannah had the ten-pound note in her saddle-bag. She could afford the best. "I'd like a bed to myself."

"There are none left," the woman said. "Everyone's stopped here due to the storm. All we have is a three-man bed."

"I'll pay four shillings for a bed," Hannah said quickly.

"I told you, there are none."

How would a man respond to such an indignity? Hannah plunked Will's hat on her head, pulling it low over her eyes. Then she stood up and crossed her arms. "It is not my custom to share a bedchamber with anyone!"

"If you can't share, you can't sleep here," the innkeeper said walking off.

Hannah yearned for a soft pillow and an hour of sleep. Her body ached, and her eyelids were heavy. She followed the woman across the room. "How much will it cost for me to sleep in the barn?"

The lady looked at her in surprise. "In the barn?"

"I'd prefer to sleep near my horse anyway," Hannah said.

The woman thought for a moment, then said. "For two pence I'll give you a blanket and pillow, but you must tender the money to me now. For all I know, you'll get up and leave without paying."

"Very well," Hannah agreed. She paid for her supper, Promise's keep, and the bed in the barn, then left the tavern with a quilt and pillow.

In the stable she climbed onto a stack of hay in the corner near Promise and was soon fast asleep.

When Hannah awoke and remembered where she was, she jumped up. How long had she been sleeping? Had she slept through the night? Would she be able to get to Salem in time? After all she had gone through to warn Salem, had she missed her goal because of sheer laziness? She ran to a window and saw with dismay that it was dawn. Angry tears spilled from her eyes.

She darted into Promise's stall and buckled the blanket, saddle, and saddlebag onto his back. She then pulled on Caleb's coat and Will's hat and led Promise out of the barn.

"We must go quickly," she whispered as she swung herself up on Promise. "Giddap, boy." She tapped her heel and Promise lunged forward into a brisk trot.

The morning was bitter, and smoky clouds puffed from Promise's nose. Hannah had no time to search out landmarks; she had to trust that Promise knew the way. She would let him have his head and find his way home to Salem. "Hurry, Promise! Hurry!"

Within an hour the sun had risen, casting the shadows of the trecs on the snowy landscape. When they crossed over a brackish inlet, Hannah caught the scent of the sea.

"I know where we are!" she exclaimed, shifting her weight forward. "We're almost to Salem! We're almost home!"

Feeling her excitement, Promise sprang forward into a full gallop. But no sooner had he changed his gait than he slipped, falling to the ground on his front legs! Hannah was thrown forward into the snow. "Promise!" she screamed, jumping up.

Promise thrashed about on the slippery ice,

trying to raise himself. Hannah ran to him, drawing off her jacket. She placed it over him and lay on the horse to keep him still, murmuring soft words. "You'll be all right," she said. "Stay quiet, Promise."

After the horse calmed down, Hannah took her jacket and placed it under his feet to give him safe footing. Then she took hold of the bridle and gave it a gentle tug. Promise struggled, and after a few attempts he was able to pull himself erect. But he was holding his right foreleg off the ground.

"Oh, my boy," Hannah cried. "I was in such a hurry, I forgot about the ice under the snow." Fearfully, she examined the horse's leg. "The bone doesn't seem to be broken. You'll be all right, my sweet, wonderful horse," she said reassuringly.

But she knew by the way Promise was holding his leg that something was very wrong.

What had she done to her beloved horse by racing him along the icy roads? Promise nickered and nuzzled his head against her as if to comfort both of them. Then Hannah paced back and forth, wondering what to do next.

"We can't just stay here!" Hannah finally said. She took hold of the horse's bridle and led him for a few steps. At first Promise resisted, but after a moment he was able to limp hesitantly beside her. "We'll go for help, Promise. It's only a little farther to get to Salem."

Hannah looked ahead and could see the church steeple. Soon the church would be filled with townspeople. If she could just make it in time!

It seemed like hours passed as Hannah led Promise slowly toward the town. She stopped several times to let him rest, but each time they began to walk again it was more difficult for Promise. Hannah could tell he was in pain. His ears drooped back, and with each step his limp became more pronounced. But he continued on obediently.

When Hannah arrived in the town, she could see the churchgoers heading into their place of worship. She guessed that the service had started already, since she could hear music and singing each time the door was opened.

"We're here in Salem, Promise," she said. "You can rest now." She tied Promise loosely to a hitching post and kissed him.

Hannah pulled her collar high around her face and lowered the hat over her brow. She did not want to be recognized, for fear no one would take a warning from little Hannah Andrews seriously. She took a deep breath and went into the church. The preacher was leading the congregation in prayer, so she waited at the door. She suddenly remembered that a man was supposed to remove his hat when in church, but she kept her hat over her face, hoping the importance of her visit would overcome any objections to her lack of respect.

The people attending worship looked up curiously as the strange boy approached Parson Barnard. "I have an urgent message for the people of Salem, sir," Hannah said clearly in Hans's voice. "British soldiers are landing in Marblehead today and will march into Salem to retrieve your cannon and munitions."

The parishioners began speaking all at once.

"On whose authority are you bringing this information?" the clergyman asked, tapping the podium for silence.

"The Sons of Liberty," Hans answered.

"Who is this?" asked a voice from the audience. "Why should we believe him?"

"Yes, who are you?" Parson Barnard asked curiously.

"My name is Hans Gibbs," Hans said privately to the minister. "I've come through the storm in place of Will Samson, who is ill."

"How can we be sure—"

Hans interrupted. "You can look out and see that I came on Will's horse. He's tied up across the street. While there is time, have the men remove the cannon and arms! You have nothing to lose by concealing the weapons, but you have everything to lose by wasting time questioning me. The British soldiers will be here soon."

"General Gage would never send his troops here on the Sabbath!" came a loud voice from among the congregation. "He knows it would infuriate us."

"Why didn't Will Samson bring this message to us? He's the messenger we trust."

"This boy is just another harbinger of disloyalty sent by those Boston Whigs!" a Tory in the audience yelled.

"If he's a messenger of the Whigs, then we should hear him out!" Members of the two factions in the congregation began quarreling.

"You have not removed your hat in the house of God," someone else called out. "Why should we believe you?"

"Remove your hat, lad," said the minister. "You and your message will be more credible if you show the respect due here."

Hannah turned her back to the assemblage

and removed Will's tricorn. Parson Barnard stared at her in amazement. "Hannah! Is it you?"

"It was safer for me to ride here as a boy," she said. "And no one would believe me if they knew it was just a girl bringing this message."

"A point well taken," Parson Barnard agreed. "Go into my parlor, and I will speak to the congregation." He pointed to a door behind him.

Gratefully, Hannah left the pulpit and entered the private room, leaving the door open a crack.

"I can vouch for the honesty of this . . . young man," said the parson. "We must rally now and remove the cannon quickly. The redcoats are on their way." He knocked on the podium for silence. "But first we must ask God for his help and protection."

After a quick prayer the meeting was adjourned. Those who were Tory Loyalists stormed out of the church angrily, while Whigs and Patriots gathered in groups to plan their strategy.

"The drawbridge!" yelled Old Skid. "The cannon and arms are on the other side of the river. Get men over there to remove them. Then lift the drawbridge! It will give us time!"

Voices joined in agreement as the groups

dispersed under Old Skid's directions. Satisfied that her trip had not been in vain, Hannah closed the door and sat in a chair.

Parson Barnard stepped inside. He was with Will's father. "My child, what a desperate journey you have taken. Tell me about Will. Is he well?" Mr. Samson asked, taking her hands.

Hannah told him about Will's surgery. "Dr. Warren himself removed two of Will's toes and saved him from losing his foot—or leg. I spoke with him just yesterday. He will be fine once the healing has taken place," Hannah assured him. "But Mr. Samson, Promise slipped on the ice—"

Mr. Samson interrupted. "I already ran out and looked at Promise. He was down when I got to him, Hannah. When an injured horse lies down and stays down, it can be a very bad sign. He's gone lame and may have torn muscles. We'll bring Promise to my farm and try to save him."

"*Try* to save him?" Hannah nearly burst into tears. "You've *got* to save him! Why, he came all this way to protect this town."

Mr. Samson and Parson Barnard exchanged

glances. "It may be that this trip was the purpose of Promise's life," the parson said gently.

"Please save him," she begged Mr. Samson. "Please."

"You don't want Promise to suffer, do you?" Will's father asked.

"No! But . . ." Hannah began to sob. "Promise is all that's left of my family. Please don't let him die."

P arson Barnard put Will's hat back on Hannah's head, dried her tears with a handkerchief, and guided her out of the church. Steeple bells clanged the warning, and young men beat the signal "to arms" on their drums. The whole community was alive with action.

Over by the hitching post a group of men had managed to get Promise to stand and were leading him onto a wagon. Hannah gasped and put her hand to her mouth.

"We've got people here who know what you've done and will do everything they can to save your horse, Hannah," the parson said.

Sarah Tarrant stood on the granite steps of the church. "I realized it was you, Hannah, once I saw your horse over there." She threw her arms around Hannah. "Come to my house, dear," she begged. "You have done us all a wonderful deed. Now you must rest and have a good meal before you go back to Boston."

Hannah was suddenly aware that she had no way to return. "How will I go?" she asked.

"Mr. Samson has already asked Mr. Greenleaf to take you back."

"Mr. Greenleaf? He's here?"

"Oh, yes. He's been in Salem for several days. He comes often. As the owner of the *Royal American* newspaper, and since Salem was the seat of government before General Gage returned to Boston, he is able to travel back and forth freely. He's only too happy to bring you back to Boston safely."

"He's an acquaintance of my good friend Catherine," Hannah said.

Mrs. Tarrant led Hannah toward the river and across the bridge. Several men were standing guard with guns and bayonets. "Just let those red lobsters try to cross once we draw the bridge."

Hannah couldn't help but smile at Sarah Tarrant's name for the British soldiers.

Sarah went on. "How brave you were to take

such chances coming out to warn us. Now stay with me awhile and tell me about your life in Boston."

That afternoon, from the window seat in Mrs. Tarrant's great room, Hannah watched the activities going on at the drawbridge. Mrs. Tarrant served Hannah beef stew and plum cake with a hot pot of tea.

"What's happening outside?" Hannah asked.

"Your alarm has given us some time to hide the arms," Sarah said. "But it will take even more time to move the heavy cannon. Old Skid brought his strongest wagon. He *is* the best carriage maker around, you know. They'll get those cannon out of here in time." She pushed the casement window open. "You'll be able to hear everything now."

Suddenly there was an outcry as a man on horseback galloped into view. "They're coming!" he yelled. "The regulars landed in Marblehead and are on the march!" He pulled his horse to a stop.

"We already know, Major Pedrick," Parson Barnard called back. "We were warned hours ago."

The messenger climbed off his horse and scratched his head. "Who warned you?"

"A young man from Boston rode most of the night in the snow to get here. Had a rough ride. His horse may be dead by now."

At those words Hannah felt tears rising again. *Please, Heavenly Father. You've taught us through the Scriptures that you care for even the smallest sparrow. Please spare my horse, Promise. He is faithful and true. And he is my own family, a precious gift from my papa.* The cold air swept through the window, bringing with it the scent of the salt marshes and the river.

The rhythmic thumping of drums vibrated from up the street, and Hannah could hear the high-pitched sound of fifes playing "Yankee Doodle." "They're here!" Sarah exclaimed. Hannah moved closer to the window and saw the foot soldiers marching straight toward the drawbridge. But the men on the other side had already begun to raise it.

The soldiers came to a stop at the embankment. They could go no farther.

Sarah burst out laughing. "Ha! They won't get across the river. No red lobster can make us put that drawbridge down until we are good and ready!"

Many of the men from the town on the other

side of the river had disappeared to hide the arms, but others had climbed onto the edge of the drawbridge. "Hey, you lobster coats!" they yelled. "Damnation to you and your government!"

Colonel Leslie, his face an angry red, dismounted his horse. "How dare you obstruct the king's highway! Lower the bridge," he yelled. "Now!"

The Salem men and boys sitting on the edge of the bridge hooted at him.

"Lower the bridge or we'll open fire!" the officer demanded. He raised his arm as if readying to order the shoot.

"Colonel Leslie!" A captain in the foot regiment raced to the officer's side. "You have no right to fire upon these people without direct orders. If you do, we'll all be dead men."

By now the soldiers were confronted with crowds of men from the town, everyone from strong, weathered fishermen to elderly merchants. Suddenly, behind the soldiers, a new group of Massachusetts minutemen arrived. "It's the Marblehead men—Major Pedrick's boys!" someone yelled. "Why, we've got them reg'lars surrounded!"

Colonel Leslie stood at the embankment and looked down at three large gundalows along the shore. "Seize those boats and cross!" he demanded.

Several foot soldiers dashed to obey his orders, but the Salem fishermen heard too and jumped into the boats. Some of the regulars charged after them, but they were too late. Already the fishermen had punched holes in the bottoms with picks and bayonets, and the boats were filling with water and sinking fast.

As one of the fishermen climbed up the bank, a furious British foot soldier ran after him with a bayonet. The fisherman opened his shirt. "Go ahead! Slice me up!" he taunted.

To Hannah's horror, the soldier pricked at the man's chest, and blood began to flow. She shrieked and put her hands over her eyes.

"It's all right, Hannah," Sarah said. "He isn't hurt badly."

At the sight of the blood, the enraged crowd closed in on the redcoats. "There's going to be a battle!" Hannah exclaimed.

Just then Parson Barnard walked calmly through

the crowd. He raised his hands for silence and motioned to Colonel Leslie to approach him. The two men spoke together quietly. Then the clergyman spoke loudly enough for everyone to hear.

"Colonel Leslie has agreed to a compromise here. He and his men are looking for the cannon. He has been advised that the munitions are near the forge, just a hundred yards or so beyond the bridge. He has given his word of honor that if we lower the bridge, he and his men will go to the forge and no farther. If the cannon are there, they will remove them. If not, they will return to their ships at Marblehead. I say, let them go search! Colonel Leslie is a man of his word."

The crowd, which was still growing in number, murmured its approval. The men and boys on the bridge climbed off as the bridge was lowered. The soldiers gathered into formation and began their march across the North River.

Sarah laughed. "They'll be back before you can blink an eye, Hannah. The cannon have been removed and all the arms hidden, thanks to you and Promise, my dear."

Just as Sarah predicted, before long Colonel

Leslie's soldiers had turned and were marching back through the town, heading toward Marblehead.

"They found nothing! They're retreating!"

And then came the jeers from the people of Salem and those from surrounding towns who had joined them. "Retreat! Retreat! You cowards!"

"Go back to where you came from, lobster coats!"

As the redcoats passed under her window, Sarah leaned out. "Go home! And tell your master he sent you on a fool's errand and has broken the peace of our Sabbath." The people cheered at her words. She called out again. "Do you think we were born in the woods to be frightened by owls?"

An infuriated soldier stopped in his tracks, raised his rifle, and took aim at the window.

Hannah gasped and tried to pull Sarah away, but Sarah jerked herself free. "Fire, if you have the courage," she screamed at the soldier, "but I doubt you do."

Another soldier pushed the barrel of the rifle down and shook his head at his angry companion. The soldier cast one last look of contempt at Sarah and continued on the retreat.

The band of soldiers marched away, their drums and fifes silent. A large group of people from adjoining towns accompanied them, shouting.

"We'll make sure they head back to Boston!"

"Give our regards to Tommy!"

"Tell King George to respect our Sabbath."

"Don't come back!"

Sarah closed the window and put a blanket around Hannah. "Just look what you achieved in coming here, Hannah. The arms are safely hidden and the regulars are heading back, defeated." She laughed. "They'd be even more humiliated if they knew that this was all brought about by one plucky girl and her steadfast horse."

"Take me to Promise," Hannah begged.

Sarah looked uncomfortable. "Let's wait until the men have had time to tend to him and we know more."

Perhaps Mr. Samson had already put Promise down. Was that the reason Sarah wouldn't take Hannah to see him? Before she could ask, there was a loud knock on the front door.

Sarah peered out the window. "It's your aunt Phoebe!" she whispered.

"Don't let her see me!" Hannah exclaimed. "She'll report me to Miss Lydia."

"Hide in my bedchamber," Sarah ordered, pointing to a door across the room.

Dragging the blanket with her, Hannah scurried into the other room, leaving the door slightly ajar.

Sarah opened the front door and Hannah could see Aunt Phoebe, who was wearing the latest fashionable clothing. "Good afternoon, Mrs. Parley," Sarah greeted her.

So Aunt Phoebe really had married the lawyer Peter Parley!

Phoebe didn't return the greeting, but pressed forward into the big room, her eyes searching.

"What can I do for you, Phoebe?" Sarah asked impatiently.

"I'm looking all over town for that niece of mine. You must have seen her at the meetinghouse today when she interrupted the service."

Sarah looked puzzled. "I didn't see any girl interrupt the service."

"She was dressed as a young man. I'm sure it was Hannah." Phoebe went to the window seat where Hannah had been watching the bridge. "You can't fool me, Sarah. I saw her again in this very window when the bridge was being lowered."

"How could Hannah be here?" Sarah asked. "She's indentured now, in Boston."

"That's where she had better be! I signed my

name to the document promising that she would be a faithful servant for seven years. If she has returned to Salem, she'll bring shame to my good name."

"Well you have a new name now, don't you? You must be happy as Mrs. Peter Parley. Is it true that Mr. Parley is thinking of moving away from Salem?"

"We've talked a bit about moving to Canada— perhaps to New Brunswick. At least there we will find people of our own high morals. People that respect the Crown. Not like those wretches out there today." Phoebe suddenly realized that Sarah had turned the topic of discussion around. "Now you listen to me, Sarah," she snapped, shaking a long finger in Mrs. Tarrant's face. "If you are hiding that child, you'll be in trouble. And if she was the one who came to warn about the cannon, I will turn her in to Lydia Perkins myself. She'll know what to do with her."

"Oh, Phoebe, you can't be serious. You surely can't believe that Hannah could have made that long trip in the snowstorm. From Boston?" Sarah burst out laughing. "Mr. Parley must enjoy your good humor, Phoebe, and I'm sure he's wondering where you are right now." She took Phoebe's arm and led her to the door.

Phoebe took a final look around the room. "You showed your true colors today, Sarah, screaming out the window at the soldiers like a fishwife."

"Yes, Phoebe, I'm a shrieking fishwife," Sarah agreed, shutting the door behind her.

Hannah came out of the bedchamber. "I must get back to Boston before I'm missed. It may be too late even now."

"Mr. Greenleaf will be here to get you shortly."

"I would like to see Promise before I leave."

"Get dressed." Sarah tossed Caleb's jacket and Will's hat to Hannah. "We'll go see how Promise is doing, but we need to hurry."

Hannah climbed into the wagon that was hitched to Sarah's big chestnut horse. When they passed the family homestead where she had lived with Aunt Phoebe, Hannah was appalled to see how deserted and unkempt it was.

Sarah's horse finally arrived at the large barn where the Samsons stabled their horses and cattle. Hannah raced inside to the stall where Promise lay. He was alive! His leg was bandaged heavily, and there was a smell of mint and other herbs about him. When the horse saw Hannah he lifted his head. She knelt by him and stroked his neck and back. "I'm sorry you are hurting so," Hannah whispered as tears slipped down her cheek. Promise nickered softly.

"I'm treating him with a dressing of herbal liniment. We'll take turns during the night with our stable hands to keep the dressing moist and get the swelling down. We want to get him on his feet as quickly as we can. The bones aren't broken, but the tendons and muscles are sprained badly." Mr. Samson shook his head. "He's gone lame. I don't know that there's much more that we can do for him, Hannah."

"Someday we'll ride again, Promise," Hannah said. "We'll gallop down among the willows and the fields. I must go back to Boston now. But you get well, and we'll be together again, my precious— you and I and Will. You'll see." She kissed the horse on his forelock, then looked up at Mr. Samson. "Please don't let him die. Please."

"We'll do our best, lass," he said. "We all love this horse."

Sarah, who had been standing quietly nearby, reached for Hannah's hand and pulled her to her feet. "We must leave. Mr. Greenleaf will be waiting to take Hannah back to Boston."

"Good-bye, Promise," Hannah said to her horse. "Get well, my sweet boy."

"Give my son a blessing from his father," Mr. Samson said.

Outside the stable, a small woman was waiting. "We finally meet," she said, kissing Hannah on the cheek. "I'm Will's mother." She looked kindly at Hannah with smoke-blue eyes the same as Will's. "How is my boy faring, Hannah?"

"He is improving, Mrs. Samson. He will soon be up and about. I shall give him your love and concern. Will is my best friend."

"I know. And you are his, my dear." Her voice broke and her eyes brightened with tears. "He is our only child. I miss him."

"He'll be back once he's better," Hannah assured her.

"Come along, Hannah." Sarah untied her horse and climbed into the front of the wagon.

"Godspeed!" the Samsons called. Sarah clicked the reins. It was almost dark as they headed back to her house by the bridge.

Shortly after they returned, Mr. Greenleaf arrived for Hannah. "I hear you must return to Boston right away. If we leave now, we'll be there before dawn."

"I'm ready," Hannah said. "Thank you!"

"Come in before you leave," Sarah insisted. "I'll pack food for the trip." She put roasted turkey legs and stuffing into a napkin and handed it to Mr. Greenleaf. Then she shoved a flask of cider into Hannah's saddlebag. "Take care of Hannah, sir," she said. "Our town owes her a great deal."

"I will get her back safely," Mr. Greenleaf promised.

the ride back was rough and cold, but Hannah sank into a pillow and slept most of the way. Now the dawn was pale in the sky as they approached the Charlestown waterfront.

"Hannah!" Mr. Greenleaf whispered when they stopped. "We're back. The boat is waiting to take us across to Boston."

Hannah climbed out of the carriage. Her legs were stiff from her long ride yesterday. She stomped her feet and shivered, hoping that no one at the Province House had noticed she was missing and no punishment awaited her. "I wonder if anyone questioned Catherine about me," she said to Mr. Greenleaf.

"If they did, I'm sure Catherine would protect you, Hannah." Mr. Greenleaf smiled. "She loves you,

you know. And you haven't been gone that long, really. Only two nights." Men from a nearby stable took the horse and carriage away as Mr. Greenleaf led Hannah down to his boat. They paddled through the ice floes, and Hannah, as before, poked the floating ice away. Boston was awakening, and smoke from newly stoked fires fell heavy on the morning air.

"How will you get back?" Mr. Greenleaf asked. "If you come to my house I can have you taken back in a carriage."

"No, a carriage will bring attention to us. I'll walk. I have my own way of getting inside the gates."

"Very well, Hannah. Be careful. My prayers go with you."

Hannah hastened up the street. Her body ached, and she was close to tears from exhaustion, fear of being discovered, and sadness for Promise.

There were no soldiers in sight when she arrived at the entrance to the tunnel. She kicked away the snow and ice from the trapdoor with a sudden anger. How she hated creeping through this damp, dark shaft! How she wished she lived in a real house with people who cared for her. She was tired of the lies, the spying, the deception.

When she slipped into the stable to change into her own clothes, Hannah noticed that most of the stalls were full. She took the clothes and hat she had worn to Salem and brought them upstairs.

"Caleb!" she called softly.

"Hannah? Is it you?" He was dressed, but he still looked pale and wan.

She told him briefly what happened in Salem.

"It was a bold and rash thing for you to do by yourself, Hannah!"

She ignored his scolding. "Have you heard anything? Is anyone looking for me?"

"No one has mentioned you to me. But I've been busy. Horsemen have been arriving during the night."

"I must appear at breakfast right away." She handed him the clothes. "Hide these," she said. "The stalls are mostly full and I don't dare leave these garments there any longer." As she left the stable, she tucked her hair under a clout, hoping no one would notice how untidy she looked.

The servants were already gathered in the kitchen, where the fires had been rekindled. Pots of coffee and tea were on the large oak table along with sweet rolls and a large bowl of cooked oatmeal.

Hannah tried to act as she usually did. She casually helped herself to a cup of tea and a sweet roll and sat on a bench. Edward, Mrs. Dudley, and Sally were already seated at the table, but Catherine was nowhere to be seen. Hannah suspected she was probably waiting for everyone to finish and leave, for fear of being questioned about Hannah.

"Well look who's up and among the living," Sally said. "You picked a bad time to be sick."

"Are you feeling better?" Mrs. Dudley asked. "We thought you might have come down with the pox or something, the way Catherine kept you quarantined. I was going to send for a doctor if you were no better today."

"I'm feeling better, thank you. Is Miss Meg back?"

"She returned last night," Mrs. Dudley answered. "I told her you were ill when she asked for you."

Caleb came into the room with Joseph. Each of them took a bowl of oatmeal.

"You're feeling better?" Caleb asked as if seeing Hannah for the first time that day.

"Yes, and you?"

"I'm fine now," Caleb assured her.

"The stables are busy," Joseph said as he sat down. "There was some action in Salem, I heard."

"Officers and soldiers were in and out all night," Mrs. Dudley said. "The general didn't have any sleep at all as far I can see."

Miss Lydia appeared and poured herself a cup of coffee, then joined the others. "What's this? There was trouble last night?"

Caleb shot a look at Hannah with lowered eyes. "What happened in Salem?" he asked Joseph.

"I heard soldiers saying it was a confidential mission. Only Colonel Leslie and one of his officers knew. Yet someone alerted the Salemites," Joseph answered. "I heard it was a young lad who rode out there from Charlestown, a boy with a gold-braided tricorn hat."

Will's hat!

Edward frowned. "There's too much gossip traveling around in the Province House. I fear there may be someone here who can't be trusted."

"Nonsense!" Miss Lydia exclaimed with a wave of her hand. "Everyone who works for the general and his wife admires and respects them. No one here would ever betray these kind people."

Hannah looked down at her tea. Yes, she had carried the warning to Salem. Yes, she had helped the cause of freedom. But it was also true that General Gage had been kind to her, giving her easier work as Meg's chambermaid and letting her keep Gypsy. Mrs. Gage trusted her with her secret letters. And what about Meg? Meg regarded Hannah as her friend.

Hannah sat in the kitchen of the Province House feeling like a traitor.

Hannah went directly to her room after breakfast. Catherine was there, sitting on the bed. Relief flooded her face when she saw Hannah. "Oh, thank the good Lord you've returned safely!" she exclaimed.

Hannah quickly explained what had happened on her trip and how Mr. Greenleaf had brought her home.

"I've been ever so worried. When people asked about you I told them you might have something contagious, so they didn't ask to see you. But I was becoming concerned that Mrs. Dudley might insist on bringing in a doctor."

"Well, I'm back, and I've already seen Mrs. Dudley downstairs. So all is well, Catherine."

"Miss Meg is back and will probably send for

you." Catherine looked worried again. "Hannah, I've heard that the general is furious that someone exposed his plan to the people in Salem. He is determined to find that person and punish him."

"Does he have any idea who it might be?"

"Lieutenant Pratt is coming to see the general today. Someone said he claims to know who may have warned Salem."

"He has no reason to suspect me," Hannah said. She wondered, though. Was he the officer who had questioned the stable hand at Valley Acres about Promise?

"You're right, Hannah," Catherine said. "No one would believe a young girl like you could have made that ride in the snow."

Curled up in Hannah's lap, Gypsy purred as Hannah stroked her. Who else could be suspected of the betrayal? Hannah handed Gypsy to Catherine, changed into clean clothes, and rushed off to Meg's room.

"Hannah!" Meg exclaimed with delight. "Are you feeling better?"

"Yes, I am, thank you," Hannah replied. "What would you like for breakfast today?"

"Oh, just toast and tea. But first let me tell you about my visit to Lady Ashby's home." She motioned for Hannah to sit down. "Lady Ashby was so kind to take me in during the epidemic. I thought I would be bored, but I had a lovely visit."

"I'm glad you enjoyed yourself," Hannah said, forcing a smile.

"While I was there, I was shown new hairstyles and her latest collection of French gowns. I don't know how she was able to get them, but she did! And, Hannah, I thought of you and the"—she hesitated— "the pockmark on your cheek. Practically everyone has pockmarks in Europe, so they cover one or two with delightful little star- or heart-shaped patches to look like moles. It's become quite fashionable. I brought some for you."

When Hannah didn't respond, Meg became quiet. "Perhaps you aren't feeling well yet, Hannah. I thought you'd be excited to hear all this."

"I'm still weak and tired, Miss Meg," Hannah responded. She stood up. "I'll bring your breakfast."

Hannah hurried down the hall to the back stairway. She didn't care about French fashions or hairstyles. Instinctively she pulled a wisp of hair over the scar on her cheek. Then angrily she shoved the lock back under her clout. She didn't care about her pockmark, either! She just wanted to be away from here and back in Salem, where she should have stayed with Promise.

While Mrs. Dudley set up a tray for Meg, Hannah listened to the other servants whispering among themselves, wondering who the boy was who had caused the British retreat in Salem.

"I heard he had a hat with a feather in it," Sally said in a voice of authority.

"It wasn't a feather, it was gold braid," Joseph argued. "I heard it myself from the soldiers who returned."

Hannah stifled an urge to run out the door. The hat they were looking for was in Caleb's room above the stable. But surely Caleb would have hidden it. Besides, they wouldn't suspect him; he'd been sick from the sore-throat distemper for several days.

Mrs. Dudley was annoyed. "Don't you have work to do? This is all gossip. We'll find out soon enough who betrayed us."

Joseph got up and left the kitchen. Sally sniffed and went upstairs. Mrs. Dudley smiled at Hannah as she handed her the tray. "You're the only one with sense around here, my dear. I never hear you gossip."

Hannah took the tray and moved hastily to the stairway.

Meg was dressed and playing with her bird when Hannah arrived and placed the tray on a table. "Thank you, Hannah," she said, sitting down. "If you're still not feeling well, go lie down. I don't want you to work when you're sick."

"Thank you, Miss Meg," Hannah said with sudden relief. She'd do just that. She'd go back to her bedchamber and shut the door on the rest of the world.

That afternoon, Catherine came into the room. "Hannah, wake up. The whole house is buzzing! Lieutenant Pratt has informed General Gage who he believes to be the Midnight Rider and the one who warned Salem. They've gone to arrest the lad for treason. They'll be bringing him before General Gage himself."

"Treason! That means death by execution!" Hannah cried. "Who have they charged?"

"I don't know, Hannah. But I'm afraid to even imagine." Catherine went to the window overlooking the courtyard and the stables. "They should be arriving any minute."

Hannah and Catherine watched the activity below. A cart pulled by two horses rattled into the courtyard from the street. There, in the wagon, sat Mr. Hubbard, and in the backseat, surrounded by redcoat soldiers, was their suspect. Will!

even from the third-floor window, Hannah could see Will's solemn and determined face as they pulled him from the cart and shoved him through the back door of the Province House. *No front-door entrance for the likes of him,* Hannah thought. *Not for a traitor.* She turned tearfully to Catherine. "But it wasn't Will!" Hannah cried. "It was me!"

"Whist. We must wait to see what happens," Catherine said, putting her arm around Hannah's shoulder. "It may turn out to be nothing."

"Of course it will," Hannah said, trying to be calm. "He couldn't have ridden to Salem after having surgery. He can show them his foot and they'll have to believe him."

"Let's go downstairs. Someone may be able to tell us what's happening." Catherine took Hannah's hand and drew her out of the room.

"They've got him in the public reception room on the first floor," Sally told Hannah as they made their way through the crowded kitchen. "General Gage has left the door open so everyone can see what becomes of traitors."

With Catherine behind her, Hannah squeezed through the spectators to the front of the building. Chester Pratt looked up with a smile as Margaret Gage and Meg descended the grand stairway with concerned expressions. Inside the room, General Gage stood behind his desk and stared coldly at Will.

"William Samson, you are charged with treason against His Majesty," General Gage said. "We believe you rode to Salem and informed them of the king's plans to remove the arms there. What have you to say for yourself?"

"I'm innocent, Your Excellency," Will answered. "I've recently had surgery on my foot, and I could not have ridden to Salem."

"Who performed the surgery?" General Gage asked.

"Dr. Joseph Warren, sir."

A plethora of murmurs and cries arose from the crowd.

"Dr. Warren! He's a rebel if ever there was!"

"Let us see your foot!"

General Gage raised his hand for silence. "Show me the surgery," he ordered.

Will sat on a chair to remove his boot. He stuck out his foot, which was swathed in strips of flannel.

General Gage nodded at Will. "Undress the wound."

Will slowly unwrapped the cloths, which stuck to the scabby lesions where his toes had been.

"Oh! It's true!" came the voices from the crowd.

"Ghastly!" Meg exclaimed.

"And when did you have this surgery?" asked General Gage.

"About two weeks ago, Your Excellency," Will answered.

"It appears to be healing well. You could have ridden to Salem."

"No, sir. I could not ride. Dr. Warren has been treating me for recurring pus."

"A strong lad like you could ride with that foot," General Gage stated.

Hannah closed her eyes. They didn't believe him!

General Gage walked away, his hands clasped behind his back. "You have a black horse, have you not?"

"Yes, Your Excellency." Will's face was pale now.

"You kept him at Valley Acres?" General Gage swung around.

"Yes, I kept my horse there."

"That horse was the one that terrified soldiers' steeds on the Common and committed other tricks, is it not?"

"I did not ride to terrify anyone's horses, sir."

"If I may interrupt, Your Excellency," Lieutenant Pratt said. "I would recognize that horse anywhere. It is ebony black, like a creature from hell."

General Gage nodded thoughtfully. Then Mr. Hubbard stepped forward and addressed General Gage. "I am this lad's employer and I can vouch for him, sir. He has been ill and not left my garret for two weeks."

"Mr. Hubbard is a staunch Yankee and has been seen attending meetings at the Green Dragon," Chester Pratt exclaimed. "You can't believe him, General!"

General Gage frowned. "If this lad rode to warn Salem, someone must have informed him of my plan." The general turned to Will. "Who was it?"

Will was silent.

"Give him forty lashes! He'll tell soon enough!" came a call from the crowd.

General Gage raised his hand for silence. "I have put up with the lapses in intelligence long enough. This young man will get forty strokes every day until he confesses and tells who his informant is."

Hannah could stand it no longer. "No!" she screamed, pushing her way into the center of the room. "Will is not the informant who went to Salem. And he is not the Midnight Rider. I am!"

The room exploded with laughter.

"She never could have taken that ride. A *girl*?"

"Impossible!"

"He must be the sweetheart she goes off to meet!" Meg exclaimed. "Poor, poor Hannah!"

"Take this girl out of here!" General Gage ordered.

"Wait! I can prove it was me!" Hannah turned and ran out to the stable.

Caleb and Joseph were busy watering and tending the soldiers' horses. Caleb rushed to her. "What are you doing, Hannah? What's going on with Will?"

"They're going to whip him!" Hannah cried.

Caleb's gaunt face went white. "No! They could kill him!"

"I've told them it was me, but they won't believe me. I have to save him. Get me Hans's clothes. Now!"

"You can't do this, Hannah."

Hannah beat at Caleb's chest with her fists. "I will, whether you help me or not! Get me the clothes I wore!" She was sobbing as she continued to strike him over and over.

Caleb put his hands up to protect himself. "All right, Hannah, all right." He went into the barn and returned with the bundle of clothes and Will's hat.

Hannah pulled the breeches on over her skirt, thrust her arms into the jacket, and donned Will's gold-braided tricorn hat. Then running back into the mansion she pushed her way to the reception hall, where Will was being bound up.

"Stop!" she called in Hans's voice as she stood before them. "I am the one who brought the alarm to Salem. I am the Midnight Rider!"

the reception hall fell quiet. General Gage stared at Hannah, his gaze moving from Will's hat down to Caleb's boots. "It's me, Hannah Andrews," she proclaimed in her own voice. Her hair tumbled out from under the hat as she plucked it from her head.

"Surely you didn't take that wild horse all the way to Salem!" exclaimed the general.

"I did, Your Excellency."

"I, for one, believe her. She's been a trouble-maker all along," said Chester Pratt. "I don't know why Miss Meg has put up with her."

"It's not your place to question my choices in friends or servants!" Meg retorted, "Besides, I prefer Hannah's company to yours!"

Chester flinched at her sharp words.

"Hannah, why did you do this?" Mrs. Gage came forward.

"I heard the general speaking to Colonel Leslie as I mopped the floors by his office. I knew I must warn my friends back in Salem. If their arms were taken away, how would they defend themselves if there was war?"

Miss Lydia joined in the assault on Hannah. "This child is disobedient and disloyal. That's why her aunt sent her away in the first place."

"She's living here in the Province House under the care and protection of our soldiers, and she's turned traitor," Edward said in disgust.

General Gage put his hand up. "Silence! I believe the girl is foolishly trying to protect her friend. She could never ride that distance alone in a snowstorm. I'm convinced this boy is the traitor."

"Yes, it was me," said Will, his eyes on Hannah. "It wasn't her, General Gage."

"They're protecting each other," someone said.

"And where is the horse?" General Gage asked.

Hannah broke in. "I left him in Salem after he foundered and fell. He is badly hurt." Hannah paused. "I may never see him again."

"After what you've done, you never *will* see him again," Lieutenant Pratt said with relish.

General Gage slammed his fist on his desk. "Let the girl ride my stallion, Gabriel. If she can get mastery over him, then I'll decide what I believe."

"No, Thomas! She's only a child!" Mrs. Gage cried out. "No one has ever been able to ride Gabriel other than you. Would you put one of our children on that animal?"

"If this girl has betrayed us, then she deserves whatever will happen." He stomped out of the room, pausing only to give orders to Edward. "Tell Caleb to saddle Gabriel and bring him into the courtyard immediately."

"Please, sir," Will pleaded, "your horse is too dangerous."

"Be still!" General Gage snapped. "I haven't finished with you . . . yet."

In the courtyard, Hannah and Will stood between two soldiers as Caleb led Gabriel out of the stable. The crowd gasped as they saw how the horse struggled against him. Hannah realized that Gabriel could very well be dangerous. The stallion had not had the freedom of the open fields, nor had he received training from anyone other than General Gage.

"I can't believe that you would do this, Thomas," Mrs. Gage said. When he replied with only an icy stare, she lowered her gaze.

"Go! Mount the horse," General Gage said to Hannah. "Show us all what a fine horseman you are."

Hannah walked cautiously to the golden horse that was pawing the ground. "Gabriel," she said in her most tender voice. "I know you're fearful out here with all these people watching us."

Gabriel pulled back, his nostrils flaring and his eyes wild. "Easy, boy," Caleb said as he reached out to stroke the horse's neck. But the horse drew away, tossing his mane and wriggling.

"Remember me, my good friend?" Hannah's words were soothing. "If you were mine, we'd ride over the fields and down to the shore. We would fly up to the clouds and never come back, wouldn't we?"

The stallion was motionless now, watching Hannah warily.

"Come, my pretty one. I'm the one who fed you apples and petted you." She held out her hand, palm up, and after a moment the horse nuzzled it. Hannah slowly reached for Gabriel's forehead and petted it. "Sweet, sweet angel horse," she crooned, "please let me ride you."

Gradually she moved to the stallion's left side, all the while stroking and whispering. She grasped the stirrup. Gabriel sidestepped with a snort. "There, there, you golden beauty, we are going to fly up to the sun. That's where you came from, Gabriel. From the gold of the sun." The horse stood silently as she mounted him.

The crowd talked softly among themselves. Hannah could see Mrs. Gage and Meg standing rigid, their hands clasped together. Hannah clicked the reins, and Gabriel lifted his feet in a high-stepped trot over to the winter-killed garden. "Fly, Gabriel!" she said with a tap of her heel. The stallion sprinted forward, galloping through the empty vegetable beds, under the apple trees, and around the entire mansion. Hannah felt his joy as he leaped over the hedges, his mane glistening like sun rays.

A few of the people who had gathered applauded at her horsemanship. Hannah could see relief flood Mrs. Gage's face. Meg laughed and cheered out loud, but then covered her mouth with her gloved hands.

General Gage stood solemnly as Hannah pulled his horse to a stop. She dismounted and handed the reins to Caleb. "I lose, even though I win," she said to him.

Hannah turned to face General Gage. "You and Mrs. Gage and Miss Meg were all kind to me, and the choice I made was not an easy one, sir. I know what I've done is unforgivable in your eyes. But it was I who was the Midnight Rider, and it was I who went to Salem. It was not Will Samson."

There was a long moment of silence and then General Gage spoke. "The boy will get forty strokes at the whipping post."

Cheers erupted.

"No!" Hannah wailed. She looked over at Will, whose face was drawn and colorless.

"Will could die from forty strokes," Caleb objected.

"What about the girl?" asked Lieutenant Pratt. "She committed treason."

"She'll go to prison for the rest of her life," General Gage exclaimed.

Hannah's legs buckled under her, and Caleb reached over and supported her. She would never be free now! Her hope of living in Salem, of flying through the willows with Promise—all of her dreams were gone forever!

"No!" Meg screamed. "Don't do that to Hannah, Uncle Thomas."

Mrs. Gage shook Meg's shoulder. "Whist!"

Mr. Hubbard stepped forward. "Your Excellency, would it not be fair to let these children have a trial?"

"They just had their trial!" General Gage exclaimed. "The girl admitted she was guilty. The boy owns the horse—what more is there to say?" He turned to walk away.

Cheers erupted. "Serves 'em right!"

"Traitors!"

Mrs. Gage grasped her husband's arm and took him aside. "Wait, Thomas. Before you make this decision—"

"I've already made my decision," the General stated, shaking her away.

"Hear me out!" Mrs. Gage pleaded. "If you do this to these children, you will be adding fuel to the fire of rebellion. The people of Boston—of all of New England—will be inflamed! They have not forgotten the shooting of that boy, Christopher Seider, five years ago."

General Gage paused, listening.

"Thomas, for the sake of peace, don't make these children into martyrs. If you do, it will result in an uprising that will surely turn into a great conflict."

For a long moment Thomas Gage didn't speak. Then he turned and faced the crowd. "I've decided not to create a possible war by making martyrs out of these disloyal and ungrateful children," he announced.

The crowd jeered. "You're letting 'em get away with it?"

"Give them what they deserve!"

"Hang them!"

General Gage pointed his finger at Hannah and Will. "You are both banished from Boston. Get out of this house and this town! I never want to see your faces again."

the rest of the day no one at the Province House spoke to Hannah. Even Catherine pretended to shun her, except when they were in their own room.

"Where will you go?" Catherine asked, her eyes filling with tears.

"Back to Salem. I want to be with Promise. The house I lived in there is empty, now that Aunt Phoebe has moved out. That house belonged to my grandfather, and my father grew up there. I have a right to live there too, though I'm sure Aunt Phoebe will object. She says I've dishonored her good name." Hannah took her mother's ring from the drawer and put in on her finger.

"The people of Salem love you, Hannah."

"I'm sure Mrs. Tarrant will take me in for a

while. Or maybe Will's family." Hannah slumped onto the bed. "I'm afraid to find out what's happened to Promise. Oh, Catherine, if he's dead I shall die myself."

Catherine sat next to her. "No, you won't, Hannah. You are strong and brave, and soon you'll be free again."

"I'm not sure anyone is ever really free."

Catherine patted Hannah's hand. "I understand why you did what you did, Hannah. I believe even General Gage understands. However, his loyalty is to King George."

"And Mrs. Gage?"

"She saved both you and Will, you know."

"That's true," Hannah said. "I wonder if Meg hates me."

"Meg doesn't hate you at all. In fact, she probably admires you and your faith in your convictions."

Gypsy jumped into Hannah's lap, purring. "Oh, what will happen to you?" she said, petting the kitten.

"I'll take care of her until we meet again." Catherine embraced Hannah. "Stay safe, my dear."

. . .

It was dusk when Hannah went to the well in the courtyard to wait for Will. Save for the ribbons Meg had given her, she had not taken anything other than what she had brought to the Province House. She wished she could say good-bye to Meg, but she knew Meg was forbidden to speak to her.

Hannah darted inside the barn and up the stairs to Caleb's quarters. "Caleb? I've come to say good-bye."

Caleb peered out at her. "You shouldn't have come. We can't let anyone suspect we're friends. I'm supposed to shun you."

"Good-bye, then," Hannah said, turning away.

"Hannah, wait," Caleb whispered. "You and Will *are* my dearest friends. Someday we'll all be free and I'll come to see you in Salem."

"Until then, Caleb, God bless you." Hannah tiptoed down the steps and out into the courtyard.

Will was pulling up with Mr. Hubbard's horse and wagon. He didn't stop even long enough to hitch the horses. He jumped out, tossed Hannah's bag in the back, and helped her climb in. Hannah wore her mother's red cloak, and she pulled the hood up over her hair. Will clicked the reins, and the horse plodded down the brick pavement toward the street.

"Hannah!"

Hannah turned to see a small figure flit out from the darkness at the side of the mansion. It was Meg. Will pulled the reins, and the horse stopped.

Meg bounded into the cart and threw her arms around Hannah. "I will miss you terribly," she said, and Hannah felt the tears on Meg's face. "I wish I could go with you!"

"I wish you could too," Hannah said, her own eyes filling up with tears. "But you cannot. Your life will take a different roadway than mine."

"I will probably go back to England before there is war here," Meg said. "But you will remain in my heart forever." She kissed Hannah's cheek, jumped lightly off the wagon, and disappeared once again into the deepening shadows.

m r. Hubbard was waiting at the cove of the river where the small boat was hidden. Once Will and Hannah were safely on board, he rowed them across the dark water to the other side.

"Go to Deacon Larkin's house," Mr. Hubbard told them as they climbed onto the wharf. "He will give you a horse to get you to Salem." He pushed off to head back to the city. "Good-bye and God bless you both," he said. "Who knows when we will meet again."

Hannah and Will hastened up the darkened street to the deacon's house by the church. A lantern light flickered in the back kitchen window.

A few minutes passed before the clergyman responded to Will's knock. "General Gage discovered we were rebels. Thanks be to God, we were not severely punished, only sent away because of our youth. We need a carriage or horse to get to Salem."

Deacon Larkin took them to the stable. "I have only one horse available, Brown Beauty, and a small cart. This should do, but you may need to change at the Great Elm Tavern. I keep another horse there."

He helped Will hitch the horse to the carriage. Will climbed into the driver's seat and pulled Hannah up beside him.

"God be with you!" Deacon Larkin patted Brown Beauty's flank, and they were off. Stars glimmered through the leafless branches of the trees that arched over the snowy roads. Hannah was afraid of what might have happened to Promise in her absence. She knew she had to be brave and strong, like Catherine had told her, but still, her heart was heavy with worry.

She thought about Catherine, Caleb, Meg, and her other friends in Boston. Would she ever see them again? If there were a war, what would become of them all?

As they passed through sleeping villages, past lonely farms and their snow-covered fields, she prayed for her friends in Boston, both Loyalist and Patriot. Then she leaned against Will's shoulder and fell asleep.

Morning had broken when Will woke her. "Wake up, Hannah. We're almost in Salem." She sat up sleepily. She vaguely recalled changing horses at the Great Elm Tavern and then climbing into the back of the cart to sleep in the loose hay.

The morning air was icy, and great clouds of steam puffed out from the horse's nostrils. Ahead were the North River and the bridge.

Hannah wondered fearfully what she would find when she arrived at the Samsons' stable. *Please, dear Father in Heaven, let Promise be alive and well. But if he is not, help me to be brave.*

In a short time they arrived at the Samsons' stable, and Will pulled the reins to stop the horse. After he helped Hannah down from the back of the cart, he hugged her for a moment. "Be strong, Hannah," he whispered. Hand in hand they walked into the barn.

Will's father was there, preparing to milk the cows. He looked up, went to his son, and clasped his arms around him. "It's good to have you back, Will."

Hannah clutched Mr. Samson's sleeve. "How is Promise?"

Mr. Samson shook his head sadly. "Alive, but not doing well. Hannah, I've nursed that horse's leg as if it were my own child's. The swelling is down, but I can't get Promise on his feet. He just wants to lie there, and sometimes he tries to roll about. These are all signs of colic, which troubles me the most. We must get him up and walking or he'll eventually bloat and possibly die, Hannah."

Mr. Samson led them to the stall where Promise lay with a poultice bandaged to his leg. "Promise!" Hannah cried as she rushed to him. "My sweet, wonderful boy. I'm sorry I drove you so hard that you fell." Promise lifted his head at her voice and nickered softly.

Hannah knelt at his side and stroked his ebony neck. "I once promised I'd never leave you and that we'd always be together. Did you think I'd forgotten when I went away? Is that why you're just lying here?" She pressed her face close to the horse's cheek and wept. "You were always in my heart, dear boy. I've never forgotten my promise to you."

"Hannah," Will said, "come along. You mustn't upset yourself like this."

Hannah stroked the horse's muzzle gently. "I'm here now, dear, dear Promise, and I'll never leave you again."

Will clasped her shoulder gently. "Come away, Hannah." Will was crying too.

Hannah took a deep breath. "You've got to get up and get well, my love." She stood and backed away from the horse. "Come, Promise. Get up, my boy."

Promise didn't move.

Will bent over Promise. "Get up, boy. Do it for Hannah."

"I've watched horses go through this before," Mr. Samson said. "The leg hurts when he puts weight on it, so he's afraid to stand. But he must get up. I've used herbal poultices—witch hazel, mint oil, oil of wormwood, rosemary—day and night to alleviate the pain. But he won't eat, either. Maybe it would be easier for you to . . . say good-bye to Promise now, child," Mr. Samson suggested gently.

"I can't say good-bye!" Hannah exclaimed. "Not yet!"

"We'll wait a while longer," Mr. Samson said soothingly, "but we don't want Promise to suffer." He patted his son on the shoulder. "Take her into the house, Will. You'll both feel better once you've had a bite to eat and some coffee. Then you can tell your mother and me why you're back and what happened in Boston."

The morning sun beamed in a clear sky. Smoke curled up from the chimney, and a rooster crowed. Will was just about to open the kitchen door when his father suddenly called from the barn. "Hannah! Will! Come quickly!"

Alarmed, Hannah dashed back to the stable with Will by her side.

"What's happened?" Will asked.

Mr. Samson waved them back to Promise's stall. Hannah and Will looked in fearfully.

"Promise!" Hannah cheered. "You're standing!" His ears perked up at her voice.

"I don't know what it is between you and that horse," Will's father said to Hannah. "See those eyes? He has that spark again."

"Oh, my wonderful horse," Hannah cried as she ran and snuggled her head against him. "You just needed to be sure that I had come back—that I'd kept my promise."

It was a late June day in Salem. The meadows were blossoming with wildflowers, and Promise grazed contentedly in the shade of the elm tree. A salty breeze from the sea whispered through the open windows of the little saltbox house. But Hannah was worried. She had heard the news of a great battle at Bunker Hill in Charlestown. Will had gone to Charlestown three weeks ago, and neither she nor his family had heard from him. Today a post rider from Boston had delivered a letter to Hannah from Catherine. Hannah was afraid to read it. She had put it on the table, unopened.

When she heard a knock on the kitchen door, she hurried to unbolt it.

Sarah Tarrant stood on the threshold carrying

a covered basket from which emitted a series of chirps and scratches. "I've brought the chicks I promised you."

Hannah and Sarah set the little chickens into an old coop that Hannah had swept and cleaned. "You'll soon be gathering your own eggs, Hannah." Sarah told her.

"Thank you, Sarah." Hannah poured two mugs of coffee and brought them to the table where Sarah was already seated.

"Things worked out well after all, didn't they?" Sarah asked. "Once Phoebe and her husband moved to New Brunswick with the other Tories, there was no question that this house should be yours, Hannah. Everyone in town agrees." Sarah smiled. "Have you heard from your friends in Boston since the battle at Bunker Hill?"

"I received a message from Catherine today, and I've been terrified to open it. But now that you're here . . ." Hannah's hands shook as she opened the letter. She read aloud.

My dear Hannah,
As you most likely have heard, the war is

upon us. A terrible battle was fought on Bunker Hill in Charlestown on June 17, and the losses were great.

I have such sad news for you, Hannah, that it breaks my heart to write these words. Your dear friend Caleb took sides with the Massachusetts militia, and was killed in battle there. I know how much sadness this will bring to you and Will. He was only seventeen years of age. Remember how strongly he yearned for liberty? He will be remembered as one who gave his life for that cause.

"Oh, not Caleb!" Hannah burst into tears. Memories of their friendship overwhelmed her: the first day she met him in the stable, with his hands on his hips and his scolding words; their daring midnight travels through the tunnel; even his clothes, which "Hans" had worn. Now she would never see him again. He would never to come to live with them in Salem.

"Caleb dreamed of freedom. Now he has died for it." Hannah wiped her eyes and, after a moment, read on:

Dr. Joseph Warren, who had just been elected president of the Massachusetts Provincial Congress and general of the Massachusetts troops, lost his life in that battle, also. The British claimed victory, but it was a questionable one, since many of their brave young men died, as well as several of General Gage's officers.

There have been strained feelings here in the Province House. I've heard rumors that someone discovered General Gage's secret plans for Concord and Lexington on April 19 and revealed them to Dr. Warren. He, in turn, ordered Paul Revere and William Dawes to carry the warning throughout Middlesex County that the regulars were on the march.

Everyone is wondering who the informant was. It's been said that Dr. Warren had a spy among the high ranks of the British and that he vowed he'd take that person's name to his grave before he'd ever reveal it.

I also heard from a knowledgeable clergyman that the informant was a woman—someone close to General Gage who betrayed him.

Such is the talk and the rumors. Mrs. Gage has been tearful, but I heard one of their sons, William, died in England, so it is no wonder that she is very sad. She does not eat at the general's table. In fact Mrs. Gage will be sailing to England very soon on that old ship the Charming Nancy *that is bringing the wounded soldiers back home. I suppose she will be nursing them.*

Hannah stopped reading. "I used to deliver letters to Miss Wheatley for Mrs. Gage. There was always an iris on the paper. Did you know that in the language of flowers the meaning for an iris is 'I have a message for you'? I thought it was strange, especially since I saw that she kept the paper in a secret drawer in her tallboy."

"There's nothing strange about Mrs. Gage writing to Miss Wheatley," Sarah said.

"Yes, but one day I saw Miss Wheatley convey one of those letters to Dr. Warren."

"You think Mrs. Gage was the informant?" Sarah asked skeptically.

"It *is* hard to believe," Hannah agreed. "But

she was terribly torn between her love for this country and her love for England. There was no writing on the messages I saw—only the flower."

"I've heard of messages written in invisible ink. But I suppose we will never know if Mrs. Gage was the informant or not," Sarah said. "So many families have been torn apart because of this revolt."

Hannah continued reading.

> *I'm sure you are wondering about Meg. She was sent to England two weeks ago.*
>
> *Here is good news, Hannah. Mr. Greenleaf and I will be married in a few weeks. He is going to war, so perhaps I shall come and stay with you, if that is possible. And of course I shall bring that little mischief maker Gypsy. We both miss you.*
>
> *Until then, dear Hannah, I send you (and Will) my affection.*
>
> *Catherine*

Hannah looked up at Sarah with a smile. "It would be wonderful for Catherine to stay with me while her husband is gone." Then tears welled up in her eyes again. "I am stricken with the news about Caleb, though."

"Such are the affairs of war, my dear," Sarah said gently. "We will be hearing of more casualties in time."

"No one has heard from Will since he left. Perhaps he was with Caleb at Bunker Hill!"

"Whist! Don't stir up a storm, Hannah. Wait on the Lord." Sarah reached across the table and took Hannah's hand. "Are you all right here alone?"

"Yes. The Samsons visit me every day with milk and butter and good things, and I eat over there often. And you've been especially kind to me, Sarah."

"I must get home," Sarah said, getting up and heading for the door. "Have you ridden Promise yet?"

"Not yet, although Mr. Samson feels Promise is well enough now. We've given his leg four months to heal."

"I'll be happy to see you riding again. Good-bye, my dear." Sarah left.

Hannah sat at the table and reread Catherine's letter. Her heart ached for Caleb and with her worries for Will. She bowed her head and closed her eyes. "Dear Lord and Father, I thank thee for answering my prayers and setting me free from bondage. I thank thee for friendly neighbors and for my grandparents' house, and for saving my own wonderful Promise.

"Now we are at war. Please protect Will and send him home. Bless thy servants, on whichever side they may be. May thy will for our country be done. In Jesus' name."

Hannah stood up and went outside to spread seed for the new chicks. As the door slammed shut behind her, Promise looked up. Hannah climbed over the small stone wall and into the pasture. Promise neighed and trotted over to her.

"You're anxious for me to ride with you, aren't you, my boy?" She rubbed Promise's ears. On an impulse she went into the shed, picked up Promise's bridle, and ran outside.

"Come, Promise," she said. The horse trotted to her and allowed her to pull the bridle on and adjust it. "Good boy. You want to run again, don't you?" Hannah stood on the wall and climbed on Promise's bare back. She grinned as she tucked her skirt above her knees. *Aunt Phoebe should see me now,* she thought.

Promise pranced about for a moment, then paused as if waiting for Hannah's command. Hannah tapped his flank lightly with her hand.

The horse ambled through the spring grass. How wonderful to be on Promise again. But she couldn't brush aside her sadness over Caleb—and the fear that something might have happened to Will. She tried not to think about it.

Hannah let Promise take her to the hillside. In the distance the deep blue Atlantic glistened in the sunlight.

Suddenly she heard someone calling. A horse and rider were heading in her direction.

Will!

"Hannah! Wait for me!" Will, on his mother's pretty roan mare, Tulip, galloped up to Promise, reached for Hannah, and kissed her sweetly and lightly on the lips.

"You are back safely. God has answered my prayers," Hannah whispered, kissing him back. "But my heart is broken because Caleb was killed."

"I was with him when he died. Caleb's last words were about freedom . . . and about you, Hannah." Will's voice broke and he took hold of her hand. "I buried him on Copps Hill, overlooking the sea."

A cloud drifted over the sun. Hannah clung to Will's strong grasp. They were silent for a long moment, remembering their friend. Then the sun broke through the clouds once more, and Hannah let go of Will's hand. "Fly, Promise!" she called. Her horse, in a sudden burst of freedom, vaulted toward the shore.

Hannah and Will raced their horses over the meadow, chasing birds and butterflies from their path. Off they flew through countless wildflowers, which bowed in the breeze before them—and then down, down the hill to the willows by the sea.

midnight Rider is a work of fiction based on historical events that took place just prior to the American Revolution. As a writer, I've discovered that history books are treasure troves of fascinating facts that can be woven into stories.

While researching the period prior to and during the American Revolution, I discovered that there were many dispatch riders who carried messages and secret information for the American patriots. The most famous of these was Paul Revere, who on the night of April 18, 1775, took the warning to Lexington, Massachusetts, that the British were on their way. But there were other warnings carried by fearless riders whose names have been lost in history. I decided to use a girl as

the rider in my story—and so Hannah Andrews
and her beloved horse, Promise, were created.

Orphan children in that era often became
indentured servants. Since I needed to put Hannah
in a setting where she would be privy to secret
information she would later carry to American
patriots, she became a servant at the Province
House in Boston. This is where the real British general, Thomas Gage, and his wife lived just before
the Revolution.

Boston was a hotbed of opposing factions in
1775, and the Province House was an ideal background for Hannah's story. History describes its
location and some of the events that took place
there. However, although there are a few drawings
and tales about the mansion, its original form is
not clearly known and much description of the
actual building has been lost.

When the Province House was demolished
many years ago, a short tunnel was discovered
that ran from Province Street to Harvard Place. No
one knows why or by whom it was built. When I
read that there had been a tunnel, I knew it would
work in very well in this plot!

Although most of the characters in my story are fictional, I have brought back real people to appear in the book, including Paul Revere, Phillis Wheatley, Dr. Benjamin Church, Dr. Joseph Warren, Sarah Tarrant, General Gage, Margaret Gage, Colonel Leslie, and Esther Dudley. These people did in fact live in 1774–1775 New England, when *Midnight Rider* takes place.

General Thomas Gage, as both commander of British forces in America and governor of Massachusetts, was in a difficult no-win situation during that period. Americans despised him, and the British felt he was ineffective. As I studied his letters, and other historical documents pertaining to General Gage, I realized that this fair and likeable man was caught up in circumstances that were spinning out of his control.

At one time General and Mrs. Gage kindly took in a motherless teenage girl who was unmanageable and wild. I smiled as I read how stressed the Gages became by her escapades. This is how the character Meg came to life, although to my knowledge the real Margaret Montcrieffe never resided at the Province House in Boston.

In the construction of my plot, I had to decide which warning Hannah and Promise would bring to the Patriots. There were many incidents that could have been used for this book. The historical event I chose for Hannah's ride is known as the Salem Alarm or Leslie's Retreat. As Hannah discovers, General Gage ordered Colonel Leslie to secretly take troops by sea to march on Salem and retrieve the cannon there. Paul Revere heard about their mission and went to Castle William to spy on their ship. He was captured and held there until after the mission had taken place. Historians feel he may have been lured to Castle William and imprisoned so he could not carry the warning to Salem.

The British regulars were brought by ship to Marblehead, Massachusetts, where they came ashore and marched into Salem on February 27, 1775, disturbing the people's Sabbath. History tells us that when Major Pedrick, a Whig leader from Marblehead, saw Colonel Leslie and the soldiers marching toward Salem, he raced ahead to warn the Salemites.

Salem Tories had told Colonel Leslie that the

munitions were across the North Bridge near the forge. When he arrived with his men to find the drawbridge raised, he gave orders to use nearby boats to cross the river. The Salem men did in fact smash holes in their boats to keep the British regulars from using them. The British came after the Patriots with bayonets, and one man was pierced in his chest, causing a superficial wound. Parson Barnard made an agreement with Colonel Leslie that if the bridge were lowered, the British would march only as far as the forge. The negotiations gave the patriots on the other side of the river enough time to remove the munitions.

When no arms were found near the forge, Colonel Leslie lived up to his word. He and his men retreated to Marblehead in defeat and humiliation. In this scene I have used Sarah Tarrant's actual words taunting the British. There are many other historical quotations throughout the book.

History verifies that Dr. Benjamin Church, a highly regarded and trusted member of the Sons of Liberty, was a spy for General Gage. In my story, Hannah is the only one who believes that Dr. Church is a traitor. I did not expose him in this book, because his treachery was not actually revealed until after my story ended. Only when, in July 1775, a coded letter was intercepted was he finally exposed and tried. On November 6, 1775, the Continental Congress dismissed him from his high-ranking office and voted "that Dr. Church be close confined in some secure gaol [jail] in the colony of Connecticut without the use of pen, ink, and paper." When Dr. Benjamin Church left America in disgrace sometime in 1778, his ship was lost at sea and he was never heard from again.

In my book, Catherine's letter to Hannah relates historical evidence that points to Mrs. Gage as a possible informant for the Americans. Some historians do not feel that Mrs. Gage was the informant. Others feel certain she was. Margaret Kemble Gage was an American aristocrat who was born in New Jersey. History indicates that Mrs. Gage feared that if there were war, her husband would be responsible for the deaths of her countrymen. It has been recorded that she did use the quotation from Shakespeare's *King John* to explain her torn loyalties.

Midnight Rider takes place in 1774–1775, just

prior to the American Revolution. My story ends with Hannah and Will riding together in a peaceful meadow. The war for independence from England was only just beginning, however, and would continue for several years.

acknowledgments

I'm much obliged to the following historical resources: The Paul Revere House; The Bostonian Society; the Boston Public Library; the Danvers Peabody Institute Library; the Salem Public Library in Massachusetts, and the Selby Public Library in Sarasota, Florida.

Much appreciation also to the reference departments of my friendly and accommodating neighborhood libraries in Venice, Florida, and Moultonborough, New Hampshire.

Gratitude goes galloping to my equestrian cousin, Janet Nakashian Sinclair, and her horse, Promise, for sharing their expertise.

Thank you, historical architect Chuck Parrott, for long discussions and fascinating information about New England's past.

Love and appreciation to friends and writers June, Carol, Elizabeth, and Gail for their kind critique and comforting reassurance over the years.

To Claire Krane, my good friend, neighbor, and my newly appointed best-ever proofreader, who checked out the final manuscript with eagle eyes—thanks, Claire. The job is yours!

Many thanks to my amazing and talented editors, Emma Dryden and Sarah Sevier, for their abiding faith in my stories.

Literature Circle Questions

Use these questions and the activities that follow to get more out of the experience of reading *Midnight Rider* by Joan Hiatt Harlow.

1. How does Hannah first meet Will and Caleb?

2. Make three columns with the following headings: "Whig," "Tory," and "Undecided." Under each heading, list the characters who are aligned with each cause at the start of the novel.

3. Which characters use the secret tunnel? Why do they use it? What do they do there?

4. In your own words, explain the meaning behind Sarah Tarrant's words on page 341: "Do you think we were born in the woods to be frightened by owls?"

5. Cathcrine says that Hannah is the best friend Meg ever had. Why is Hannah such a good friend? Give four or five examples.

6. Why does Hannah feel like a traitor to the Gage family? To whom else might she feel like a traitor?

7. What would you say to Mrs. Gage to convince her to completely support the Whigs' cause?

8. This story is told from the perspective of a young servant girl. In what ways do Hannah's gender, age, and position help her? In what ways do these factors limit what she can do?

9. Explain the significance of the name "Promise" to Hannah and to the story.

10. Hannah and Catherine each have one prized possession from their homes. Explain why these items are significant to each girl.

11. When she is angry or frustrated, Hannah sometimes mimics people's voices. How else might Hannah have used her talent for mimicry in this story?

12. Imagine Hannah is a student in your school. What classes, clubs, and activities might she be interested in? Pick one other character from the book. What school activities would he or she be interested in?

13. Decide whether or not it was wise for Hannah to disrupt the British soldiers during her midnight rides with Promise. How might Hannah's actions have helped the Whigs' cause? How might her actions have hurt their cause?

14. On page 249, Mrs. Gage questions Hannah about Meg's activities. Argue why you think Hannah made the right decision in her response or why you think she did not. What would you have done in her position?

15. Hannah and Lydia respond differently to authority and instructions. Justify the behavior of each character. Which way of behaving is most similar to yours?

Note: These Literature Circle questions are keyed to Bloom's Taxonomy as follows: Knowledge: 1–3; Comprehension: 4–6; Application: 7–8; Analysis: 9–10; Synthesis: 11–12; Evaluation: 13–15.

Activities

1. Create a menu for a restaurant in the year 1775. Be sure to include a variety of meal options and prices. Give your restaurant a name and a theme or a logo.

2. Create a timeline of significant events in Hannah's life.

3. Choose one character in the novel and write a help wanted ad to which he or she might respond. For instance, Meg might answer an ad to work in a boutique, while Phillis Wheatley would be more likely to answer an ad seeking an English teacher.

Other Books by Joan Hiatt Harlow

Joshua's Song
Shadow Bear
Shadows on the Sea
Star in the Storm
Thunder from the Sea